MW01167238

LINDEN FALLS

JOSHUA HERSHEY

ARCHWAY
PUBLISHING

Archway Publishing books may be ordered through booksellers or by contacting:

Archway Publishing
1663 Liberty Drive
Bloomington, IN 47403
www.archwaypublishing.com
844-669-3957

ISBN: 978-1-6657-3245-1 (sc)
ISBN: 978-1-6657-3250-5 (hc)
ISBN: 978-1-6657-3246-8 (e)

Library of Congress Control Number: 2022920459

Print information available on the last page.

Archway Publishing rev. date: 05/11/2023

CONTENTS

CHAPTER 1

THE DRAGON AND
THE DREAMER

L et me in!" The hooded girl was nose to nose with the masked
priest, but her voice was drowned in the roaring crowd behind
her. He made no move. She stood on her tiptoes to peer over
the mass of prophets a short distance beyond him, all wearing scarlet
cloaks, heads shaved, and covered in worm-sized veins. The gates to
the graves of Esettvi, shining in the afternoon, were closed. "They
just buried her this morning!"

"Mabel, we can come back!" said the teenage girl standing beside
her. She had a soft face, long dark hair, and heavily lidded eyes. The
crowd roared again, and the prophets began passing their hands
across their chests.

"I don't care about your Dazæn Day!" shouted Mabel, ignoring
Issy and waving a flippant hand. "Or your curses!"

Issy threw a pleading look at the handsome boy on Mabel's left,
his blond hair stirring in the wind, shoulders wrapped in the snowy
fur of the Linden bear. Jay glanced down the dusty street lined with
merchants. People were staring now. An armored guard turned his
head in their direction.

"Hey, Mabe . . ."

But the girl had realized it was no use and was about to turn away when the priest raised the Regada pole as though he too would issue a curse. Anger exploded in Mabel's heart, hatred licking her insides like flames, consuming her pain, and filling her mind so she couldn't think.

Mabel clubbed his arm, and the golden rod clattered to the ground. Jay grabbed her around the waist and pulled her back as a yelling tide of red cloaks rushed forward. Issy looked mortified as Mabel kicked the priest, who had lunged for the pole, and knocked him flat on his back. Jay let go and rammed the first prophet who arrived, Mabel snatching up the pole and taking a swipe at the next, just missing him as he jumped out of the way.

"Come on!" Jay seized Mabel's hood and yanked it back, revealing an ivory face with high cheekbones and dark almond eyes. She wheeled around, caught Issy by the wrist, and they were off.

Jay led the way as they ran toward the city, whose earthly tones made the buildings appear to be rising out of the ground. Within seconds, they were snaking their way through the throng, many of whom were facing away from the ocean and chanting with a nearby group of singers. Issy looked over her shoulder at the red cloaks muscling their way after them.

"Give it back, Mabel!" she cried into the mane of auburn hair flying in front of her.

"No!"

They squeezed between bodies wrapped in dark cloaks and furs, ducked around horses, and hopped over wagon tongues. In a minute's time, they had lost their pursuers, whose shouts could not rise above those of the crowd. Another minute passed and they were through, walking briskly down the paved streets of Port Majoris, which was still crowded but thinning enough to allow Mabel to pull Issy alongside her as she took the lead.

"Those were the prophets of Mog!" said Issy, glancing at the glittering pole in Mabel's hand. "They were cursing you!"

"Not now, Izz!"

Mabel avoided the square and turned down a dismal lane with few doors and no balconies, the brown walls blocking the slanted rays of the sun. The number of people lessened, and Jay drew even with Mabel, who handed him the Regada pole as she shifted the leather bag slung over her shoulder.

"What are you gonna do with it?" Issy asked nervously.

"Melt it down and sell it," said Jay, stuffing it under his coat.

Mabel felt a pang of remorse, knowing that her grandmother would have been heartbroken to see what she had become. But hadn't Gigi known? It was as though her grandmother had seen the stolen clothes stashed at school and listened to Mabel's fights and had watched the girl on her own, as she slipped into the nights.

"At least we're gonna get paid," said Mabel in a louder voice. She turned south onto another lane.

Issy drew her coat tightly around her neck. "At least I don't have to worry about the gods."

"They're not real," said Jay in a low tone.

"You know what, Izz?" said Mabel fiercely. "I'm glad you came, to see what I have—*nothing* . . ." Her voice broke, and Jay looked away.

"I didn't mean—"

"This"—Mabel held out her bag—"and whatever crumbs my aunt left." The bag fell to her side as she sped up and flung the hood over her head. "Let's keep moving . . . I wanna get my stuff and be back in time to catch the last ship."

Some thirty minutes later, they were enveloped in a world of white birch trees. No cries rose from its depths, and the stones that littered the floor were covered in moss. Mabel shivered as they walked on, wordlessly, the girl becoming more isolated by the day, afraid to let others know what she craved. If only she had parents to lift the world off her shoulders, people to love her without wanting anything in return. There had been Gigi, but like the leaves drifting from the branches around them, her grandmother's life had withered and fallen into the shadows. *I never should have gone back to school*, thought the girl of seventeen. A serpent of guilt slithered through her veins. *I should have stayed.*

Her insides smoldered. Mabel had come as fast as she could when the news came of her grandmother's death, believing her aunt would wait for her so that she, Mabel, could give Gigi one last kiss. But her aunt had not. Mabel's stomach growled, reminding her that she hadn't eaten for days, but the girl didn't care. Looking at a tree on the horizon, weathered and pale, she felt as though she were staring at herself.

The sound of running water interrupted her thoughts, and her eyes fluttered. "We're almost there," she said. The path turned north along a shallow river, and soon they reached Gigi's house, timbered with stone-filled sides, nestled in a clearing. They mounted the steps and entered the cabin. Jay moved over to the small window by the door and peered out at the trees. Mabel lowered her hood, and her brow furrowed as she looked around the sitting room. Everything was gone.

"You can sit there," Mabel said to Issy. She nodded at the raised stone hearth by the closet. "It won't take long." But Issy was eyeing the Regada pole that Jay examined in his hands. It looked like a wand, with two curved horns rising from a shapeless skull on its tip. Her eyes flickered to Mabel, then to the pole, and back again.

A sense of pity stirred in Mabel. No one cared about her more than Issy—rich, yet small and innocent. Even with her money, Mabel wondered how the girl would make it through this world. She reached out, and Issy stepped forward, Mabel putting an arm around her and pulling her close.

"I'm sorry," she whispered, and Issy pressed herself against Mabel's chest. "Come on."

"Let me know if you need anything," said Jay. Mabel led Issy down a short hall and through the kitchen. The girls reached a door on the other side and were about to cross into a sunroom, the narrow windows pierced by copper rays when Mabel stopped. A strange feeling was spreading through her.

She gazed down the flagstone steps on her left, where the sculpture of a boy peering into a jar stood at the bottom. The girl knew she must keep moving, to collect what little remained in her room, and be on her way. But something was falling upon her. Believing the torment was coming from the memories of a girl long ago, hiding behind the statue, and calling for Gigi to find her, Mabel let go of Issy's hand and descended the stairs. It was as if touching the figure would somehow break the spell.

Mabel reached the bottom and brushed the boy's face with her fingers. Issy joined her and gestured at the stone door beside the statue.

"What's in there?"

"Just the cellar—"

Mabel gasped and clenched her hands.

"What is it?" said Issy in a quivering voice.

But Mabel wasn't listening. The new feeling was owning her and driving everything else away. The girl couldn't breathe; her eyes darted around before they rested on the door, and the sensation was gone. Emptiness took its place.

"I dunno," panted Mabel. And they exchanged fearful looks, each driving the rumors from her mind. "Something I never felt before."

"You haven't eaten."

"It's not that. . . ."

Mabel stepped forward and laid a hand on the door. Her heart shook. *There's nothing in here*, she thought angrily. *What's the matter with me?* She tried deciphering the feelings inside her, but they were legion. Her eyes narrowed, and she shoved open the door, hoping the sight of the empty room would appease them. The girls stood in the doorway and poked their heads inside, musty air filling their lungs as they scanned the stone walls lined with empty shelves. But the misery would not relent.

They were about to leave when Mabel froze. A shimmering olive-green book was tucked in a crevice along the back wall.

"What's wrong?" said Issy. She had felt the shudder pass through Mabel's frame and was unable to ignore the stories anymore. There were whispers around school that Mabel was a witch, a possessed dreamer who used magic to enter shadows and speak with the dead, who could draw power from the stars, look through the eyes of animals, and turn people to dust. She was a waymaker for demons. There were more like these that Issy had refused to believe, but the girl was looking scared.

"I saw that book last night," said Mabel slowly, "on the ship."

"How?"

"I wonder why my aunt left it. She took everything else. . . ."

"But how did you see it?"

"If I read it—"

"Mabel! *How* did you see it?" said Issy and grabbed her by the shoulder.

"In a dream," said Mabel, the vision playing in her mind.

She was in a temple that shone like the sun, rainbows crisscrossing overhead, with the spirits of men. They had translucent bodies, filled with brilliant, sparkling lights. They couldn't see her as she walked with them onto a terrace. A god stood with his back to them, facing another sea of spirits, his cape soaked in blood. His hair struck her eyes like lightning. A spirit was standing beside him, and it read from a book that burned but was not consumed.

"How long will the light be hidden?" he said, closing the book, and the fire vanished. "How long until the sixth nation falls?"

The god held out his arm, covered in flesh with HE MAKES WAR written on his skin. "The time has come," he said, in a voice that made her sink to her knees, "for destroying those who destroy the Earth. A thousand days will pass, and the girl will stand again. Ten thousand more, and your bodies will return."

The spirits roared.

"Let's go!" said Issy and jerked Mabel's arm. She felt panicky and didn't know why, but something about the book made her feel worse.

"I have to look at it," said Mabel, shaking her head. "It's the one I saw in my dream—I have to know."

"Know *what*?"

But Mabel wasn't listening as she slipped through the door and stalked toward the book. She hated the stories about her, but they weren't without reason: she had had dreams before, some that blessed her and others that haunted her mind, visions that left her collapsed on the ground with no way of knowing if they were real. Until now.

Mabel pried the book loose and was startled by its weight. "It feels warm," she said musingly and caressed the hard, icelike cover.

"Don't open it!" said Issy, who crept closer for a better look. "Something about it makes me, I dunno, afraid."

"It's just a book," Mabel murmured and released the iron claps. She opened it to a place in the middle and found golden characters written on pages that seemed to have been fashioned from clouds. "Izz, look at this. It's perfect."

Issy stiffened as Mabel flipped a page that rose and fell without a sound. "Yeah, but we can't read it. What language is that, anyway?"

Mabel shrugged.

"It's weird, but I think I know what it says. . . ." And something in her heart flooded her mind. The girl began to read the words aloud, slowly at first, then faster until she was speaking the language as fluently as her own.

"How can you read it?" said Issy anxiously.

Mabel didn't seem to hear, her voice becoming more powerful with every word that fell from her lips. Dazzling beams of light suddenly flashed from the words and flowed across the pages like water.

"Magic!" cried Issy, leaping back as the winds howled outside.

Mabel was spellbound, held by a book that would not let her go, by a warmth that broke upon her spirit in waves. The light thickened and became like fire, birthing flames that neither burned the book nor gave her fingers any pain.

I'm a witch! thought Mabel frantically. This must be why Gigi, who had scarcely mentioned Mabel's parents, had told her they died during the plague and no more. Was this why her grandmother had always dismissed her dreams? Had she been protecting Mabel from herself? A scream coiled in the girl's throat: *Anyone who practices magic, apart from service to the queen, must die.*

But the scream never came, her fear slipping away as she read of things in another world: gods and prophecies, angels and demons— and the one who is to come.

And without warning, the book floated before her.

"Mabel!"

But Mabel wouldn't stop. She held her hands under the hovering book and felt the flames as they poured like a waterfall onto the floor. The light swirled around her feet, gaining speed and rising like a funnel around her body.

Outside the sky grew dark, and a gust of wind screamed through the trees and lashed the house.

"Mabel! Izz!"

Jay's voice sounded from somewhere above.

"Stop!" said Issy as the house shuddered and groaned, watching Mabel in terror—her hair whipping round her face, caught in a whirlwind of light, never pulling her eyes from the book.

The funnel thickened until Mabel could hardly be seen, and the girl extended her arms as though to push the light away. Expanding away from her body and passing over Issy who flung her arms over her face, it roared around the room, consuming the shelves and leaving no ashes. The doorway erupted in a blaze.

Issy dropped her arms and saw the light of the book feeding

what had become a cyclone, moaning and growing stronger by the second, pulling the mortar from the walls. The girl lunged forward and swatted the book shut; its weight instantly returned, and it crashed to the floor, glowing, then went dark.

Mabel looked like she'd been startled out of a dream, and Issy backed away breathing quickly. The vortex weakened, a few rays still zipping around the room like tiny comets, and vanished. But the fire still burned in the door, and the storm continued to rage—alive with shrieking voices, the wind screaming as though it were giving up its soul. Mabel's heart grew cold as she glanced down at the book, gleaming in the firelight. She had a moment to decide whether to keep it and knew that she was never coming back. It was a powerful book, one that could both save and destroy; it had shown her another world and something about herself, that at least one dream was true. What else could it do? *Had it belonged to my parents?*

She had no sooner scooped the book into her bag than a tree smashed through the sunroom above, and the girls screamed as mortar rained down from the ceiling.

"Jay!" yelled Issy, who appeared to have lost all faith in Mabel. *"Help!"*

"I don't think he can hear us!" Mabel shouted over the wind, her hands trembling, eyes fixed on the burning door. "We gotta go through the fire!"

"What?"

Mabel swung her bag over her shoulder and grabbed Issy's arm, but the girl ripped it away.

"The flames won't hurt!" said Mabel, this time seizing her wrist. A beam toppled into the house, and mortar trickled on their heads once more. Issy inched closer.

"Let's go!"

They closed their eyes and leaped through the door.

Their hearts stopped. They were standing in darkness, bathed in a crimson glow that soaked the air like a shadow. There was no storm, no noise, and nothing moved. The air was strangely warm. The girls spun away from each other and faced the cellar door. The fire was gone.

"What's happening?" said Issy woefully. She stared at her hands where a satin light glittered and was gone. Her skin was like ash.

Mabel didn't speak as she gazed at the head of the statue, lying broken at her feet. Something like a large branch had crushed the sculpture, but it was bits of stone, not wood, that littered the steps. She looked up, and her mouth fell open. A stone tree had split the roof, revealing red stars that flickered like candles in the midnight sky.

The girls turned and faced each other.

"*Your eyes!*"

They clapped their hands over their mouths, each stifling a scream as one stepped back from the other. Their eyes were gone, and dark voids had taken their place. A tarlike substance oozed from their sockets and drizzled down their smoke-colored cheeks.

Mabel touched her face; her skin was cold and her body shutting down. What had she done? To Izz? And Jay . . . where *was* he? But something about the helpless look on Issy's face unraveled the chains in her stomach, and she fought to pull herself together.

"Izz, look, you know me!" said Mabel earnestly. "I don't know what's going on, but you know I'd never hurt you. *Right?*" she added when Issy didn't move. The girl gave a weak nod, and Mabel gazed into the cellar, which looked like a tomb. "Let's get Jay, and we'll figure this out."

Mabel took Issy's limp hand and climbed the steps, the pieces of stone crunching like seashells under their feet. The girls squeezed through the kitchen door, nearly pinned shut by a fallen tree; picked their way over a broken beam in the hall; and moved carefully into the sitting room. Scarlet light seeped through the window by the door that formed a pool over the hearth. It sat alone but for the

Regada pole lying on the floor, no longer golden, but warped and wasted like a burned match.

"Where is he?" Issy whimpered, and she clenched Mabel's arm with both hands.

"Probably hid from the storm—"

"Jay!"

Issy's voice reverberated throughout the house, but there was no answer.

"Jay!" they shouted together.

Mabel shut her mouth, seized by the sinking feeling they were giving themselves away. Issy was about to yell again, when a low and distant voice breathed within the forest.

"The girl readssss. . . ."

It came and went, a little more than a passing breeze. Issy deflated.

"Lavian comessss. . . ." sighed another voice, and Mabel felt a thrill of dread that had nothing to do with the nauseating tone nor her inability to determine from whence it came but from the name itself: Lavian.

"Mabel," said Issy as she began to cry. "W-we're cursed!"

"It's not because of those prophets," Mabel hissed. "Jay wouldn't have left us, and wherever we are, it's not our world. Let's just get out of here."

They walked through the front door and stopped dead. The forest was lit with that bloody starlight, the river was dry, and the trees were made of stone. The floor was no longer covered with leaves but marred with cracks, deeper than a sword, which whispered of an earth that had never tasted rain. Their hearts were hammering as they stood a moment longer then bounded down the steps and hurried up the trail. They were nearing the first bend when a cloud layer rolled across the heavens, though there was no wind, and veiled the stars in seconds, hurling the forest into utter darkness.

The girls slowed their pace to a crawl but refused to stop, tripping over cracks as they inched along with outstretched arms, feeling their way, then screaming as lightning struck the house with an explosion that rocked the atmosphere.

They spun around and watched in horror as violet flames incinerated the ruins like chaff. "There's something inside!" said Issy, who was pointing to a tall dark shape that moved in the fire. It burst into the open and sent them crashing on their knees.

The massive creature had the torso of a man and the head of a snake. Milky scales with jet-black streaks covered its skull, and orange eyes, split with vertical pupils, peered into the gloom. His muscles looked as though they were rocks fitted tightly together, wrapped in ashen skin. The beast wore no clothes, his body adorned with markings written in blood. He was Lavian.

"It has the wings of an angel!" whispered Mabel in terror, gawking at the enormous black-feathered wings that arched over his shoulders and flowed majestically to the ground. She grabbed Issy, and they scooted behind a stone briar patch.

"It doesn't look anything like an angel!" hissed Issy, peering through the stems. *"Oh!"* She clawed her hair so forcefully that Mabel could hear it tear. Instead of legs, it had the tail of a snake.

"Let's go!" sobbed Issy, but her words were overpowered by another blast of lightning. Having no eyelids, the girls covered their faces with their hands and then lowered them at once: the flash had caused no pain. A second figure was standing beside the first.

"That *is* an angel!" said Mabel emphatically.

But he was nothing that she imagined one to be. The being had the full body of a man, with black wings and long hair that was darker than the grave. His gray skin was covered with names, symbols, and signs, and the grooves that lined his muscles were filled with shadows in the firelight. Animal skins were tied about his waist, and his veins were black.

"His eyes look like ours—"

"Shh!"

The angel turned, his empty sockets looking aimlessly in their direction. Mabel froze; they should have been out of earshot, but the darkness was thicker than air. Weak sounds traveled far. Then a symphony of lightning crashed from heaven, the lines splitting like veins in the sky before striking the earth. This time, the girls didn't cover their faces and watched the storm until it ceased. More than two hundred Dark Angels stood around Lavian, awaiting his command.

Mabel was riveted by the figures. Despite their ghastly appearance, she saw glimpses of perfection. They were powerful and moved with precision, as though they had been wonderfully made yet fallen from destiny.

"It's a girl," rasped Lavian, his voice sounding like a swarm of flies. His fangs flashed in the blue light that emanated from his mouth. "She passed through the fire and stands with us in the Unseen."

"Does she have the book?" said an angel in hollow tones.

"*Yessss . . .*"

"We must hurry!" called another. "She's a Reader!"

"She's afraid!" shrieked Lavian, rising on his tail. "Fear owns her, which means I own her!"

He stared intently into the trees, his forked tongue gliding out and then in.

"D'you think he sees us?" whispered Issy.

Mabel said nothing. She knew their worst fear was about to be confirmed. Though they were hidden, the monster seemed to be in control, as if the darkness itself gave him the information he desired.

"She is near!" said Lavian savagely. "Bring her to me!" He spread his massive wings and took off, looking like a dragon with his tail dangling in the air. A moment later, his angels flew after him through the trees.

"Oh God!" cried Issy.

"C'mon, *c'mon!*" said Mabel, who seized a fistful of Issy's coat and yanked her to her feet. Mabel spun around and ran into the forest, pulling her friend behind. The only light came from the burning house, and she knew it wouldn't be long until they were lost in darkness.

CHAPTER 2

WAR WITH THE FALLEN

Mabel was electric, expecting the Serpent to slice her back at any second. Issy's breaths sounded more like muted screams as she stumbled after Mabel, who never let her go. The firelight faded, and they lost the path. Mabel tripped, the bag nearly flying off her shoulder, and the girls tumbled to the ground. They had no sooner clambered to their feet than a line of seething golden flames erupted fifty yards ahead. Distant voices screamed then ceased. The fire towered through the trees.

"It's the same light as the book!" cried Mabel, though for some reason it was stabbing her brain. "Let's go!"

"No!"

Issy looked paralyzed. "This is all happening because of that light! And it hurts!"

"Are you crazy?" Mabel yelled, her voice breaking as she seized Issy by the collar and struggled to pull her toward the flames. "It's either the light or those *things!* Maybe if we go through the fire . . ."

Her voice trailed away, and she let go as hundreds of the most glorious figures she had ever seen appeared in the flames. They were angels in loincloths with bodies of topaz, sapphire, emeralds, and rubies, covered in markings that glittered like gold. Their crystal wings were furled behind their backs, and their long hair shone like the stars. They stood like statues, faces set, eyes filled with fire.

Mabel was about to call to them when a shriek made the girls spin around to find Lavian hurtling through the air. Issy threw her arms around Mabel as the Serpent landed in the distance with a thud that shook the ground. The markings on his body were easier to see now, illuminated by the flames. LAWLESS was written over the winged snakes carved in his chest, LIAR was burned on his side, and SERPENT and DRAGON on his arms. Dark Angels poured through the trees and landed on either side of Lavian, forming a line opposite the angels of light and trapping the girls in between. FALLEN was etched in their chests.

"The girl belongs to me!" Lavian shouted to the angels in the fire, and Mabel and Issy shivered: The black liquid that had been seeping from his angels' eyes filled their sockets and froze, forming scales. "She has not chosen the Morning Star!"

There was silence.

A jasper angel with Aurèle written on his chest and a tiny star tied around his neck stepped toward the Fallen. The angel extended his arm and clenched his hand—a line of fire erupted in his fist like a sword, forged in the sun, its core made of light. The angels with him came out of the fire, and the flames vanished, the pain in Mabel's head with it. The Light Angels raised their arms, swords of fire flashing in their fists.

"So be it, sons of God!" yelled Lavian, and he closed his hand. A bluish-white bolt of lightning burst in his fist. His angels did the same, and the girls shrank back as the bodies of the Fallen changed from flesh to obsidian, the feathers crystalizing on their wings. Within seconds, the creatures looked as though they were dressed in armor, reflecting the lightning at their sides.

"Vur draaken cy hvis angeli!"*

---

* For the Dragon and his angels!

They shouted as one.

The Light Angels said nothing, but their burning swords whispered their defiance. Lavian looked more like a machine than ever, and Mabel knew that it was useless to beg. Thinking fast, she looked for an escape, but there was none. To her horror, Lavian slithered closer but was looking off into the distance, as though aware of something no one else could see.

"Go!" shouted Mabel, and she shoved Issy toward the angels of light. As they sprinted through the trees, Mabel keeping her back between Issy and Lavian, fire exploded over Aurèle. A feathery golden raptor soared out of the flames, screaming as it rolled to avoid a lightning bolt thrown by Lavian, and struck the Serpent, sinking its talons through his shoulder.

Mabel glanced back and saw Lavian thrashing, unable to shake the great bird as the forest erupted, Light Angels yelling and vaulting forward as the Fallen flew to meet them. Fire and lightning and peals of thunder filled the sky. The lines collided over the girls who never stopped running until a Dark Angel plummeted through the crisscrossing bodies and threw his bolt like a spear, just missing Mabel. A new bolt flashed in his hand, even as the first blasted the ground and sent Issy flying. But the assassin was cut in half by a ruby-red angel before he could strike again, his body shattering like glass and releasing a green light that disappeared into the earth.

"Get up, Izz!" screamed Mabel, who had miraculously stayed up and hoisted Issy to her feet. The red angel landed nearby, his back to the girls, and a shield of light flashed in his fist that smashed a lightning bolt with a blast of blue sparks. A black shape pelted through the Light Angels that circled the girls and drew back its arm.

"LOOK OUT!" shouted Mabel and Issy together, but it was too late. Lightning struck the angel guarding them, and he crumbled in a pile of glittering gemstones, a white light rising into the sky.

At that moment, the ground split, and the earth turned into sand. The girls were swept down a slope, screaming, toward a chasm that was opening at a terrific speed. Mabel grabbed Issy around the waist, dug her feet into the sand, and brought them both to a halt before a precipice that plunged into oblivion; but she knew they were dead at the sight of demons, rising from the chasm on translucent wings. They appeared more like insects than men, covered in purple exoskeletons with drooling mouths, mouths that issued pink vapors, and were filled with needlelike teeth.

"No!" shrieked Issy, who flipped onto her stomach and clambered up the slope. And this time it was Mabel who was paralyzed, her heart exploding as the demons flew toward them, but the chains that trailed from around their necks tautened. The monsters raged against the shackles that bound them to a place far below the earth as the Fallen came to set them free, but two brilliant bodies racing down the chasm brought Mabel back to the fight.

"We gotta get down!" she yelled. "They're coming for us!"

"I know!" shouted Issy, slipping and sliding.

"I mean the angels!"

Mabel seized Issy's coat and pulled her back down the slope. Bolts of lightning rained through the atmosphere and smashed the demons' chains. Burning swords fell with them, spearing the beasts who burst into flame.

"Get off me, Mabel!"

A tremor shook the earth as the chasm ground to a halt, its walls locking in place, and a second landslide ensued that dragged the girls closer to the abyss. Mabel's bag slipped off as the girl let go of Issy and completed a somersault, her heart pierced with despair—the book, the only potential link to her past now gone—and she was back on her feet, surfing down the slope as an emerald angel scooped Issy in his arms and rose into the air. Light Angels sped toward the last of the demons and drove them into the chasm as Aurèle zoomed underneath them. He reached Mabel as she jumped off the precipice, unable to stop herself, the girl landing on his back and snapping her arms and legs around his steely frame.

More Light Angels plummeted and flew over the girls with light shields in their fists. Thunder roared as lightning pelted the shields, sparks flurrying into the chasm below. They climbed higher and hovered as Light Angels swarmed around them.

The fighting intensified, and Mabel looked down in horror as angels piled on top of angels where she had lost the bag. A Dark Angel came away with the bag and rose into the air, but was blasted out of the sky by a sword that impaled his back. The bag fell as his body disintegrated, but was caught by an angel of light before it hit the ground. The amber figure dodged two lightning bolts and sped for Mabel, the angels around her parting to make way.

"Take it!" he shouted, his voice ringing like steel. Mabel grabbed the strap and flipped it over her head.

"Fly with Hamal!" Aurèle said over his shoulder and spun his back to the angel that had just given Mabel the bag. The girl reached out, hooked an arm around Hamal's neck, and was glued to his back a moment later.

Aurèle swung his arm over Issy's head and flashed a shield that obliterated a lightning bolt. "Capella!" he shouted, and the turquoise angel carrying Issy moved in behind Mabel. "Dagenn se!"

The company bolted, flying in V formation with Mabel and Issy in the middle, Aurèle leading the way. They put on a burst of speed as they zigzagged through the trees, apparently able to see through the darkness. Mabel looked up and saw a tide of fallen angels that raced to cut them off, illuminated by their electric blades.

Her party halted as Aurèle continued onward, a sword in each hand. A moment later, he jetted into the throng as it dove through the trees ahead, swords flying with such fury they became blurs. Gleaming angels plunged from the sky and came to his aid, spearing the Fallen through the stone trunks, which split and toppled to the ground. Gaps opened in the melee, and Hamal and Capella were off, the girls pressing their faces into the necks of their angels as lightning zipped overhead. There was a series of earsplitting blasts, a shower of sparks that rained over their bodies, and a second later, they were free.

Mabel could both feel and hear the trees whipping by, the wind rushing over her body like a river that tugged at her hair and clothes. The explosions faded in the distance. She lifted her head and watched Capella weaving through the trees on her right, Issy latched to his back. Hamal glanced up as though he wanted to climb higher, and Mabel followed his gaze: hordes of Dark Angels had them hemmed in from above. A fresh shower of lightning began to fall as the angels flung their bolts, Hamal banking to avoid two flashes that sailed overhead and blasted a tree. Issy screamed as Capella rolled on his back and threw his sword at an angel diving behind them; the body exploded as soon as it was hit, another sword flashing in Capella's fist. He flipped facedown and pulled alongside Hamal, the angels bobbing and weaving and doing everything they could to stay alive.

We're not gonna make it! thought Mabel, who was trying not to imagine what it would feel like to be blasted to bits.

Suddenly, the sky shook, clouds melted, and the forest came to light, the darkness pierced by a million diamond rays. Mabel looked up and gasped. The sky had been torn above the red stars, revealing a higher heaven that was laden with snow-white stars. Their light was alive and unafraid, causing Mabel to relax just enough that she nearly flew off Hamal's back as he swerved to his right.

"*Shit!*"

"Are you hurt?" he shouted, reaching back and shoving her waist toward his spine.

"No—sorry!" Mabel bellowed and clenched his body with all her might.

The barrage of lightning intensified, bolts hammering the forest but wildly missing their marks, thrown by predators who knew their time was short. The white stars plummeted, mysterious stars that grew no larger as they came and merged over the trees. Within seconds, legs as tall as the ten towers of Killbron emerged, with a head as large as the moon. Mabel cried out as she watched Leo come alive, the constellation bounding forward and launching itself into the fallen angels who abandoned the chase and swarmed the lion like bees.

Seeing their chance, Hamal and Capella arched their backs and soared over the forest and into the atmosphere as Leo shredded the Fallen. The green lights of their souls plummeted through the sky and disappeared into the earth below and Mabel's insides with them: the crimson stars churned and became one body.

"What is it?" cried Mabel.

"Scorpius!" yelled Capella. *"Kæ nä!"*

The angels leveled off and raced away from the bloody mass that transfigured behind them. Mabel looked around and saw a new constellation rising, a scorpion with pincers the size of bridges and a wicked tail that arched over its back. Scorpius smacked Leo with its tail, and a shock wave rocked Hamal and Capella. Slivers of crushed stars littered the sky like confetti as Leo rallied and mauled the scorpion, ripping the stars from his body and dragging him into space.

The angels had no sooner resumed their ascent than a bright light appeared over the molten moon, streaking toward them like a comet.

"Don't look at the light!" shouted Capella, and in the next moment, Mabel felt as though her head were on fire. She thought she heard Issy crying in despair. "The pain will end inside!"

Soon the orb was upon them, pulsating, but Mabel forced herself to look through the pain. A golden castle was suspended where the comet had been seconds before. The angels sped toward the fortress, a blur of battlements, towers, and spires, flying for those gates of fire. The girl looked away and shouted, "Almost there, Izz. . . . *Look out!*"

Mabel leaned hard and pulled her angel sideways, a bolt narrowly missing their heads. The girl looked back and saw Dark Angels pouring from violet flames beneath the moon.

Another bolt whizzed past them, then another as the fortress drew nearer. Throngs of jeweled angels dove from the parapets and sped toward the Fallen, the sound of their wings like rushing waves as they flickered over the girls. Rapid explosions broke out as the armies met somewhere above them, angels slaughtering each other and decorating space with the flashes of their souls. A Dark Angel with bladelike wings dove beneath the battle, fired up at Hamal, and hit him in the chest. Mabel hurtled through the air and wrapped both arms around her bag, her angel crumbling as the light of his soul was released.

"*Aaaaaaah!*"

The girl was caught by a trailing sapphire angel and was off again. More angels came to her aid with flashes, shouts, and shields of light. Gasping, Mabel glanced back and saw Dark Angels covering their faces against the light of the castle and falling away, then she looked ahead. The gates were growing larger at breathtaking speed, the doors beginning to open, the pain so great in Mabel's head that she screamed. There was another beat of her angel's wings, and she knew no more.

CHAPTER 3

THE LONGING TO LIVE

Mabel was cradled on a hard surface, wisps of light slithering over the hand that covered her eyes. The sockets were streaming as the light sought to enter her quivering body, poison to the darkness within. Something was pressed against her lips, and a liquid forced itself into her mouth that tasted like blood then rain. For a short time, Mabel couldn't breathe before she gasped as though she had been pulled from beneath the sea.

The pain let go, and the hand departed from Mabel's face. Her vision returned, her eyes no longer empty voids but filled with a white and swirling mist. The girl found herself in the arms of Aurèle, the star burning cheerfully on the strands of light around his neck. He lowered a diamond cup from her mouth. The angel looked different now, his body no longer jasper but covered in skin that shone like the moon. Soft feathers clothed his wings instead of crystal, and his eyes were like water. A large number of angels surrounded him, staring into Mabel's face.

"Where am I?" she murmured.

"In the Citadel, our fortress in the middle heavens," said Aurèle, and the cup melted into nothingness. The angel stood, lifted Mabel in the air, and dropped her deftly on her feet.

"We are suspended above the Earth, yet beneath the stars."

Mabel shifted her bag unconsciously as she looked around. They were in a golden chamber with a procession of sunset flames that rose like pillars from the floor. Archways were stacked high into the walls like those of a coliseum. A stream of angels emerged from a tunnel overhead, soared across the room, and disappeared down another with the sound of a passing breeze.

"Issy!" said Mabel with a start. "Where is she?"

"She has passed from the Unseen to the Seen and walks in the world of men," said Aurèle. "Her path is not your path. Her cross is not the one you will bear."

"And Jay?" Mabel said, having no idea what he meant.

"I know him not."

"He's my friend. . . . He was with me, at my grandma's house."

"Did he pass through the light?"

"No."

"Then he remains in your world. No one can pass from your world to ours unless he walks through fire."

Mabel stared at him, wanting to believe that she was having a dream. But her visions had never come without warning, her own world falling away and another taking its place. Although they were full of people and creatures that she'd never seen before, they could never see her. The girl was afraid, not because she was having a dream, but because she wasn't.

"I just want to go back," she pleaded.

"Mabel—"

"You know my *name*?"

"My god has revealed it to me," said the angel and laid a hand on her shoulder. "It's your time now."

"Time for what?" she said fearfully. "And why did that Snake and those things that look like you . . . but aren't like you . . . come for me?"

"They did not come for you, but for the book."

Mabel held out the bag. A dull ache squeezed her heart, the one that plagued her every time she thought of her parents, when she realized that she was poor and would never have a wedding, a father to give her away; when she was alone and wondered what might have been had they lived. The one that made her feel like she was cursed.

"Did it . . . did it belong to my parents? Did you know them too?"

"The book belongs to no one. I never knew them."

Mabel dropped the bag as though she had been stabbed through the chest. Time stood still as another convoy of angels glided from a tunnel high above, the draft of their wings rocking the fires below.

"Aurèle," said Mabel vaguely, her eyes fixed upon his chest. "It's a beautiful name. . . . The others, what do they mean?"

"Our names are given to us. Some can only be known by the one who wears them. Others can be revealed."

I'm christened a Cherub
And Captain of Light,
An Archangel Divine
That's fearless of hell,
And a Rival of Evil
That clashes with hell.

The angels were chanting now, joining Aurèle as he read the names on his body.

Mi Ka El? Who's like God?
Of chief princes, Great Prince
By whose king I am awed—
Head of Armies I fight
FOR THE PEOPLE OF GOD!

The angels had belted the last phrase, and then a heavy silence reigned.

"That's magnificent," said Mabel, but the girl no longer met his eyes. She was nothing like him. What names did she possess? What feats, what worth had she ever had? Mabel felt like a tramp as she looked down at her reflection on the floor. Her tunic was little more than rags in the glory of this place, and pitch still marred her ashen face. Worse, the external decay reminded her of an internal darkness—the things she had done, the thoughts that she had had, all the hate that she harbored—and the girl despised herself.

"Daughter!" rang a clear voice.

Mabel lifted her eyes as Capella landed gracefully beside her, his body no longer turquoise, but dressed in skin that sparkled like snow. His eyes were the color of the dawn.

"Capella," she said quietly. "What happened to . . . you know?"

"Hamal?"

"Yeah."

"He still lives. Though his body is fallen, his spirit reigns in Zaphon."

"The city of God, in the highest heaven," added Aurèle, moved by the confusion on Mabel's face. "Fly with Capella, and he will take you with me to Demacci Tower. There I will tell you the story of the worlds, and you will choose your path."

Aurèle unfurled his wings and climbed straight for the lofty ceiling as Mabel hoisted herself onto Capella's back. Within seconds, they were rising after Aurèle who banked left and flew through an arch, soaring down a passageway of gold so bright that Mabel was sure they had entered a furnace. Four angels whipped around the bend ahead of them, flying single file in the opposite direction. Mabel flinched as they blew past, and Capella drifted around the turn, out into a chamber where angels crisscrossed through the air amid a network of halls. Aurèle rose higher, pitched left once more, and disappeared through the highest arch. They were speeding down another passage, beyond which Mabel could see the darkness peering back at them. It was a few moments before the three of them plunged into the starry sky, flying over spires and around towers where angels stood guard with flaming swords. They descended toward the highest tower of the northern wall, where more angels made way for the trio as they landed.

"Degasi, Eyewing," said Aurèle to the ones nearest them. He extended his arm toward Mabel. "The daughter who reads what the Morning Star has written." The two carnelian angels faced Mabel as she slid off Capella's back and bowed. But before she could ask Aurèle what he had meant, the angel put his arm around her and steered her past a series of large crystal rings, upright on the floor, to the parapet beyond. He pushed her body gently against the wall, the girl looking over the gleaming barrier at the world below.

"Behold the Earth."

"Oh my . . ."

Mabel forgot everything else, awestruck at the Earth lying beneath them. She recognized the rectangular shape, whose sides dipped toward the center before sweeping out to the four corners like a giant bow, but it was unlike the maps she'd seen at school. The landmasses were covered in pearls and emeralds, lilac valleys that ran among sapphire mountains, peppered with onyx, and wrapped in seas of gold.

"What *is* this?" Mabel breathed.

"Your world as it truly is," said Capella, who peered over her shoulder at the gleaming canvas.

Mabel's mist-filled eyes roved over the northern edge, but she could not make out Linden. Her nation was hidden by impenetrable darkness that made a qualm come over her, and the longer she stared, the more its shadow crept over her heart. Magón was veiled by the same darkness to the east, though the others—Tavar, Neo Padosta, Arraphna, Veldesh, and the Highlands—could all be seen.

Mabel opened her mouth to speak and stopped. What looked like a green comet had fallen out of nothingness and was speeding toward the western rim of the world. The body slowed and floated beside the sun, which vanished as though it had been swallowed. The emerald light flashed a moment later and plunged out of sight.

"What just . . . What happened to the sun?"

"The sun is an angel," said Capella, "and has passed through the Western Gates. In your world, you cannot see him for who he truly is—Estelle, the one who walks through the heavens, casting light from the Unseen."

"The what?"

"There are two worlds," said Aurèle. "The Seen in which you live, and the Unseen realm that permeates the heavens and Earth. Where there is one, you will find the other, and the other the one. Many call our world the spiritual, and believe that it is nothing more than phantoms and fantasy. But now you see that ours is as real as yours, though we have our own laws of nature. Your body is sustained in the Unseen, wherever you go, from below the sea to the stars above. You will never grow tired, never need food or water."

"But you can still feel pain," said Capella, a note of sadness in that clear, metallic voice. "You can bleed and die in this place."

"There are two worlds," Aurèle said again, "but it was not always so. The Seen and Unseen were one, and all angels burned with the light of Zaphon. We lived with my god, his son, Jezul, and the Raptor—the one that you saw fight Lavian."

"The bird?" said Mabel. She turned away from the wall and gazed at Aurèle. "Is it still alive?"

"It lives forever."

"And Lavian?" said Mabel, forcing the name from her lips.

"The Serpent lives until the last nation falls."

"When it *falls*?"

"Peace, and it will be revealed to you," said Aurèle and continued his story.

"Next to my god, Jezul and the Raptor, there are none more powerful than Lavian. He too lived in Zaphon, but was different then. His body was cut from the dawn and framed in gold. He became proud and desired to rule the nations. Jezul knew the darkness in Lavian's heart and warned the kings of men not to serve him, but Lavian deceived them with his beauty. They laid stones in the center of their countries, built temples upon them, and the people of Earth worshipped Lavian."

"They wanted to become like him," said Capella, dropping his voice, "and so they did. The darkness in his heart became the darkness in theirs, and his death became their death."

"Why didn't anyone stop him?" said Mabel.

"My god will not force the heart of the creature," said Aurèle. "He allows us to choose. Some, like Lavian and his angels, and many of the stars, have chosen evil."

"The stars too?"

"Our stars are not like yours," said Capella. "Here they are spirits. Those filled with blood belong to Lavian."

"Your race chose Lavian," Aurèle resumed, "and his darkness reigned over them. Their hearts became like stone and death coursed through their veins. They became blind, unable to tell right from wrong, preying upon each other like animals—killing, destroying, and lying with ease. They loathed what they had done, but were unable to free themselves from Lavian's grip.

"Jezul was grieved, came to Earth, entering the temple in Tavar where Lavian sat on his throne, and struck him before the nations. His face split and the darkness of his heart poured out so that Lavian transfigured and became the Serpent. His angels kept their form, but were severed from light and became the Fallen.

"Jezul tore the Seen away from the Unseen, separating angels from men so that any who wish to cross from one world to the other must walk through the light that burns like fire. Lavian created his own fire to enter the world of men, but Jezul cursed the Serpent and his angels so that any who pass through it will burn."

"So it's over then," said Mabel with a tremendous wave of relief, not caring how the light came out of the book in the first place. She would never open it again.

"I promise never to pass through the fire again," she said hurriedly. "I never wanna see that—"

"It's far from over!" said Capella. "Lavian holds your people in his hand, for the Darkness remains hanging over Linden, day and night since he deceived your first king. It corrupts the hearts of men. Every lie and murder—depression and emptiness—all that is evil, stems from the darkness in the Unseen. In your world, you cannot see it, but you can *feel* it. Until it's broken, they will never be alive."

"What do you mean? You're acting like they're dead."

Capella reached out, touched Mabel's face, and pulled the hand away. The black substance from her eyes was sticking to his fingers.

"Death lives in your veins. That is why your eyes are dark and your skin is cold. The drink that we gave you allows you to function in the light, but darkness still reigns in your body. You exist, but are not alive."

"It's just a dream!" said Mabel, not wanting to believe.

"No!"

The other angels spun their heads and watched Aurèle, no longer the ambassador, but Head of Armies defending his truth against a lie.

"I know you've had visions before—"

"You know them!"

"Only that you've had them, but cannot reveal their meaning. Your visions are like windows that allow you to see into our world, but now you stand with me in the Unseen. It is here that you see things for what they truly are! Your rivers have no water, your trees are like stone—a desolate land with no life and no light. Soon you will return to the world from which you came, and your body will look as it did before. But do not be deceived! Death lives in your veins and the veins of all in your country. You and they belong to Lavian."

Mabel remembered the Snake screaming that she was his and watched a drop of the thick liquid fall from her eyes and spatter on the floor. *It's true*, she thought. *I've never been alive.*

"There is hope, daughter," said Aurèle in a different tone, and the girl looked into his eyes. "Though the darkness can only be broken by the voice of men—for it was men who pledged allegiance to Lavian—and though their voice is powerless, the Raptor carried seven books to Earth, one for every nation, whose words contain the Light. When a book is read in the heart of a land, its light rises into heaven, and the light of heaven descends to Earth. When the two unite, the darkness is destroyed, and that nation falls from Lavian's hand. Tavar was the first to be set free, then Neo Padosta, the Highlands, Arraphna, and Veldesh. Linden and Magón remain."

"This is one of them, isn't it?" said Mabel, not bothering to look down at the bag. "How did my grandma get it?"

"I do not know all things, and that is one," said Aurèle. "Lavian's life is forfeit the day the last nation falls, and so he hunted the books. He sent spirits into Linden that deceived people into believing the book was cursed, killing thousands with plagues and terrorizing them with signs and wonders. Men tried to destroy the book to appease the spirits but mourned when they saw that it was indestructible. The book was hidden until it was lost."

"But why did my aunt leave it behind?" Mabel mused.

"She was blinded. The book was meant for you and no other."

"But enough of the past," said Capella. "Only the future matters now. Jezul will slay the Serpent when the last nation is set free, and the Seen will join the Unseen once more. Zaphon will descend to Earth, and the sons and daughters of men will shine like stars forever."

"That sounds amazing," said Mabel quietly, staring into space.

"But it won't happen without you."

The girl looked dumbfounded. "Why me?"

"You have been chosen," said Aurèle, "to break the darkness over Linden."

"By who?"

"The one who wrote the book," said the angel. "Why? I cannot say. It is for him to know and he alone. But there's something in you that he sees. The book is written in our language, and you've been given the wisdom of our tongue. It will release its light at the sound of your voice."

> *Of you, it is said,*
> *"Hear the voice that comes from the dreamer,*
> *From the daughter that needs a redeemer;*
> *She stands and cries on the white stone,*
> *She stands in death, but not alone."*

"You have been chosen," Aurèle repeated, "but the calling is yours to accept."

He gestured for Mabel to follow and headed for the crystal rings, each large enough for two angels to pass side by side and removed the star that was tied to his neck. The cords sparkled as they gave it into his hand. Aurèle opened the star and tipped its light that poured like water onto one of the rings. Flames erupted around the crystal and filled the opening with fire. He released a trickle onto a second circle, which burned like the first and closed the star.

"When you pass through the light," Aurèle told Mabel as he stood between the rings, "you will leave this world and enter the Seen." At these words, a worried look crossed his face. "You haven't eaten. Though your body is strong in this place, you will be weak in the world of men."

He stretched out the star and pressed it to her lips. An ecstasy thrived in Mabel's being, recharging her every fiber with feelings whose meanings she couldn't fathom, and she came back to herself as though rising from the sun.

"You have been restored."

"Th-thank you," Mabel murmured, her mind lingering on the star that he returned to the cords around his neck.

"When you pass through the fire on the left," said Aurèle, "you will continue the path of your calling, but not alone. You will arrive in Carnecia, the king's castle by the sea—and find those who will love you as their own. Break their chains, and they will fight for you."

"Who are they?" said Mabel numbly. The peace from the star was fading, and it was sinking in that she had nothing to return to.

"Those whom the Raptor reveals. When you find the weapon fashioned against you, you will find yourself. Seven is your number."

"And the other ring?"

"You'll return to your old life. The book will be taken from you and given to another."

Mabel watched absently as a meteor plunged into the depths of space. How suddenly it appeared, and how brightly it burned. Yet no matter which way it chose to fly, darkness would be its fate. How quickly it vanished.

"Thank you for what you did, for me and Issy," Mabel whispered, and her curved lips trembled. "But I'm not like you." She held the bag loosely in her hand and stepped toward the ring on her right.

"Mabel," said Capella softly, "why do you say this?"

The girl stopped a few feet from the fire and looked back over her shoulder. "Because you're perfect, and I'm not. All your names . . . You're not afraid of anything and I'm—"

"—priceless. We fought and died for you, Mabel. And would do it again."

The girl said nothing, seized by the burning feeling in her throat.

"This tower is called Demacci, which means 'tomorrow,'" said Capella. "We come here to pass through the rings, into the universe, to accept our callings and never look back. Tomorrow is the only thing that matters. We must forget the past and all that lies with it."

"Easy for you to say," said Mabel hoarsely. "There's nothing you've done, nothing you have to forget."

She had fought off the tears for days, vowing to be strong. It's what Gigi would have wanted. But she could fight them no longer, and clear drops of rain fell from the clouds in her eyes. She cried for herself. There was no one left to cry for her.

Mabel told the angels about her past through feeble sobs; once they saw who she was, they would realize that she could do nothing.

"None of that matters," said Capella after a while.

"How can't it?" said Mabel, angry at the hope that was sweeping through her. *I know what I am*, said a voice in her head. *Let me accept it.*

"Even if you were perfect, it wouldn't matter," said Aurèle. "Lavian was perfect, and see how he fell? He loved himself and dwelt on his feats, his triumphs, and how he shook kingdoms with his power. But he became proud and chose a path of destruction. Even a perfect creature can fall. Forget what is behind—good or bad, perfect and imperfect—and press ahead. There is tomorrow, daughter, and no yesterday.

"Look at the rings! You have two different tomorrows. One will take you back to the way things were before, the other will give you life."

Mabel retreated a few steps and looked at the ring before her. She would return to school the outcast, more so now than ever, certain that Jay and Issy would be terrified of her. And that made it hurt the worse. She and Issy had made plans to live together after they finished school. But Mabel knew that would never happen now. She had seen the terror in Issy's eyes, a deep-seated fear that went beyond everything that had happened—it was a fear of Mabel herself. The girl had become an orphan with nowhere to go. It was the life that never was.

Mabel looked at the ring to her left, afraid as she watched it burn, not knowing what would be her fate. *But if it offers the chance to live, wouldn't it be worth it? To feel alive and not simply exist?* The girl slung the bag over her shoulder, turned, and walked toward the other ring.

"Mabel," said Aurèle.

"Yeah . . ."

"These are the twilight days of time, the hours before the night gives way forever. You will face spirits, demons, and fallen angels, the gods of this age and their magic. They will war against you, but where there's death, there is life and where there's darkness, there is light that's greater still."

There was a long silence, and the way the angels stood reminded Mabel of the first time she had seen them in the forest. She held their gaze a moment longer then drew herself up and walked through the fire to Carnecia. The flames vanished, and she was gone.

Aurèle walked over to the ring on the right, placed his hand in the fire, and the flames disappeared. Capella came to his side, and Degasi and Eyewing joined them. Together they strode to the wall and peered down at the Earth as though searching for a jewel that was brighter than the stars.

CHAPTER 4

RISE OF THE TITANS

Clouds ebbed along a stone fortress floating in the heavens, battlements lined with Dark Angels that looked like flies in the rays of a silver moon—one with a light of its own. The stronghold rose like a mountain, culminating in a throne room perched on its summit. Lavian stood inside the chamber, illuminated by the molten moonbeams that fell through long, narrow gaps in the wall. The floor was littered with crowns that were cursed, orbs and weapons of magic that were strewn among the altars. The Serpent's upper body was flesh once more, blood oozing from the gashes in his shoulder. He was staring through one of the slits into space, and the angels with him dared not speak.

"The girl will walk again in the Seen," said Lavian at last. He turned his orange eyes away from the opening and faced the angels, assembled before columns of violet flame that ranged the length of the chamber. "*Yessss*, and will carry the book. . . . She is worthless and has nothing to live for. . . . *tssss* . . . She will do the will of Jezul."

"Have the spirits seen her?" said an angel, whose voice whipped like the wind. The fire burned brightly behind him, but his body did not glow in the reflection of the flame.

"Yes . . . she goes to the house of the king. But why has she been sent? Do I not know? Jezul cannot break his promises . . . *tssss* . . .

and this makes him predictable, and this will be his undoing. He has given Eva his word—'Yava ilys A avi yú; yava ilys A vurstel yú,'"* said Lavian in a quiet, seething voice, "and so the girl comes for Eva."

"The girl is weak," jeered another. "Too soon will the book be taken from her."

"*Yessss,* too soon," said Lavian, slithering to a black crystal ring that towered upright in the center of the room. "I will raise the Titans, and they will give the book to me."

There came a long hiss from the angels, mingled with low and venomous curses.

"Time is short," snapped Lavian. "The queen would slay the girl, but my spirit will deceive her . . . *yessss,* with the truth that speaks a lie. But deception will only give us until nightfall of the morrow."

The Serpent scanned the line of angels, his tongue flickering in and out, as though he could see clearly in the darkness. His head turned in the direction of his throne. "Antares!"

A dark figure, outlined by his sweeping wings, stepped away from one of the fires and came to the Serpent.

"Summon the Titans," Lavian told the angel. "Send them to the waters at the northernmost edge of the Earth. *Yessss,* tempt them with power, and they will do my will. Now take mine."

The Snake grabbed Antares behind the neck, pressed his forehead against the angel's, and said,

> *Leave my domain*
> *And pass through the pain,*
> *To the place of the living tomb.*
> *Show the world the Dragon's authority,*
> *Lifting the Titans' gloom;*
> *You will, commanding my authority,*
> *Unseal the Titans' doom.*

---

* Never will I leave you; never will I forsake you.

Antares opened his mouth, and Lavian breathed out, releasing a pale vapor the angel inhaled. The Serpent let go, wheeled around, and touched the crystal. "Dên e lleyag wei näkunse lavium,"* he said, and the ring was engulfed in a purple blaze.

"Go quickly!" said Lavian. The angel bowed, walked through the ring, and disappeared in a swirl of flame.

The Serpent stared at the cold and vacant ring, glittering, drunk on its own magic.

"My lord," called an evil voice, trembling as though it could not contain itself any longer. "We beg you, kill the girl before the Raptor—"

"I will not yet take her life," said Lavian quietly. "The books cannot be destroyed, and seizing them only delays the hour of judgment. To be truly free, we must break the prophecy."

"But it is written, 'Deos raima jores etorum.'"†

"*Fools!*"

Lavian had risen on his tail and was shrieking at them all. "I know what is written . . . and more! Did I not live in Zaphon and climb Mount Deo? Do I not know the secrets of light? Listen, you villains, devils, and blackhearted rakes!

> *The words of Jezul have been spoken,*
> *They live as one and never lie.*
> *But Fallen sons! If one's broken—*
> *Each prophecy ringing truth will die!*

"I will play the girl," said Lavian in a low and violent voice, his fury subsiding as quickly as it had come. "*Yessss,* I have my plans for her—I will deceive her into giving me the crown, and when I wear it upon my head, the word will be broken."

"But the prophecy of our doom . . . Will it break with it?"

---

* To the place our offspring lie.
† God's word endures forever.

Lavian only hissed, but the angels shouted at the gleam in his eyes.

———•◆•———

The moon glared coldly over the Desert of Cusas. The mists had been vanquished from the sky, and a few clouds hovered like ghosts beneath the stars. Images of gods, carved into cliffs that overlooked the bone-colored sand, were gazing into the night. Fires flickered in the caves beneath them, the homes of witches, soothsayers, and spell makers of old.

Suddenly, a wall of violet flame roared across the desert and Antares emerged. His body flashed as though it had been struck by lightning, and the angel burned, screaming before he became like a stone. Trails of smoke rose from his frame, and a vapor, darker and thicker than the rest, escaped through his mouth and was swept away by the wind.

The vapor traveled east, separated from the winds, and entered a viper that was so white it seemed to be glowing in the sand. The snake's eyes changed from yellow to black, and a blue light radiated from its mouth. Winds swirled around the snake that became a whirlwind, lifted the creature, and carried it toward the cliffs.

"Vora!"

A young witch, seated by a fire in a cave, pulled back her veil and raised her eyes. A hideous and gray-bearded man, wearing a black coat covered in charms, beckoned her. The woman rose and joined him at the mouth of the cave.

"Tonight, the Titans rise," said the man and pointed to a whirlwind that was following a moonlit path across the desert. "They will take vengeance upon the nations."

"Are you sure, Amangar?"

"Yes, or I am not the Enchanter of Savér."

"Praise the stars," said Vora. But she clutched her mantle, even so, unable to mask the fear in her voice.

The enchanter murmured as he read the stars, and a twisted smile quivered beneath his beard. "Tonight, the tragedy unfolds," he said softly. "The phantom lives and the puppets die."

Soon the howling funnel could be heard, and Vora shrank back as it climbed the slopes.

"It's coming for us!" she cried, but Amangar snatched her wrist and dragged her even closer to the edge.

"Be still!"

Something had flown from the whirlwind with a spark of blue light, something that had not avoided the enchanter's eye, now slithering among the rocks below. The storm halted, seething, its walls full of sand. Once more, Vora stepped back, but Amangar would not release her. The viper glided inside the cave along a crevice in the wall.

"Kneel with me and worship!" shouted the enchanter in Vora's ear. He threw a forearm across his face as the winds tore the charms from his cloak. "Appease the god within, or he will destroy us!"

The pair fell to the floor, and Vora bowed before the funnel. Amangar hesitated and watched the viper strike the witch, sinking its fangs through her leg. She screamed as Amangar pinned her to the ground, the serpent slithering under her clothes, toward her head. It coiled itself around her neck and plunged its fangs through her spine.

Vora stopped moving, and this time, it was Amangar who was afraid. He scrambled off the witch as she began to rise, floating, her body as stiff as a wooden beam. Within seconds, she was standing upright, sand pelting her as she embraced the whirlwind. She turned toward Amangar, her hair snapped wildly in front of her blood-smeared face. In one powerful stride, Vora seized Amangar by the throat and lifted him with a strength not her own. She flung him into the vortex and moved into the cave, where magicians and mediums cowered against the wall.

Vora walked through the fires, whose flames fluttered on the floor. The wind tossed their smoking ashes like fireflies as she swore, "Do not warn the king or you will die!"

It was not her voice that sounded, but that of Antares. A blue light shone in her mouth, and the viper tightened its grip around her neck. "Let this be a sign to you!"

She stared at the only magician that faced her in defiance, held out her arm, and yelled,

> *Cut down, in the name of the Serpent,*
> *This worker of darkness and lies!*
> *Drag him to the pit, you vermin—*
> *To the place where the worm never dies!*

Worms burst from the magician's belly, mouth, and ears. Those around him pressed themselves harder against the wall, as though by doing this they could pass through the stone. Spiders fell from the ceiling as beetles rushed across the floor, smothering the magician who collapsed in a quivering heap.

"You are under a curse!" shouted Vora to the rest. "Reveal the Titans have risen, and you will suffer the same!"

They fell to worship Vora, but the witch only hissed as she spun around, ran through the cave, and jumped into the arms of the storm.

It was hours before the vortex had crossed the desert and dissipated in front of the boulders at the base of the Na Fa Cliffs. The sand that it had been carrying drizzled to the ground. A shadowy figure emerged that looked anxiously at the red horizon. Lowering her gaze, Vora raised her arms and shouted over the fallen rocks, "Nomtîya od Extruzzan . . . Evaci cre!"

The boulders rose, suspended ten feet in the air, as the witch gave a long, continuous breath. A pale mist came from her lungs and passed beneath the rocks, where it thickened like fog and entered the earth. Minutes passed; the desert quaked, and the sand peeled back in waves to reveal what looked like the figure of a man. He got slowly to his feet, his naked body lined with scars, dressed in the muscles of an animal, and clothed in human flesh. His eyes and teeth were those of a lion. A mane, woven in braids, hung past his waist.

The sands shifted again. More bodies rose with faces resembling the predators of the Earth—lions, hyenas, wolves, and jackals. Those who were the first to rise pulled more to their feet, and soon three hundred bodies were standing before the witch, caked with earth, swords clenched in their fists. They appeared to be unaffected by the cold, and despite their heavy breathing, no steam escaped from their mouths.

"Titans!" cried Vora. "Come forth!"

No sooner had the creatures moved out from under the boulders into the impending dawn than Vora dropped her arms and the rocks fell with a mighty crash. The masses came to a halt, but several Titans continued forward and closed in around the witch.

"How long has it been?" said Raine, a growl fluttering in his throat. He was the first to have risen and was nose to nose with Vora.

"Nine years—"

"Years!" shouted Raine, his voice rising in a catlike howl. "You were to hold us until the judgment passed and no more!"

"Cut her down," snarled the Titan on his right. Raine stepped back and raised his sword.

"*Beasts!*"

Lightning flashed in Vora's fist, and the Titan froze. "I'm not the witch you see with your putrid eyes!" she shouted and leveled the bolt under Raine's chin. "I am Antares, angel of Lavian! That night the Destroyer came for your lives and you groveled for the stargazers to save you, Lavian answered and hung a new star in the sky. They used its power to hide you with the dead, but he kept the star from returning so no one could release you until he needed—"

"I don't care what he needs!" Raine fumed. His muscles twitched as if he was about to pounce on the witch, lightning and all. "We serve no one!"

"Arrogant fools!" shrieked Antares through the witch. "You thought you were strong and could rule the Earth! But when you faced the Destroyer—yes, my brother from the Abyss!—you were powerless against him. Why? Because your mothers were human animals, and dust flows in your veins!

"I came to give you power—to war against angels and become like your fathers. If it were not for my god, I would let you slay me . . ."

Vora lowered her arm and relaxed her hand. The lightning was gone.

"And watch the power slip through your hands."

The Titans said nothing as Raine glowered at the witch, who cast a feverish glance at the eastern sky. Twilight was slipping into dawn.

"I don't have much time!" said the desperate voice of Antares. "Enter the fire and go to the northernmost edge of the Earth. There you will drink from the water that calls you and become like us."

"At what price?" Raine demanded.

"Go!" cried the witch. "Go now! Or become the hunted once more!"

The first rays of the sun struck Vora's face, and her body exploded into a pillar of purple flame. The viper crashed to the ground. The Titans gazed into the fire, waiting for Raine to determine their fate.

"Come, Andromede," he said finally, facing a Titan with a pantherlike skull. "Into the fire."

"We know not the price," said Andromede in a cold, cruel voice.

"There's a price either way! Reject the power and live as slaves beneath the angels, or take it—"

"And do the Serpent's will," finished Andromede. "But what is that?"

"It doesn't matter!" snapped Raine. "We drink from the water and become like our fathers, then do the bidding of the Serpent. For a time. But we will war against him and break his chains, for I will serve no one."

He turned and bellowed to the rest, "Today we become gods!"

The Titans shouted and thrust their swords into the air. Raine bolted through the fire, and the rest sprinted after him in single file, shrieking as though expecting to be set ablaze. The viper waited until the last was gone, entered the fire, and vanished with the flames.

CHAPTER 5

IN THE CASTLE OF CARNECIA

F ire erupted beside a fountain in the middle of an empty
courtyard, and Mabel emerged from the flames, which
disappeared the moment she stepped out onto the marble
floor.

The girl shivered in the cold November air, still immersed in
the world from which she had come. The Citadel had vanished the
moment she stepped through the ring, and a company of angels had
escorted her through space. There had been no stars, only planets,
and something like ice had popped beneath their feet, sending
moonbeams that marked their path through a network of gateways,
doors, tunnels, and columns of fire that hovered in darkness. Some
were guarded by angels and others by demons that looked at her
with hungry eyes. On and on they had walked, Mabel with the wild
feeling they were moving through time until they reached a column
of fire, where a bloodstone angel had gestured them to halt. The
flame swayed, and the angel made way for Mabel to pass through
the fire.

The cry of a seagull shook the girl from her reverie. She could
hear crashing waves in the distance and inhaled deeply as though
noticing the smell of salt for the first time. Mabel scanned the
perimeter of the yard, surrounded by archways and walls and turrets

beyond. An imposing bell tower was lord over them all, crowned with golden spires whose windows and arches were filled with stone. A few servants stirred somewhere in the halls, the rhythmic sounds of their brooms echoing around the courtyard. Mabel put back her face, searching for the Citadel in the heavens, but found only a clear sky kissed by the dawn.

She looked down at her hands and gasped. Her skin was shining with soft light, and she patted her face, feeling the warmth again in her cheeks. Mabel touched her eyes and nearly shouted; the voids were gone. But a chill was creeping over her as the light faded away.

She was in the house of the king with no idea what to do. Legends flooded her mind of a ruthless man that fought for power and called for the heads of whomever he pleased. Isn't that how he, Sören, made Hadesha his queen, by hanging his wife on these very walls? What would Mabel say? That angels had sent her to break someone's chains?

"And look at me!" Mabel groaned. Although her body had been restored, her cloak was ruined by the sparks and debris in the forest. Her hair was a mess. She was angry with herself for not asking the angels more questions, for being so desperate that she had come to Carnecia in utter disarray.

Mabel glared at the fountain where a sculpture of Centrum Stella stood in the middle of an enormous stone basin, right arm broken off, face contorted. The tail of a crocodile came from the back of his head, descended into the water, and rose out of it again like a curling wave. A shark's mouth was carved in the tip of the tail, eels dangling from its jaws like tongues. Statues of what looked like slave fighters stood around the edge of the basin, each facing Centrum Stella and wielding swords of *fire*. Mabel's heart leaped, and she edged closer to get a better look, noticing that each of the men had the same series of scars on his forearm.

She had reached out to the nearest statue when a voice sighed like the wind.

"Sheeee . . ."

The blood pounded in Mabel's ears, and she glanced around. Crows flew over the western wall and filled the sky, their hoarse caws ricocheting off the walls as the flock split: masses zoomed across the courtyard and disappeared through the windows of the palace while the rest attacked Mabel, tearing at her hair and clothes.

"Get off!"

Mabel sprinted for cover down a nearby hall, the birds ripping at her bag when a woman's voice yelled over the throbbing cries. "Dov nesul!"

Instantly, the birds left the girl, who slumped to the ground, clutching her bag.

"The girl!" said the same voice. Mabel looked up to see the queen fly around the corner with her king and guards in black armor. Mabel had never seen either before, but there could be no mistaking the monarchs of Linden as they charged down the hall: Hadesha was tall and fair, with a flawless face and black paint along her eyes that made her age impossible to guess. She wore a tight dress, adorned with ostasi leaves, black hair falling in a single braid past her waist. Sören had golden hair and was dressed in white linens, covered in diamonds that sparkled with every move that he made. They both looked livid.

Mabel scrambled to her feet, her face turning pink, but at least she had an excuse for looking like a wreck. *I'll blame it on the birds!*

She slung the bag over her shoulder, ran her fingers through her hair, and had just dipped into curtsy when Sören seized her by the arm.

"Come!" said the king in a brusque voice.

Mabel winced at the pain from his steely grip, shocked at the frail man's strength, then did her best to smile. "Your Maj—"

"Silence!" hissed Sören, with a squeeze that forced Mabel to bite her lip. "We can't speak here!"

Hadesha clapped her hands; and the guards stepped back for

the king who nearly dragged Mabel up the hall, into the courtyard, and down another, the rest marching behind them as they made their way toward the bell tower. The girl wanted to know where they were going but was afraid to ask as they hurtled toward a stone door beside the statue of a hydra, a sword through every skull. Hadesha shot past them all and cried, "Engorii!" She threw a hand at the door, which opened by itself.

Magic! thought Mabel frantically. *She's a witch!*

Hadesha stepped aside as Sören shoved Mabel through the opening, guards at her heels, then passed and closed the door behind them.

Mabel struggled to see as they sped down a narrow corridor, dimly lit by torches along the wall. Hooded figures came out of an adjoining passage ahead and faced them through the veiling shadows. Sören stopped with the girl whose stomach churned at the sight of the wasted white noses and wrinkled chins, poking out from beneath their hoods. Hadesha shoved her way through the entourage to meet them, muttering under her breath as they put their heads together. The figure nearest the queen had a bone-white vulture perched on his shoulder that stuck its head among the rest as though it too were part of the council.

They suddenly grew quiet and looked up together. "Let's go!" barked Hadesha. The company moved forward, joined by the hooded figures, where the corridor curved to the right and ended in another stone door.

The queen halted, grabbed a torch from the blackened wall, and spoke to the one burning beside the door. "Keep watch!"

"Either souls in the Seen or spirits in a dream," said a voice from the flame. Mabel's heart was pounding harder than ever, the girl wondering if she was going mad. But no one else seemed fazed as Sören spoke to the door that opened at his command. There was no light on the other side. The hooded figures filed through the opening, black cloaks flowing behind them. One looked over his

shoulder at Mabel before entering the darkness, and the thought of being trapped with them in what looked like a dungeon brought the girl out in such a sweat that her clothes stuck to her body in seconds.

"Your Majesty, where are you—"

Sören shoved her again and sent her flying through the door.

"Wait here," Hadesha said to the guards. She followed Sören through the door, which was thrown shut behind them.

Inside, Mabel jumped up as Hadesha flung her torch against the wall. Flames rushed around the circular room in both directions, and the temperature dropped. They were standing in a damp dungeon, empty but for the scattered chains, and Mabel wondered why the queen was scanning the area so carefully. Apparently satisfied, she faced Mabel and stretched out her hand.

"The book," she demanded.

How does she know I have it? Mabel wondered, her hand dropping to her bag.

"Now!"

Mabel wrenched out the book and thrust it in the queen's hands. The figures behind her backed away until their backs touched the wall, flames licking their bodies but their bodies not burning.

"Worthless prophets!" The queen looked over her shoulder at the one with the vulture. "You too, Ruel? Come here, coward!"

The man stepped slowly toward Hadesha, the firelight revealing his deeply lined cheeks, though his eyes remained hidden by the shadow of his hood—one that Mabel prayed he would not remove. Her eyes shifted to the vulture and widened. It had the head of a fish, and its skin was split along its chest, revealing scales underneath. It peered at her intently then gazed down at the book.

Hadesha's lip curled at the look on Mabel's face. "The spirits need bodies," she said, stroking the bird, "and take those they may."

Hadesha relaxed slightly, apparently satisfied with the book in hand, but frowned at the girl. "There are spirits everywhere," she said in a different voice. "They pass unimpeded through our world, through sea and sky—"

"Except through stone," murmured Sören.

"But I know their secrets—that an unbroken ring of fire allows me to look into their world and see what can't be seen. . . ."

Her hand slid down the back of the vulture once more, and then fell at her side.

"What's your name?" she said abruptly.

"Mabel, Your Majesty."

Her curtsy ended with another jerk from the king.

"How did you get the book?" he said, twisting her arm.

Mabel hesitated. *But what if they think I'm a—*

"Don't lie to me!"

And the girl spewed her story, afraid the queen could read her mind. "But I'm not a witch!" she said desperately when she told them how she had read the book. "I mean, I don't think I am. I don't know how the light came out, I never practiced magic or anything, and nobody in my family—"

"Go on!"

"Then we jumped through the light. My friend and I ran into the woods when we saw lightning strike my grandma's house, and Lavian came out of the—"

"The *Snake* came for you!" said Hadesha. The flames shrank, and the temperature dropped further in the chamber.

"Yeah—"

Mabel gasped as Sören tightened his grip.

"Impossible!" he breathed, sounding more scared than amazed. "How were you not destroyed?"

"Because of the angels," said Mabel hurriedly. "The good ones. They came for us."

"Did they?" said Hadesha tersely, casting a meaningful look at Sören who released the girl. But Ruel advanced and seized her wrist, just as the blood was returning to her fingers, and rammed back her sleeve.

"I'm not hurt!" said Mabel, wanting him to let go. But the prophet examined her forearm, decayed fingers creeping across her skin like the legs of an enormous spider. "Really!"

"And what, pray, did the angels tell you?" asked Ruel in a waspish voice. He let go and stepped back to the queen's side.

"They said that our country's held in darkness. I mean, you can't see it because it's in the Unseen . . . this other world that you have to walk through fire to get to—"

Hadesha's face darkened with the look of one who's being told what she already knows.

"Anyway, this darkness holds our people in death, and that book," Mabel said, pointing to the one in Hadesha's hand, "is the only thing that can break it—"

"Enough!" boomed the queen. "I've heard this fairy tale before!"

"It's true!" said Mabel. "I've seen the darkness and light of the book!"

The queen drew so close that Mabel could feel her breath. "I too have seen the darkness," she whispered, her eyes boring into Mabel's, "but never the Light."

A tremor went through the prophets. An outbreak of gurgles and whimpers came from beneath their hoods.

"Your Highness!"

Hadesha whipped around and slashed the air with her arm. "The next who speaks dies!" A sphere of violet light welled in her hand, and she held it out threateningly before them. No one moved, but the rasping grew louder.

Hadesha turned to Mabel again. She snapped open the book and almost threw it in Mabel's arms. "Release it!"

Not knowing what else to do, Mabel looked down at the words

and began to read. "Yeul raima id enå sollum dên moj pette cy lunan vur moj gatai . . ."[*]

The writing came alive with the same golden light that Mabel had seen at her house, and the girl no longer felt alone. She let go of the book, which floated before her, the light spilling from the pages onto the floor, splitting into threads and snaking out to the walls. The prophets pulled their hoods down to their chins; the lips of the queen tightened. Then without warning, the light exploded into a cyclone that devoured the queen's flames and the room became like the sun. Mabel could feel its power as her mind slipped into another realm, unable to see the prophets stumbling or hear the monarchs gasping. There were only the words of the book and nothing more. "A vor pumë diyadi . . . conseron moj atim, O Deo. . . ."[†]

"STOP IT!" shrieked the king, who had grabbed Mabel by the collar and was shaking her violently. The girl's eyes were torn away from the book, and she came back to the room. The light was screaming, shredding the walls and consuming the prophets without a trace. The green lights of their souls vanished through the floor. Instinctively, Mabel swung a fist and smacked Sören in the jaw. He let go and stumbled backward, and Mabel panicked at what she had done. A thousand apologies raced through her mind, but her tongue wouldn't move.

I'll make it stop. . . .

But the queen rallied first, snatching the book where it hovered and closing it with a *crack*. The light slowed, the dungeon stopped trembling, the screaming sounds weakened, and soon there were mere flecks of light that circled the room and melted away. The eyes of the queen smoldered a moment longer and then went cold.

"Lunan od jørnesh," she said, stowing the book under her arm. The violet light in her hand turned pale, separated from her palm, and hovered in front of her face. Sören stood frozen beside her. Ruel

---

[*] Your word is a lamp to my feet and light for my path.
[†] I have suffered much . . . preserve my life, O God.

crept up to the light, his head against the vulture who appeared as calm as before.

Mabel's eyes darted between the king and queen and then to the place where the prophets had died. How could she have known that would happen? The light had never hurt anyone before. The girl felt faint; the chains seemed to be swimming on the floor. Mabel opened her mouth to beg for mercy when Hadesha spoke into the shadows.

"The book can end the Darkness," she said in a toneless voice as though her mind was not her own. "Lavian will come for it and destroy us. . . . The gods are powerful, and we cannot stand against them. Our only choice is which one we'll serve."

Hadesha looked at Mabel as though she had just realized she was there. The queen dropped the book and drew a dagger from her waistband. "Weak and helpless dog! You've brought a curse upon us!"

"No!" screamed Mabel, throwing out her arms and leaping back.

But before Hadesha could strike, the vulture sank its talons through Ruel's shoulder, and the prophet grabbed the queen by the wrist. Mabel relaxed enough to breathe, her eyes glued to the knife. "Listen!" hissed Ruel when the queen jerked her arm. It was no longer the prophet that spoke, but the bloodcurdling voice of another. A wild light flickered in Sören's eyes, but he made no move. "She has not brought a curse upon us. Far from it! She is the key to the crown."

Mabel watched, light-headed, as the bird controlled Ruel. Sören said nothing, and Hadesha yielded, her white knuckles loosening around the hilt. "I've tried everything," she said bitterly, "but anyone that's tried to remove it has died. No blade can kill her, no spell . . . You know what it says!"

"Yes," said Ruel darkly.

The life by no means can be riven,
Under the crown that's freely given,
Willingly, and not—

"Silence!" said the queen. "Must you tell me the words I can't get out of my head?" She jerked her arm free and pointed the blade at Mabel. "How's the brat going to give me the crown?"

Mabel wanted to tell them that she didn't know anything about a crown, but was afraid to set the queen off. She had lowered her dagger as Ruel whispered in her ear.

"So," she said softly to Mabel, "for whom did the angels send you?"

"I don't know," said Mabel quickly. "They didn't tell me."

"But they gave you power?"

"I don't know what you mean! They just told me I was gonna help someone else."

"Break their chains, isn't that so?" said Ruel in the same hideous voice.

Mabel swallowed. Hadesha looked as though she wanted nothing more than to wrap one around her neck.

"See how the gods favor my queen? The girl has been given the power to remove the blade." The vulture was staring into Hadesha's eyes, who looked spellbound as the voice pressed on. "You can release Eva and offer her the one thing—the only thing—that she'll take for the crown."

Ruel picked the book off the ground, the bird never pulling its eyes away from the queen's.

"With the crown Eva saves herself, but with the book she gives life to many."

"I will become the goddess of the Earth," said Hadesha distantly, her face void of expression, "and take back what is mine."

"But you must first wear the crown!" said Ruel. "Eva will not give it to you without the book *and* the girl. It's useless without the one who can release the light."

"We will use the girl," Hadesha conceded, and the vulture looked away. The queen batted her eyes and sheathed her dagger.

An invisible fist let go of Mabel's throat, but not for long.

"Rochet analu!" said the queen and blew through the floating light. It became smoke, and the room went black. Mabel could feel it forcing itself into her lungs though she tried not to breathe. She heard Hadesha's voice from far way, but had no idea what she was saying. Poison was coursing through her veins, her heart beating slower.

"I don't have . . . any power . . . ," Mabel muttered and fell to the floor. A trail of smoke came from her nose and returned to Hadesha's hand, glowing once more. A slow time passed before the king spoke.

"If the darkness is broken," he said in a cold, unsteady voice, "our power will be destroyed."

"Without the crown, Eva dies," spat Hadesha. "Once she has the book, Lavian will come for her and kill her before she can set Linden free." The queen shot a revolted look at Mabel. "And the one who reads."

"Kamaci," said Sören, and Mabel's body rose into the air. She hovered on her back, eyes closed. Hadesha took the bag that had fallen on the ground, dropped the book inside, and slipped it over her shoulder.

"Let's go." The queen waved a hand at the door, which gave way, and disappeared into the corridor. The others followed, Mabel floating behind.

Hadesha dismissed the guards, walked back down the corridor, and turned up the passage from which the prophets had appeared a short time before. There were no torches along the walls, but the light of the queen drifted like a breeze ahead of them. They reached a spiral staircase, which they took to a landing that was halfway up the bell tower, and a door opened to reveal an empty chamber with stone-filled windows. The others stood back as Mabel's body glided into a place in the center of the room, followed by Hadesha who opened an arm toward the wall. A stream of fire shot from her hand and enveloped the room in a blaze. She looked around, clapped her hands, and the flames swirled out of sight.

"Tonight we return," Hadesha said to Sören and Ruel as she returned to the landing, "and take the girl with the book to Eva. Tonight, when Jupiter rises."

"Why did you give yourself to him?" Ruel grumbled, who was speaking in his own voice again. "Now we must wait."

"What else was I to do? Lavian lusts for the crown as much as I. Our magic was not strong enough to keep him away."

"We're wasting time!" said Sören. "Lavian's forces are nigh!"

Hadesha cast another look at Mabel, closed the door, and led them down the stairs.

The sun had just cleared the walls of Carnecia, the parapets glittering under a heavy layer of frost. Soldiers filled the yard outside the armory, their breath rising like smoke around their helms, decked with purple crests. They wore raven-black cuirasses and carried shields marked with the Linden bear. Before them stood the king and queen.

"A sword will rise against us!" shouted Sören, his words echoing over them. "But it will fail!"

The men roared and pounded their spears, no one noticing the eyes of the king, eyes that betrayed an all-consuming terror of the mind. The general raised his shield, and the men grew still.

"Tonight!" shouted Hadesha, "I will wear the Crown of Creation! I will hold the wind and the sea. . . . The mountains will bow to me! Now let's stand together!"

And the men chanted, "A sword for the queen and for Sören!"

The king nodded to his general, who began dispersing the troops.

"Go to Mount Dominion," said Sören to a messenger on his left. "Summon the warriors from the nine tribes of Múl."

"My lord!" said the soldier, and he bowed and turned away.

"*Tell them!*" the queen yelled after him. "Not to be deceived by the spirits of Lavian, those that say I will fall! Tell them to come to me, or I will send them to Avaddon!

"You!" she bellowed to another. "Go to the glaciers and bring the barbarians of Erenbedi, they that bow to Krone!"

He gave an affirming shout, wheeled his horse, and sped off, a purple cape streaming behind.

"I will summon the descendants of Zoridian," said the vulture through Ruel, "those with the spirits of Molek." The bone-colored bird let out a chilling shriek, spread its wings, and climbed over the battlements as Ruel took a long and shuddering breath.

"Lefilt ånepratus . . . balé von mocce!" cried Hadesha. Several winged creatures dove from the spires, soared across the courtyard, and alighted on her outstretched arms. They were falcons with the heads of lizards, wings covered in scales.

Ruel took two of the sinister birds, one on each arm, and said to the first, "Call the horsemen from Phycum, and they will rise from desolation." He brought the second to his quivering lips. "Fly to Cusas and bring my brothers and sisters from the caves. Tell them their time has come. They are outcasts no more." He raised his arms, and the creatures screamed as they vaulted into the air, the first soaring upward to the east and the second flying west.

Sören sent falcons to the Islands of Aeragos, for the raiders of Tar-Saul, and to the ghouls of Vatarii.

"We've summoned all who thirst for blood," said Ruel, watching the last of the reptilian birds as it faded into the horizon. "All who can arrive by nightfall."

Somewhere to the east, a bird vanished through a sunbeam, leaving ripples in the sky.

CHAPTER 6

MALEFICENT POWER INFERIOR

The Titans were kneeling on a black rock shore, panting beneath a rust-colored sky. Glacial waves pounded the rocks and sprayed the creatures in a world with no hills, earth, or sand. A veiling fog floated toward the coast and immersed the pack, whose breathing slowed and green eyes brightened. They grabbed their swords and picked themselves up from the ground, indifferent to the bitter chill.

Raine headed toward a canal that was flowing away from the ocean, the others keeping their distance as they padded after him, gazing warily from side to side. Within minutes, they had arrived at the channel and turned north where small craters marred the surface, none of which could have been larger than a pond. The figures wended their way among the gloomy depressions, some filled with water barely thicker than air, others with clouds that would shrink as though something inside had taken a sudden breath. A few were covered with black ice, impenetrable as the rocks around it. The Titans' nostrils widened, the smell of the sea overridden by a fetid metallic scent.

They were soon overcome by shadows whose origins could not be determined, shadows that mixed with the fog until it darkened like a storm. Every now and then, the creatures would venture into open skies, grasp their skulls, appearing to scream but giving only whispers, and plunge into the shadows ahead: darkness would envelop them as they gulped the swirling mists, their minds clearing in seconds, navigating the craters and leaving their world further behind. The sound of the surf weakened.

A drizzle began to fall that rinsed the dirt from the Titans, but no water ran along their swords which seemed to lengthen and bend toward space. The shadows darkened and the half-bloods could no longer tell where the sky ended and the ground began. The pack stopped as two Titans stumbled into a crater and let out airy shrieks, the water entering their skin and flowing out of their mouths like fountains. Their bodies froze, and a rotting smell emanated from a column of yellow steam.

Shining emerald eyes flickered as the Titans looked around. They began moving forward when several more fell into the pools around them, unable to see in the darkness. There were more shrieks, and the rotting smell overpowered the air.

"This is madness!" shouted a cougarlike figure with *Bloodscar* written on his neck though his voice was faint and shrill. "If we don't die in the shadows, we'll fall from the Earth. The end is near!"

The others howled their assent, their cries sounding more like muffled screams, and Raine whipped around.

"If we fall from the Earth, so be it!" he yelled savagely. But his voice too was high-pitched and hollow, and the Titans strained to hear him. He thrust his sword in the air, but only his eyes could be seen. "The sons of god are stronger than us and control our fate! We must become like them . . . their power *our* power . . . no matter the price! The next who defies me dies!"

The growls sank into silence.

Raine turned and moved forward, edging along the canal. The half-bloods narrowed their ranks to avoid the craters and hugged the bank of the channel, barely visible as the water had become darker than the atmosphere. They could no longer hear the waves hammering the shore, and their padded feet issued no sound. Nothing disturbed the silence, save the water gurgling beside them. How long they wandered, no one knew. Their minds faded. They wondered whether it was day or night.

The Titans no longer scanned their surroundings, each staring miserably at the one in front of him when the mist softened with a pale blue light. Five minutes later, they saw what appeared to be fluorescent blue veins, crisscrossing the terrain beneath their feet. The narrow streaks were filled with a clear liquid that carried millions of glowing particles. The beasts picked their way, stepping over the lines whose energy flowed through the rock like blood.

Suddenly, there was a whispering cry, and the procession stopped. The shadows fled, and the mist began to fade, allowing the Titans to gaze into a sea of stars. The heavenly orbs gleamed like diamonds and sapphires, appearing so close that Bloodscar stretched out his hand as if to pluck one from the darkness. Silence ruled with an iron fist. A hush had fallen over the water streaming down the channel. It spilled over the horizon like a waterfall, crashing into space.

The Titans left the edge of the channel and huddled together, no longer fearing the craters for they were easily seen—menacing abysses, tucked among the glowing rocks—and murmured to each other.

"An end comes to all things," said Andromede, his eyes following two comets that arched across the cosmos. "Even the Earth."

"There are secrets in this place," said Bloodscar, who leaned over and dipped his finger into a vein in the rock. The light dimmed, and the earth began to shake.

The Titans crouched and bared their fangs as Raine kicked Bloodscar's hand away. The stream instantly brightened, and the ground became still.

"We stand on the edge of worlds unknown," said Bloodscar, who got to his feet and ignored the glaring eyes that floated to full height, "in darkness everlasting."

"And where there is darkness," said a figure behind him, "there is magic."

"Which means nothing!" Raine snapped over his shoulder. "If it gives no power—"

The earth trembled and screams obliterated the silence that made the Titans cover their ears—voices magnified by a power that carried them through space. They vied with each other and came together as one.

"Titans!" said the voice. There was a fleeting silence, and the Titans lowered their hands in time to catch a dying breath.

"*Titans . . .*"

Their ears twitched as they looked at a crater beside the waterfall. Its frozen surface flashed and shattered like a mirror. A crimson light shone in the depths of the pool, its rays passing through the cracks in the ice and forming runes on the surface of the water.

"*Come, you who are blood of the Fallen . . . and dust of Earth's dust. . . .*"

The half-bloods made no move, afraid to leave the dissolving mist. But the haze stirred and formed thin wisps that slithered through the air, which Raine followed as they glided toward the pool. The rest hung back to watch, but could no longer breathe and ran to catch up with the ghostlike vapors. In less than a minute, the pack had circled around the perimeter of the pool, the mists swirling over the Titans who gazed at the signs and knelt on the edge of the crater.

"Spirit—"

"Call me god!" shouted the voice, spiking to a pitch that caused the Titans to drop their swords and let out muted howls. A column of black and bloodred water burst through the ice and showered the Titans, their bodies glowing in the crimson rain. The unchained waters thrashed.

"You are god!" cried Raine in that same thin voice. "We have come for you . . . If you slay us, so be it!"

"Give me your blood," said the voice, suddenly hushed and weak. The waters grew calm. "Do this and worship me."

The Titans cut themselves, and their blood flowed into the pool, screaming through stricken voices that made them sound all the more wretched. A trail of water rose out of the crater like a tentacle and wrapped itself around the ankle of a sallow-skinned Titan, his face like a jaguar, who fought madly as he was dragged forward until Bloodscar plunged a sword through his chest. The victim splashed into the pool and was swallowed in a plume of yellow steam. The Titans raved at the smell of death and fell facedown, calling on the water and blaspheming all other gods. And so they worshipped the water and the voice that came from it.

The Titans grew still and waited, foreheads pressed against the rock, and the voice came again. "Speak, devils. What do you desire?"

"To become like the sons of god!" Raine said feverishly. "To have their power and make war against them!"

The water churned, and a cold blue light came from within. "That which that has been given to me, I give to you. The stars of my god will heed your command. I will give you the power of the Serpent."

"We are willing!"

"Drink from my water."

The liquid in the pool rose until it was level with the rim of the crater. The Titans crawled forward, and those nearest the water placed their mouths in the pool and drank. When their bodies could hold no more, they fell back and made room for the ones behind.

The last of the beastlike men had barely finished drinking when the Titans convulsed and began writhing on their sides, vomiting between spasms. Their skin split and their bodies expanded, each growing a head taller than before. Scales appeared beneath the gashes in their flesh. The skin melted from their heads and exposed yellow fangs, but their manes held fast, sinking into their skulls that became stone. Spines thickened and eyes grew dark and scaly. Shoulder blades burst through their skin and widened like shields.

Minutes passed and the Titans got slowly to their feet, not bothering to retrieve their swords. The vapors entered the pool, but the beasts could breathe as easily as before.

"We have become like our fathers," growled Bloodscar triumphantly, a blue light proceeding from his mouth. His voice was stronger and had become the chilling sound of steel on steel. Arrogance flashed across his scaly eyes as he stretched out his arms and looked over his body. The veins had risen through his skin, and his streamline frame was swollen now, studded with muscles that were sculpted by the gods. He raised an arm and formed a fist. Lightning burst in his hand.

The others did the same and exalted themselves under the stars. Before the howls had drifted into space, however, the skin on their abdomens smoldered. The Titans grated their teeth, folded their arms, and staggered as if their insides were being incinerated. The horror subsided, and the Titans lowered their arms: numbers had been burned in their skin, just above the navel.

"Now, dogs!" said the Water. "You have not only drunk my power, but also my death. A curse flows through your veins. Give the book to the Serpent"—here the voice rose to a scream, and the ground trembled—*"or your blood is forfeit me!"* The voice subsided until it was a little more than a whisper. "Every day that you fail to deliver the book, one of you must die at dawn's first light. Each according to his number."

The water suddenly went dark, and the crater looked like a black hole. The few Titans with lightning in their hands relaxed their fingers, and the bolts vanished.

"What book?" said Andromede, staring down at the number 2 that glimmered on his body.

"Gaze into my waters!" said the voice. The surface of the pool became like a mirror, and the book that Mabel found shone in its reflection. Moments later, the water thrashed, and the image disappeared.

"Where does it lie?" called a Titan.

"In the house of Sören it lies. Kill the king and queen of Linden." The water again became a mirror, and this time, the faces of the monarchs appeared. "Spill their blood, and the earth will open to receive them. Throw the book into the earth, and Lavian will find it in Avaddon. Throw the book into the earth, and you will live."

Before the voice had died away, a pale bird appeared out of thin air, some forty feet above the Titans. Dark ripples followed the creature as though it were gliding through water, ripples that quickly disappeared. The bird let out a screech as it circled the crater once, then twice, before diving into the pool and shattering the faces of Sören and Hadesha. The surface grew calm and slowly turned green, the soul of another bleeding through its essence, and the bird was seen no more.

"Speak, spirit of mine," said the Water. A lone, cold, and somewhat-broken voice answered from its depths.

"Hurry!" it said. "I was in Carnecia. . . . Hadesha was about to slay the girl, so I told her the girl can remove the blade."

"Fool!" shrieked the Water. Its voice split into thousands, each screaming to be heard. The water churned as the Titans covered their ears, howling. "The queen will use the girl to wear the crown!"

"It was the will of the Serpent!" said the lone voice. "But I did not tell her the secret of the girl!"

A gruesome cry gurgled deep beneath the surface and was suddenly cut off. For a few seconds, everything was still.

"Go now, Titans!" seethed the Water. "You must reach Carnecia before Jupiter rises, before the one who wears the crown is released. For she is more powerful than you."

"But you've made us like gods!" shouted Raine. "Who on Earth is greater?"

A freakish roar erupted, legions laughing over legions with

hatred and glee. "Fiends!" they screamed wildly, vacillating in and out of pitch. "There is a power you know nothing about, one trapped in Carnecia. A power you cannot overcome. Run for your lives, arrogant half-bloods! Arrive before Jupiter rises, or face the wrath of the crown!"

Another round of maniacal laughter shook the air.

"Enter the waters of the sea," said the voices before dropping to whisper, "and they will carry you to Carnecia."

The green light dimmed, and the water froze.

The Titans were breathing hard, nostrils flaring, incensed at becoming slaves for a power inferior to another. No one made a sound as they left the crater and dove into the canal. The current in the waterway reversed its course and flowed toward the sea. Faster the current raced, hurling their bodies like arrows shot from a bow. They began to glow crimson as the stars descended and lent their powers to the Titans. Minutes later, they zipped out of the channel, into the ocean, and the half-bloods were carried away.

CHAPTER 7

THE FACES OF MEN

Visions flitted through Mabel's mind as she floated over the stone floor, her eyes closed, arms hanging by her side. She was standing in the courtyard, drenched in a heavy black rain that was so cold she felt like she wasn't wearing any clothes. Sören's head rose out of the fountain. Laughing screams rang out as the head fell into a chasm, one that grew until it swallowed his castle, soldiers, and power. A bright light flashed, and the rain became like snow.

The silhouette of a woman appeared in the storm, and Mabel couldn't shake the feeling that she knew her from another life. The girl longed to be with her and called out, but could make no sound, tried to hold her, but the figure slipped away. Voices echoed, some cursing her and others begging for her to come. The voice of the queen rose above them all, crying, *The gods are powerful, and we cannot stand against them. . . . Our only choice is which one we'll serve. . . .* Darkness crashed over her mind.

Mabel! a celestial voice whispered in her soul. The girl stirred, but the magic fought to keep her asleep. Her mind drifted further into darkness.

A bird screamed, and Mabel opened her eyes to find a glorious sparkling light that licked the walls of the room. She sat up, no longer hovering but resting on the floor, and gasped: the Raptor stood in a window that was no longer filled with stone, but with fire.

Mabel was captivated by the magnificent bird of prey, whose beak glittered like a diamond and feathers glimmered like a star. Its head was lined with crimson streaks that flowed down its golden body. The girl felt its power and knew that it could see all things: her doubts, failures, and the darkness within. *He knows everything about me*, Mabel thought and dropped her head, but a soft chirp caused her to lift her face. His eyes left nothing unsaid. He had waived all judgment, for he had the power to do so, and accepted her. She need not thank him for anything, for coming for her and saving her life, because he already knew. Tears gathered in her eyes because his said that he loved her.

The bird let out a second cry, and Mabel jumped up as flames streamed into the room and rose over her body. A fiery glow ran through her spine, and wings burst from her back, tearing through her clothes and growing instantly until they brushed against her feet. Mabel glanced over her shoulder, her jaw dropping at the sight of the moonstone feathers, then looked imploringly at the Raptor as though he would offer an explanation. But the bird simply turned and dove into the sky.

"I don't know how to . . ."

Mabel broke off, and a look of determination crossed her face. *No way I'm staying here . . . and I wanna be with him.*

She stepped forward and hoisted herself up onto the sill, squeezed through the window, and passed through the fire. The girl crouched in darkness on the other side and glanced at her ashen hands then peered into the courtyard below. The figure of Centrum Stella was smoldering in the fountain, the eels swaying in his tail, covered in slime: streams of lightning emanated from their eyes and bore into the surrounding fighters, each gleaming with an inner light that made him appear softer, almost alive.

Mabel looked up and saw the Raptor climbing toward a

golden-white star that she had never seen before, suspended over the stars of blood. The Raptor did not deviate from its course, and Mabel knew that she must fly or be left behind. The girl held her breath, hesitated, then jumped from the ledge.

Mabel spread her wings and drove them toward the ground, again and again. She felt as though a giant hook had been lodged between her shoulders and was reeling her into the sky. The tightness in her stomach gave way, and she zoomed over the wall in a blur of hair and streaming clothes. Everything that had ever plagued her shattered inside as Mabel shouted, flying higher and faster and farther into the darkness.

She followed the Raptor toward its star, and how long they flew she could only guess. They were soaring high above the Earth, just beneath the red stars, and were about to climb higher when the Raptor vanished and the heavens tore in two. Mabel flung an arm across her empty sockets as a blinding light pierced the darkness. The light dimmed, and she peered over her arm to find herself surrounded by cities. Absolutely stunned, the girl landed on glass steps that led to an enormous temple, upheld by opal pillars that shimmered like the sea. The sky burst into violet flames beneath her.

"Reader of the book!" rang a voice from above, and Mabel pulled her gaze away from the fire.

A coral star had emerged from the temple and was floating toward her, down the steps, transforming into a goddess with a shadow veil, dressed in the skins of the monsters of the deep. Her white arms were bare, blasphemies were written across her skin, and every magic charm hung from her body.

"Wha . . . who are you?"

Mabel had nearly shouted, but the figure did not seem to be listening as it landed beside her.

"You have been given the knowledge of our tongue and a dreaming eye that sees," said the intoxicating voice. "But I will lift you higher, for I am Vøge, the goddess of magic, signs, and wonders.

I will give you the power to deceive the people of Earth, and they will worship you through me." She held out a golden amulet, forged from the furnace of the Deep. "Wear my chain about your neck, and your mind will be opened."

"Fair creature!"

Mabel whirled around in time to see a star land on a pinnacle of black jagged rock that had risen from the fire. Emerald winds swirled around the star as it became a human figure with the head of a wolf. He was clad in shredded armor, and parts of his body were missing.

"Serve me!" he said in a high-pitched and howling voice. "I am Krone, who will make you a witch of divination. You will see things to come, and your king will eat from your hand. Come now, child." A black star the size of a fist passed through his body and floated toward her. "Gaze into my crystal, and you will be mine."

"Give yourself to Chemosh!" shouted a bleeding star that fell beside Mabel. She sprang back and collided with Vøge before backing up the stairs. "I will give you vengeance, and you shall bathe in the blood of your enemies," it called after her, taking the form of a man with no eyes and a headdress of bones and crow feathers that descended over his body. He held out a cupped hand filled with blood. "Drink the blood of the slain, and it will be yours."

Mabel looked away, but the stars continued to fall, offering her the world and all that lie within. Asherah presented riches, and Dagana the souls of men. But the girl rejected them in her heart and retreated further, saying, "Look, I don't want any of you!"

The temple behind her exploded as lightning struck. Mabel ducked, a downpour of glass hammering the stairs and pelting her wings, then straightened and turned around. Lavian slithered from the ruins and descended the stairs.

Mabel couldn't breathe as she stumbled back down the steps in a daze. The Snake moved no faster to close the distance between them and no slower for her to get away. She stole a terrified glance at the writing wrapped around his arm—𝕬𝖉𝖆𝖒𝖐𝖆𝖎𝖑𝖑 𝖘𝖊𝖒 𝕴𝖓𝖟𝖊𝖓𝖌 . . . 𝕷𝖊𝖇𝖆𝖗 𝖈𝖞 𝕷𝖊𝖇𝖆𝖗𝖘 𝕿𝖍𝖆𝖉𝖆*—then stared ahead as his voice broke the silence.

"Daughter," he breathed, his tongue flickering. "I came for you . . . *yessss* . . . but not to harm you. You are most esteemed, for the Morning Star has chosen you to read what he has written. But he will only use you, and after you achieve his will, can you trust him to be there for you?

"And these other gods . . ." He opened his arms and rose on his tail. "Do I not control them? Do they not bow to me? I have given them power, and all they offer belongs to me. For it is mine, and I give it to whoever I please. They offer kingdoms and fame, power, and a great name, but I offer what they cannot—I will make you like God. *Yessss!* Mabel"—she shivered at her name coming from his mouth—"if only you worship me."

The girl lifted her eyes and saw the star to whom the Raptor had flown, brilliant and beautiful. *Surely you must be a god!*

Lavian hissed as he followed her gaze.

"Choose this day whom you will serve!" said the Snake. "But know *thisss*. Should you choose any god before me, you will face me again. I will hunt you from the corners of the Earth and strip your skin from your body. I will slay you from the ashes, and to the ashes you will return."

Where are you? Mabel cried in her mind, searching for the Raptor. She knew the Snake was a liar. There was one who was not afraid of him, for she had seen the Raptor fight him and not be defeated. But what was more, she had seen that it loved her . . . and Mabel realized that love was what she desperately needed. And love, none of the gods could give.

Suddenly, the heavens quaked, and the stairs collapsed. Mabel and Lavian took off as an avalanche of glass poured into the flames, which spiked with a chilling *whoosh* that made the girl's hair stand

---

* Murderer from the Beginning . . . Liar and Father of Lies.

on end. The pinnacle on which Krone had been standing crumbled into the fire, with the dominions, gods, and their glory, and the flames parted to reveal what looked like a jet-black mirror beneath. There was a flash of ice down Mabel's spine, and her wings were gone. The girl gave a shout as she fell and crumpled onto the surface, surrounded by a vast ring of fire. Mabel leaped to her feet, the flames whispering in her ears, searching for Lavian but to no avail.

The reflection of the flames vanished, and the predators of Earth flashed in the mirror: sharks and kraken, jackals and dragons, followed by the kingdoms of the world. The people of Earth cried out in one long voice, and everything was swept away. Only the image of a child remained, close enough for Mabel to see that it was a girl, her face full and smooth, innocent eyes gazing through the mirror.

And then—was it an illusion?—the little girl rose out of the floor as Lavian emerged from the flames on the other end. He had come to destroy the child. Thunder cracked and a black cloud swirled around Lavian's right hand; it became long and narrow and crystalized into a sword whose name was *Death*.

"No!" Mabel yelled, reading the fear in the child's face, one who was aware of the danger, but not the fate. A number of fallen angels appeared through the fire as Mabel rushed toward them, having no idea what she could do but consigned herself to die with the child. She had seen herself in her eyes.

"What are you doing? *God no!*"

But a star fell in front of the child before Mabel could reach her. It pulsed and became a man, god, and king. His skin shone like the rising sun, spiked white hair, dancing in a vortex of wind, and a raging fire was in his eyes. He bore no armor, for he needed none, wearing a midnight cloth about his waist. 𝕯𝕰𝕱𝕰𝕹𝕯𝕰𝕽 was burned in his chest, and magnificent names covered his back and arms that looked as powerful as Lavian's. The king stood over the child as the Fallen crept forward like wolves; a sword flashed in his fist whose name was *Life*.

Mabel stopped short. He looked into her face, and a sword burst in his opposite hand.

"Fall back!" he said in a voice that shook the air and calmed her heart. Lavian and his angels obeyed.

"I am Jezul," he called to Mabel. "The one you've seen in dreams and creation, whose words you've read and whose spirit speaks in your heart. But now you see me face-to-face. I am the Morning Star, the one who made you and chose you. Now choose me!" He flipped the second sword, caught it by the blade, and extended the hilt toward Mabel. 𝕳𝕰 𝕸𝕬𝕶𝕰𝕾 𝕎𝕬𝕽 was written on his arm. The sword burned, and its name was *Truth*.

"I offer no riches, kingdoms, or fame. I give power to defend the innocent, fire to destroy the destroyer, and rage to save the faces of men."

Mabel came forward, pulled by her heart, not knowing what to expect, but trusting the one who called. She walked past the Fallen and refused to look at Lavian, who watched her through his venomous eyes. And Mabel seized the hilt with all her might.

Jezul held the blade as fire flooded her veins and destroyed the darkness within, transforming her innermost depths, turning her ashen skin to light, and filling her eyes with fire. The Raptor came out of nowhere and landed on Mabel's arm, talons sinking through her skin. The girl trembled from the pain, but the bird poured its strength into her soul and the weak became strong. The Raptor took off with a shriek as Jezul let go of the blade. Mabel stood with blood running down her arm, but didn't care. She had never felt so alive.

"Stand with me," said Jezul, "and be not afraid!" They stood back to back, with the child between them. Jezul raised his sword with both hands, holding the blade across his forehead, gazing beneath it at the Fallen. Mabel lifted her arms in one sweeping motion. She held the hilt by her face and rested the blade on the opposite wrist, staring down the sword like an arrow, flames streaming from her eyes, lips tightened in rage.

"So it *issss*," rasped Lavian in a low voice. He looked at Jezul then at Mabel. "You have chosen."

There was a blinding flash, and Mabel found herself alone with Jezul. They walked weightlessly over the Earth, which scrolled beneath them, faces flickering before their eyes—men and women, children, and the weak from every tribe, tongue, and nation. And evil came to destroy them. Phantoms rose from the River of Ob, and horrors from the Abyss. Devils stormed Escanaba, and ettins descended on Med la Grëv. Beasts came out of the grave and armies with them. But Mabel and her god fought them to the end, and the more she slew, the more she dared to come.

At last the enemy fled, and though Mabel searched for Jezul, she could not find him. The girl fell to her knees and cried as she had a thousand times before. But it was different now. She no longer cried from the pain of simply existing—having no reason to live, with emptiness ruling her heart—but because she was alive. She had not found something to live for, but someone for which to die. She clung to her sword, and its name was *Truth*.

CHAPTER 8

A SWORD AGAINST SÖREN

The sun was sinking over Carnecia, the castle an awesome silhouette of spires and walls in the crimson sky, a stronghold the world itself could not stand against. The air was raw and still; there were no clouds, no birds, no whitecaps across the calm black sea. Low neighs and murmuring voices mingled with the breaking waves.

"Where are they?" said Hadesha for the umpteenth time. She was standing on the Northern Tower facing the sea, dressed in black armor that glistened as though it had recently rained.

Sören gave no answer. The king had transformed over the waning hours and become something other than his queen, save the matching armor. His expression was detached and lifeless—hers, fanatic and burning. He stood limp and confused while she roamed without restraint. The king said little, and the queen was losing her voice.

"Well?"

"Peace, Queen," said Ruel, who had run out of reasons why the forces had not yet arrived but was afraid of saying nothing. Hadesha had just killed another officer, this time for loading the catapults with sacrastone instead of ravenrock though she had called for sacrastone minutes before.

"The spirits will carry them," the prophet rambled on, inching closer to the king. "Perhaps they're waiting—"

"FOR WHAT?"

Ruel was about to beg for patience when his ears twitched beneath his hood. The vague sound of thunder was seeping through the air.

"The horsemen!" said Sören in electric tones. He turned and hurried to the opposite wall, Hadesha, Ruel, and the guards running to catch up. They looked to the south where the sky darkened by the second as though to hide the approaching horror. But the riders from Phycum would not be denied, hundreds of them rushing across the grasslands on horses with bronze hooves and ember eyes, hair streaming in tangled masses from their helms, visors drawn, bodies wrapped in scales like the serpents in their hands.

The cry of a watcher caused Hadesha and her party to wheel around and face the sea. An unnatural wave was storming toward the shore with a dozen ships, bloodred flags whipping from their masts.

"The spirits of the deep are with us," breathed Sören feverishly.

The queen clutched Mabel's bag, strapped tightly over her shoulder. "Where are the others?" she said coldly, looking into the setting sun. "The sword draws nigh."

"My brothers!" said Ruel, pointing at the dunes that covered the Delgeron Peninsula. Some fifty magicians had emerged from the sand (by what sorcery, the prophet couldn't tell) and were walking single file toward the Western Gates. Lilac and emerald auroras snaked behind them as they came, the tunnels of light swaying back and forth like seaweed beneath the waves.

If Hadesha was any more relieved, she didn't show it. "What about the rest, *minion*?" she hissed into the prophet's hood. "We need them all! Even then, we cannot win without the crown."

"We need only to stem the tide, long enough to reach Eva—"

A cry erupted, and they looked east. The warriors of Múl were marching from Mount Dominion with a sword in each hand, the last sunbeams glittering in their torsos of ice. Fur as dark as the looming night covered their arms and legs, and their human faces, wrapped in snowy flesh, had eyes that could see things far away. They knew they had been spotted and gave mournful howls, now running toward the gates.

Ruel let out a triumphant laugh, low and leering, and the queen softened at last. But Sören was looking in the opposite direction, murmuring as a vivid orange liquid snaked its way down the Xmasseux River. The lava seemed to be flowing out of the last sliver of the sun along the horizon, and the river fled to the sea.

Within seconds, all eyes were fixed on the lava as it surged down the empty riverbed, into the sea, steam rising as molten rock married the water. It was minutes before the ghouls stepped from the billows, their skeletons dripping and skulls crystalizing without jaws, though fangs descended from beneath their empty nasals. Their fingers lengthened and flattened like blades as they clambered up the slopes for the fortress.

"Your Majesty," said the general's voice. He had surfaced on the tower with two knights that trailed him like machines. The three of them strode toward the king and queen and went down on a knee. "I beg you, release the men. The gates must be closed before nightfall."

Sören looked at his queen, who nodded stiffly.

"Release them."

"Your Majesty!"

The general and his knights rose and left. Soon, there were shouts from below as the soldiers began moving through the gates, and the queen's face became stony. She had kept them as long as she could, drawing strength from a thousand men at her command. But they were leaving her now, empty and bare. The infantry marched through the eastern gate, and the calvary rode through the western wall. Against the sea, the soldiers looked scattered and weak.

The gates gonged as they locked in place, and Sören looked as though his doom had been sealed. The queen stood motionless, her armor hiding the tremors in her frame until a gale slammed the castle from the south. Those on the tower leaned into the wind and shielded their eyes, Ruel clutching his hood with both hands. No fewer than a hundred figures soared out of the twilight on foul flesh-covered wings like bats.

"Barbarians!" cried Hadesha and lifted her arms. "Fall on me!" The winds ceased a few minutes later as the sons of earth alighted on the battlements, scythes in their hands. Corrupted by Crel, their bodies were covered with iron feathers, hair flowing from their skulls like the tails of a horse. Numbers were cut into their faces, illuminated by silver eyes.

"And the descendants of Zoridian?" Hadesha said to Ruel, the muscles flexing in her jaw. Her voice dropped, laced with acid. "Your beast of a bird—it will be your heart or his."

The prophet bared his teeth as the queen stalked over to the parapet and watched the ships of Aeragos run ashore. Raiders jumped from the decks and tramped across the beach like an army from the dead. The human forms had scorpions that clung to their bodies like armor, white stone faces, and tentacles that dangled from their abdomens. They approached silently, armed with harpoons, shields, and spears and took positions along the Western Gates. Horsemen circled the castle while the magicians stood at the base of the Northern Wall. Warriors guarded the Eastern Gates, and the king's infantry walled off the south with half the calvary, the rest of whom joined the raiders to the west. The ghouls issued dismal screeches as they stood with the magicians who were convinced the enemy would rise from the sea. Forming the last line of defense were the barbarians, crouching on towers and gatehouses like gargoyles. And the buildup of forces was complete.

Night thickened. Venus had not yet risen, and Hadesha looked for Jupiter, her lips moving silently as screeches rang throughout the atmosphere. The waves ceased, and the ocean became as smooth as the tide pools among the rocks. The horsemen reined their beasts. There was another outbreak of screams, louder and closer than before. A heavy fog rushed from the north and obscured the ships on the beach.

Bluish glows appeared in the fog, as though rising out of the water, and moved toward the castle. Within moments, they emerged from the mist to reveal bodies in the night. Lightning flashed in their fists.

"Gods, it cannot be!" cried Hadesha and grasped her head as if to trap a nightmare in her brain so that it would not be birthed into reality.

"Titans," murmured Sören, swaying from side to side and staring into the night. "Devils at the door."

The predators stopped. Raine, Andromede, and Bloodscar came forward, the rest looming like a wall behind them.

"They're no more than several hundred," sneered Ruel, but his face darkened at the sound of Raine's voice.

"Maggots!" shouted the Titan. His voice echoed. *"Maggots . . . 'aggots!"*

"We are gods! Give us the book . . . send us your king and queen . . . then you will live!"

"Live . . . 'ive!"

"If not," howled Bloodscar, pointing his lightning bolt at the castle, "you will die with them!"

Death was written on Sören's face. He was a king stricken down in his mind, trapped in a world where he already ceased to exist. But the queen shrieked, *"Send them to Avaddon!"* And she fired a jet of red light from her hand. Andromede threw lightning at the missile, and the forces collided with a blast that showered the beach with sparks. Cries rang out from the king's commanders. The ghouls, warriors, and horsemen stormed down the slopes as archers released a cloud of arrows that whispered high into the air, coming alive with white-hot lights before falling like a collapsing dome. But the Titans smashed them with the blue-light shields that flashed in their fists. Sparks sizzled in the sand and faded.

And the Titans came, walking with heads held high. They were that ancient race, born before hell had been wrapped in the gates of death. They had faced every foe that had ever walked the earth, plagues and famine, kings and kingdoms, wars, magic, and terrors of the soul. Like a virus, every weapon raised against them had only made them stronger. And the Titans came as one.

"Ravens!" yelled Hadesha, and the catapults fired clusters of ravenrocks as the ghouls and horsemen reached the shore. But lightning fell from a cloudless sky and obliterated the rocks, whose shards rained on the king's forces. Within seconds, the air was stained with the sounds of breaking bodies, shrieks, explosions, and flashes that turned night into day.

The ghouls spewed lava from their sockets, and the Titans fought back with lightning that thundered as it struck. Magicians released auroras, the electric currents crackling as they glided through the air from the castle to the sea. Their ends split and opened like giant mouths. But Andromede howled to the stars, and the gods answered: cyclones suddenly formed beneath the auroras and swept them into the sky, scattering their particles to the ends of the Earth.

"For me!"

Sören came alive and shot his hand into the air. A fiery beam of light rocketed high over the castle and burst into a luminous shadow that became the image of the king. The ghostly figure was as tall as a steeple and threw an arm across its body, beckoning the forces of Carnecia. Those defending the castle left their positions, save for the magicians and barbarians, circled to the north, and plunged down the slopes, jumping over the rocks that lined their way and slamming into the Titans. Arrows rained from the walls. There were more light shields and endless peals of thunder.

But no one could break the Titans. The half-bloods shattered the warriors like glass and slaughtered the soldiers until their blood trickled down the slopes into the sand. Hadesha, Sören, Ruel, and the magicians fired unending jets of light; but the Titans marched shoulder to shoulder behind their shields.

Bloodscar spotted the king and queen of Linden and went rigid: a guttural noise escaped his throat as his eyes locked on a star that released a jade teardrop. Instantly, a burning orb appeared in Bloodscar's hand. The Titan lowered his gaze, his body returned to him and threw the tiny star at the Northern Tower. The orb gained speed as it soared up through the air, but Sören blocked it with a shock wave that rocked the tower, fissures running throughout its frame.

"Jupiter!"

Hadesha grabbed Sören by the collar and swatted Ruel's arm, causing his yellow ray of light to veer and strike one of the soldiers who burst into flame.

The prophet swore and wheeled around, oblivious to their impending salvation.

"He's come to open the tower!" yelled Hadesha, jabbing a finger at the rising planet. "Get the girl!"

The queen faced the captain of the guard, her eyes wild.

"Ilix eyam!"

Strands of light flew from her hand, wrapped themselves around his body, and pinned his arms to his sides. Another glittering thread spun around his neck and choked his pleas for mercy.

"Bring him!" Hadesha bellowed to the barbarians beside her. They seized the captain as she jumped on the back of another beast, clamping an arm around its neck while trapping the bag against her body with the other. Sören and Ruel clambered onto the backs of two more barbarians, grabbing the horselike hair that dangled from their skulls.

"To the bell tower!"

The entourage took off, lightning bolts streaking past them, and another flaming globe blasted the tower off the wall.

Chapter 9

Reign Fall

Mabel felt a cold stone floor and knew that she was coming to. Her heart burned for Jezul. She wanted to stay asleep, to see him again, but fiendish shrieks were flooding her mind. There was an explosion, and she opened her eyes.

The girl struggled up from the floor, vaguely noticing the blasts that rattled the sky beyond the window where the Raptor had been. There was a light flooding the room. She glanced over her shoulder in confusion, certain there was no fire, then looked down, pulled back her sleeve, and gave a stifled cry. Three gashes were burning in her forearm where the Raptor had sunk its talons. She stared at the gold-glittering light and rolled her wrist to find a fourth hole underneath.

The light was just beginning to fade when the door flew open. Mabel's head spun around, and she froze at the sight of Hadesha.

"What!" The queen stopped so suddenly that Sören slammed into her back.

"How could the spirit enter?" stammered Sören, gawking over her shoulder as Ruel passed through the door like a shadow. "She was surrounded by stone."

"Yes," said the prophet in a dark voice, "but the Raptor is stronger than you know."

No power contains,
Or prison restrains,
The love of his Spirit,
For the soul he unchains.

Strongholds he devastates,
Demons annihilates;
Through his conquering love,
The fatherless advocates.

No incantation,
Shall impede the salvation,
Of those in need of
His life and his love.

"It doesn't matter!" said Hadesha. "She doesn't know how to use her—"

The tower shuddered with an earsplitting blast but did not crumble. "*HA!*" cried the queen, looking at Ruel. "See why I gave myself to Jupiter? Even *they* cannot overcome him!"

She pointed at Mabel and yelled, "Let's end this now!"

"What's happening?" said Mabel. But the queen didn't answer; she grabbed the girl by the wrist, Sören seizing the other, and fled with her through the door.

The king waved his hand, and a light flickered in his palm. Mabel shrieked and pulled back at the sight of the barbarians, holding the captain who struggled to escape. Sören and Hadesha tightened their steely grips. Another blast rocked the tower.

"Take us to the belfry!" Hadesha shouted at the barbarians.

"No!"

Mabel's voice vanished. A barbarian had choked her from behind, his scythe inches from her face, and grabbed her around the middle.

Hadesha flashed a light in her hand, climbed onto a barbarian, and was flying up the spiral staircase, the rest soaring behind. Mabel looked sideways as they went round and round but could see nothing until Hadesha cried out and a door opened in the wall above them. The party shot out into the cold and starry sky, spiraled higher, and landed on a ledge outside the belfry. Mabel was thrown against a stone-filled arch and her barbarian let go, the girl pressing herself against the wall as he landed beside her.

"Come on, ape!" Hadesha shrieked at a barbarian, who slammed the captain into the wall at her side.

Mabel's insides melted as she looked down at the lightning storm. What looked like a tiny comet flashed over the wall and struck the tower below, the girl screaming as she slipped, but the barbarian grabbed her by the shoulder and pulled her back.

"God of fortresses!" Hadesha shouted to the heavens and Jupiter flashed. "Open the belfry that I may take the crown! I will become powerful and make your name great across the Earth! Open what you have closed. Reverse the spell. . . . *Let me pass!*"

A lightning bolt zoomed up from the ground, toward the belfry, but was blocked by Sören. Ruel shattered another bolt with a silver jet of light, the Titans howling with their prey in sight. More bolts came. Jupiter did not answer.

Hadesha shattered two incoming bolts and shrieked every syllable so that Mabel knew her vocal cords would tear. *"Will Jupiter heed my cry for nothing? Take the blood, the life, the captain of my guard!"*

The queen drew her dagger, slit the soldier's throat, and slashed Jupiter's number in the wall with the steaming blood-covered blade. She seized the captain by the collar and yanked him forward, out of the hands of the barbarians, Mabel's brain reeling as she watched the lifeless body plunge over the ledge.

A ray from Jupiter illuminated the number, and the wall opened beside the queen. The stones floated away from the belfry, and a brilliant light spilled out into the night.

It's the light of the book! thought Mabel as Hadesha, Sören, and Ruel destroyed a barrage of incoming bolts. A barbarian crumbled beside Hadesha, his silver eyes gleaming as they fell from his skull into the courtyard below. The rest of the beasts dove downward and spread their wings, except for the one beside Mabel. Hadesha had flashed a hand in his face, daring him to flee. The queen fired light waves down at the Titans and jumped through the opening. The barbarian scooped Mabel across his body, threw her inside, and lunged after her with Ruel and Sören at his heels.

Mabel picked herself up from the floor, never noticing the stones that sealed the wall behind her or the lightning that peppered the belfry. She was taken by the figure before her.

Hovering upright in the center of the chamber, beneath the bronze bells, was the most breathtaking woman Mabel had ever seen. Her eyes were closed, and a crown of uncorrupted light, shaped like a crescent moon whose tips had been pressed together, rested on her head. Her hair was white, dyed by the light on her head, and her mystic beauty—the contour of her face, eyes, and the shape of her lips—conveyed the royal blood in her veins. Power resonated throughout her frame, clad in a black gown. Unlike Hadesha, there was no pride in her being.

The queen slipped the bag off her shoulder, threw it to Ruel, and was marching toward the figure when Mabel noticed the dagger in the lady's body, just above the navel, though no blood was flowing from the wound. Hadesha grabbed the golden hilt, fashioned like the skull of a snake with glowing eyes, and twisted the blade. The lady moaned, and her eyes fluttered open.

How can she be alive? thought Mabel, and her heart went out to her.

"Eva!" Hadesha spoke in the woman's ear, sounding more like a man through her shattered voice box. "I have the book written by the Morning Star. Look!" She grabbed a fistful of Eva's hair and jerked her head so that it was facing Ruel, who dug the book out of the bag and held it high. "And I have the Reader."

Hadesha turned the woman's head so that she could see Mabel and whispered in her ear. Mabel caught the light in Eva's eyes. "Now listen!" said Hadesha. "The Titans are here. They will kill us and give the book to Lavian. Hand me your crown, and I will give you the book and the girl. With them, you can break the Darkness." Hadesha twisted the blade until Eva cried out, arching her head toward the bells. "Don't be a fool! Your crown for the book!"

"Just take it!" said Mabel angrily. "Leave her alone!"

"Shut up!" rasped Hadesha. "You would love to see me take the crown, wouldn't you? The crown that can only be given. Anyone who takes it will die." She reached out toward Mabel, light welling in her hand.

"No!" Sören and Ruel jumped in front of Mabel as the barbarian backed away.

"We need the crown!" said Ruel. "She won't give it without the girl!"

"*Think!*" yelled Sören. "What are we to do? Stay locked in the tower until we starve? We die if we leave without it and die if we stay!"

Hadesha lowered her arm, but the light was dancing between her fingers.

Then Eva spoke in a whisper. "Have the gir—" Her voice faltered as Hadesha pressed her head against Eva's. "Have . . . the girl read . . ."

"*You don't believe me?*" cried Hadesha and pointed violently at Mabel. "She's the one!"

"Let her read!" begged Sören. "Enough to prove she can release the light!"

Hadesha shot a look at Ruel, who had no sooner extended the book toward Mabel than the barbarian swung its scythe in terror, severing the prophet's hand and sending the book crashing to the floor. Mabel leaped back as Ruel aimed a light wave at the barbarian, who deflected it with his scythe.

"So help me!"

Hadesha let go of the knife and sent a stream of black light at Ruel, though not before the prophet had flashed a shield. Mabel felt the blast and knew her ears should have been ringing, but her mind was clear in the presence of the light of the crown. Sören staggered backward, not bothering to try and stop his queen who hit Ruel in the chest, black flames consuming his body.

The barbarian retreated as Hadesha stormed over to the book, eyes burning. "Must I do everything?"

Eva groaned and twisted her body. Her right arm rose and fell, but not before Mabel had seen the scars on her forearm, identical to her own. The girl sprang forward, jammed Hadesha with her shoulder, knocking the queen to the floor as she bent to retrieve the book, yanked the dagger from Eva's body, and threw it across the room.

"*Wench!*" screamed Hadesha, her broken voice whistling in her throat. She gazed up in horror as Eva fell and landed on her knees. Light flashed in Eva's fists, which she drove through the floor as though it were sand. Far beneath the belfry, the earth heaved. The tower tipped.

Hadesha jumped to her feet and stumbled into the barbarian who panicked, caged in a falling tower, and threw her against the opposite wall. The floor pitched up, and Mabel crouched, her eyes darting toward the sliding book.

"*C'mon!*" Eva yelled. She got to her feet, grabbed the back of Mabel's coat, and heaved her forward as they ran toward the wall like a pair of leaning trees along the sloping floor. Eva slashed her hand, firing a light wave that blew a hole in the wall and hurtled through the opening with the girl.

Mabel screamed as they fell, and Eva shouted a command. Clouds of ice formed instantly beneath their feet, flattening into wings. There was a sudden updraft beneath them, and the women glided through the air, followed by Sören who had managed to jump onto the barbarian before it escaped. The tower crashed into the northern wall with a symphony of bells. The Titans surged through the break in the wall, clambering over the rubble as Eva and Mabel landed softly on the ground, the lady pulling Mabel behind as she ran to the fountain in the middle of the courtyard.

"Can you release them?" said Eva, running her fingers over the statue of a fighter, bathed in the light of her crown, looking for something.

"I don't know what you mean!"

When the barbarians saw that it was Eva, not Hadesha, who wore the crown, they flew away with screeches that caused the rest of the queen's forces to flee while the Titans descended into the courtyard. Andromede hurled a lightning bolt that killed Sören's barbarian, sending the king crashing to the ground before he had cleared the wall. Sören shrieked as he pushed himself up on his knees, spattering the tiles with his blood.

The king issued a flurry of light waves. Bloodscar blocked them with a shield. A deadly silence ensued as Raine stepped forward and towered over the king, a growl fluttering in his throat.

"Your day has come," he said. Sören reached forward, but no light would come from his hand. It was as though his power had been taken from him. Raine severed the king's neck before he could plead for his life. The earth opened, swallowed his body, and closed as before.

The Titans turned toward the fountain, and the dread was more than Mabel could bear. She caught Eva's arm and pulled her toward the archway behind them. "Let's go!"

"No!" Eva wrenched away from her and stared at the Titans. "We can't leave without the book—and without them!" She jerked her head toward the statues.

The Titans crept closer but did not get far.

"Ärra dên cosmos!" Eva shouted and whipped her arm across her body. The earth exploded under Bloodscar and the Titans around him, sending them spinning into the air. Eva swung again and issued a thin river of light. The beasts burst into golden flame and were dead before they hit the ground.

Mabel's mouth fell slightly open. The hunters had become the hunted, and the Titans backed away.

"What have we to do with you?" Andromede growled to Eva, the Titans eyeing her crown, despising its light but lusting for its power. "We are the Titans, descendants of angels, once held in dungeons and risen from the living tomb. You have power but cannot overcome us all. If you love your life, witch, you will not war against us. We have not come for you, but for the book and the queen."

"Then take me!"

They all turned their heads and saw Hadesha walking toward them, away from the rubble, carrying the book. Mabel's hand flew to her mouth. The queen's flesh had been ripped away from parts of her face and arms, exposing a golden frame.

"Chemosh!" Eva breathed.

"Yes!" said Hadesha. "I drank from his hand and hid you from Lavian. I coveted your crown, now the Serpent comes for me!"

"You can't stop them!" said Eva, who kept an eye on the Titans, their heads darting back and forth between the women.

"Fight for me," said the queen. She stopped twenty paces from the fountain, "or I will fall into Avaddon and the book with me!"

"Give me the men!"

"Fight for me, or I will kill the girl!" Hadesha leveled her arm at Mabel, but Eva stepped between them.

"Enough!" Raine shouted at Eva. "Cut her down"—he waved a lightning bolt at Hadesha—"and you will live."

"Fools!" shouted Eva. "It is I who will destroy *you*! I know who you are! I've heard the screams of those you've slain—the innocent . . .

children. For nine years I've heard them! Without the queen, you will terrorize the land and rule it for yourselves."

Hadesha laughed wildly, but no one moved.

"Leave us!" said Eva. "Gonjechas unim yú wostitum!"

The earth quaked, and fissures spread through the walls of the fortress. The Titans howled and several fell on their knees, but the ground was calm beneath Eva and the girl. Lightning flashed in the hands of the Titans. Bolts flew at Eva who smashed them in midair. Raine threw a jet of lightning through the head of a Titan on his left, and the onslaught ceased.

"No one strikes without me!" he howled. Another bolt erupted in his fist. The fountain fractured, and water began trickling into the courtyard. The arm of Centrum Stella crumbled, and Eva cast a fearful glance at the surrounding statues. She murmured and the tremors ceased.

The Titans looked around at Eva and the queen, then at Raine, and back again.

"Give me the book," Eva said coldly to Hadesha, "and I will destroy them."

"Destroy them first!"

Raine growled and looked Eva in the face. "You are strong," he said in a low voice, "but we are many. Only one needs to find his mark for your queen to fall."

Lightning burned in the hands of the Titans who stood at a distance between Eva and Hadesha, her arm still raised in Mabel's direction. Then slowly, the Titans began to move, fanning out in both directions, the girl hating herself for being weak, for standing there as Eva faced the world. But when the lady glanced at the fountain once more, Aurèle's voice rang in her head. *Break their chains, and they will fight for you . . . Seven is your number.*

Instantly, Mabel knew what she had to do. The five statues had the same scars as she and Eva, and it was Centrum Stella that was holding them in stone, the eels staring into their eyes.

But any hope of getting Eva's attention was gone. Raine threw a bolt at Hadesha, who dropped the book and flashed a shield. A second later, the courtyard was filled with lightning. The Titans unleashed on Eva and Hadesha, though Mabel scarcely felt the electric charges zipping through the air for the fire in her veins. Instinctively, she made a fist, the scars opened beneath her sleeve, and a weightless blade of light, smothered in flames, flashed in her hand.

Mabel leaped onto the basin, ran around the perimeter, and swung the blade with both hands, chopping the tail just beneath the shark's mouth. There was a shriek as the eels plunged into the fountain, and wisps of green smoke rose into the air. Lightning sailed for Mabel that was blocked by Eva's light wave, the blast knocking the girl into the water.

The sword vanished as Mabel thrashed beneath the surface, the icy water stabbing her like a thousand knives. Hands plunged through the surface, grabbed the front of her cloak, and yanked her out of the fountain.

"Get up, girl!"

Mabel gasped and stared into the dark and chiseled face of a slave fighter, no longer a statue, metal plates covering his shoulders, his arms as defined as they had been in stone. His fellows had already formed a wall between them and the Titans, flashing light shields that blocked a series of bolts with earsplitting blasts. The bronzed bodies jumped down from the basin to give Mabel and her savior room to climb out of the fountain.

Seeing that Mabel was guarded, Eva moved nearer Hadesha who kept fighting on the spot where the book had fallen. The Titans grew desperate and converged on the queen, firing everything they had.

"J'san!" shouted Eva. The tallest, most muscular fighter ran to cover the queen from behind. Eva sent a light wave that smashed three Titans. Raine countered with two lightning bolts. Hadesha blocked the first, but the second blew a hole through her chest.

The frame of the queen stood upright and lifeless, blue flames devouring her flesh, a pool of blood forming at her feet: only the skeleton of gold was left, draped in armor. The earth opened to receive her.

"No!" Mabel shivered, watching in horror as the book tumbled into the abyss, which closed a second later. No sooner had the ground closed than snakes burst from Raine's body and the Titan was no more. Eva looked stunned.

The Titans ended their assault and backed away, fearing Eva and the men standing with her. "We've done what we've been called to do," said Andromede. "The book has fallen into Avaddon, into Lavian's hand. Now let darkness gather unto darkness and light unto light."

"What have we to do with you?" said Eva in a chilling voice. "You've sown the wind and will reap the whirlwind."

Andromede flashed lightning in his fist, and the Titans stopped retreating. He was their alpha now, and they hung on his every word.

"You've lost your queen," he hissed, his arrogance restored. "You weren't strong enough to save her. . . . All magic has its weakness. You fight to save the weak." Andromede turned his gruesome head toward Mabel and raised the lightning in his fist. "She is the next to fall."

Eva looked toward the ocean and spoke in the same chilling tones. "Flö ka stalla, jaur mái raisa, sai yeul lome mái phume cy neysa."* She hadn't shouted, for the winds carried her voice.

The Titans had not understood her words, but the earth began to shake and cries rang out from beyond the wall. The half-bloods fled over the bodies that lined their way and scrambled frantically up the rubble and over the wall.

Eva commanded the water in the fountain, and it spiraled upward, forming steps that froze in a staircase of ice. She looked at

---

* Flood this castle, sea that crashes, in your mouth that foams and gnashes.

the girl and waved a hand. The water in Mabel's hair and clothes became a heavenly steam, warming her body before evaporating in a puff.

"C'mon!" said Eva and grabbed Mabel by the elbow. The women clambered up the staircase to nowhere, followed by the men as the sound of thunder filled the air. Mabel could just see over the southern wall now—the Titans were fleeing across the plains—but never stopped climbing until she reached the platform at the top and looked north.

Her stomach flipped.

A black tidal wave had rushed over the beach, scooped the ships like toys, and was surging up the slopes. It smashed through the northern wall and filled the courtyard almost at once, foaming and hissing beneath the platform on which they stood. Mabel dug her fingers into Eva's arm as the waters knocked over the southern wall and marched across the plains. A hand closed over her shoulder.

"Don't be afraid," said a low voice.

Mabel glanced back at a man with a smooth face and clear blue eyes. The wind swept his long blond hair, and she guessed him to be not much older than herself. The girl looked away and, for some reason, could breathe freely again.

Eva reached out toward a bobbing warship that was about to float by, closed her fingers, and pulled her hand to her chest. A riptide pulled the ship to where they stood, froze, and held the ship in place. The staircase beneath them rose higher until Eva climbed over the rail, onto the deck, with Mabel and the men.

A raider emerged from behind a mast and threw a harpoon at Mabel's head. The girl shrieked and swung a fist across her face. A light shield erupted in her hand and shattered the harpoon with an explosion that sent a shiver down her arm.

"Watch her, dammit!" shouted Eva. She killed the figure with two blasts to his chest and stalked toward the middle of the ship as J'san threw Mabel behind him. More raiders descended from the stern and forecastle but were quickly destroyed. Eva summoned winds that formed funnels around the dead bodies and flung them into the sea.

"Sai jaur!"

The ice melted around the ship, and a current drew them out into the ocean, against a rising tide that flooded Carnecia without mercy.

"Zane, grab the tiller!"

A fighter with short black hair hurried toward the stern.

"Sail for Gogehan!" Eva called after him as he climbed the wooden steps to the helm. Moments later, the ship angled toward Orion, and Eva murmured into the darkness. Winds filled the sails until the masts creaked and groaned. The stars shone in the western sky, and Mabel refused to look back as the ship rushed into the night.

The fighter that had pulled Mabel from the fountain crossed the deck and joined her. His head was nearly shaved, and he looked to be thirty, though his supreme condition made it difficult to tell. "Thank you for coming," he said in husky tones.

Mabel struggled to hold his gaze, wanting to tell him that she could have done nothing without Eva. But the look on his face was so earnest.

"You're welcome," she said softly, her teeth chattering in the bitter wind. "Thank you too for saving me."

"I'm Luther."

"Mabel," said the girl.

"Let's get you someplace warm."

She nodded shakily, and he led her to the center of the ship then stopped and stepped aside as Eva neared. The fire still burned in the lady's eyes, and Mabel was intimidated, filled with fear and awe. Eva was in control, her every move filled with purpose, and she looked divine under the light of the crown. Mabel saw why the men would die for her.

"This is Mabel," said Luther, looking at Eva as he put an arm around the girl's waist. "Mabel, our Lady Eva."

Mabel tensed as Eva embraced her and then relaxed; the fury was gone.

"Bless you," said Eva in low and mystic tones, and a strange feeling spread through Mabel. It was as though her heart had been stirred by a memory of long ago, one that she couldn't see but only feel, giving her the sensation that she'd heard the voice before. Eva stepped away, and Mabel shivered as the wind took her place.

"What year is it?"

CHAPTER 10

ECHOES OF THE PAST

I t's the nineteenth year of Sören's reign," said Mabel. She barely noticed Eva's face tighten as a curtain of spray showered the deck or Luther's sigh as he turned away. Seized with sorrow, her thoughts had strayed to her country, wondering what would happen now that Linden was leaderless. Despite their brutality, Sören and Hadesha had been her rulers nonetheless and had died like dogs.

Eva steered Mabel to a clearing on the deck, just beneath the mainmast. "Sit here," she said dismally, and the girl sat down and drew her legs to her chest. A lean, defined figure approached them with a flaming sword (Mabel recognized him as the one who had stood behind her on the frozen staircase), stopped in front of Eva, and bowed his head.

"My lady."

The fighter plunged the sword into the deck, three feet in front of Mabel, where it burned like a torch. Fire streamed from the talon scars on his arm, and instantly he was holding another beam of light, surrounded by hissing flames.

How do they do that? Mabel thought, rubbing her forearm as he drove the sword into a plank beside the first. *How did I?*

"I'll be back with something to eat," Eva said to Mabel. She looked at the fighter and opened her mouth as though to speak then turned and strode to the bulwark.

"I'm Mercilus." The man crouched beside Mabel who tried in vain to keep the hair out of her face. She was tired—the flames issued a mesmerizing heat that seeped through her skin and warmed her to the bone—and her eyelids were growing heavy, but her heart was beating faster.

"I'm Mabel."

"Thank you for setting us free," he said firmly.

"It was Eva, really."

"Nothing would have happened if you hadn't come," said Mercilus. There was an emptiness in his voice. "We were frozen, but sometimes could hear ourselves. Sometimes we would see your face."

A movement near the bow caused them to look up, and they saw J'san moving toward them, followed by another.

"How long were we held under the spell?" said Mercilus hurriedly. "We were struck during the Φfèimiga—the first under Sören."

Mabel's eyes widened.

"It's all right," he coaxed after she kept silent.

"Seventeen years then. That's the year I was born. . . ." Her voice trailed away as the man turned pale. His eyes darted back and forth, searching her face in disbelief.

"Thank you again." He avoided her eyes as he rose and headed for the stern, brushing past J'san who reached Mabel a moment or two later.

The large man threw the black folds of sailcloth he was carrying onto the deck, and the shape behind him stepped out into view: a small fighter with dirty-blond hair, who bent over the linen and began cutting sections with his dagger. Mabel marveled at J'san who looked at her through steady eyes, his body as powerful as that of an angel, his long brown hair streaming in the wind.

"I'm Haden," said the smaller of the two. He straightened up and draped a large cloth over Mabel's legs.

"I'm Mabel."

"Thanks to you, we're on this lovely ship," he added with a boyish grin then nodded to the one beside him. "That's J'san."

J'san didn't move.

"Accommodations are rough," said Haden. He returned to the pile of linens and slashed another piece. "No food or beds . . . Raiders aren't really human, you know."

The deck suddenly grew brighter as Eva appeared, her crown lighting the way, carrying a bucket that she nearly threw beside the burning swords. The sound of smacking tails mingled with the wind. She looked up at the sky and touched an empty barrel by the rail. A cloud descended through the night, hovered above the drum, and filled it with rain.

Eva snatched the dagger from Haden and cut a narrow strip of cloth, which she tied around her head to obscure the crown. Mabel couldn't believe that a simple cloth could hide something so divine; she was as sure the crown had restricted itself, as though it knew it was not to be seen.

Without the light of the crown bathing her face, Eva looked human now, though Mabel was still taken by her beauty. She couldn't have been older than twenty years. Eva cut another strip and gave it to the girl, who gladly accepted, having given up on taming her hair. Eva held out the blade to Haden as Mabel wrapped the cloth around her head, but he waved it away.

"They got nothing else on this ship," he said and drew another from his waistband. "But there's a ton of weapons below. Here."

Haden threw Eva a wad of cloth, which she caught and unfolded in a single motion. There was a hole for her head, and she flipped it over her shoulders, the cloth falling to her feet like a dress.

"The girl eats first," said the lady, shooting him a resentful look before she walked off, and the cloud vanished over the barrel. If it were possible, the air felt even colder.

Mabel glanced at Haden, who stared after Eva and resumed

slicing the cloth as J'san gutted a fish. Soon, he was grilling a fillet over the flaming swords, the meat skewered on a dagger. The girl felt hungry for the first time in days. There was a dull *clunk* as Haden's shoulder guards landed on the deck. Mabel's catlike eyes flickered in his direction, the fighter pulling a section of cloth over his head, then back to the steaming meat.

"Here," said J'san with a heavy accent. He stretched out the dagger toward Mabel.

"Thank you," she said, burning her fingers as she attempted to slide the smoking fish onto her hand. He smiled slightly and nodded at the hilt.

"Keep it."

Mabel smiled back, leaned against the mast, and began picking the meat from the blade, trying hard not to look like she was starving.

"Where're you from?" said J'san

"Port Majoris." Mabel swallowed her first bite whole and burned her mouth. "Well, born in Rahmais. You?"

"Kravê."

"Let her go," said Haden, as he came over and gestured Mabel to lean forward. The girl obeyed, and he stuffed two rolls of cloth behind her back. "She's gotta be tired."

Mabel sank back and stifled a yawn, her face glowing in the golden flames. Haden returned to the bucket and grabbed a fish. There was another *clunk* as J'san shed his armor and threw a linen over his head. A minute or two later, Mabel had cleaned her dagger, driven the blade between two planks, and closed her eyes.

Her mind had been teeming with questions; but strangely, the book, the powers of the crown, and all that she had seen no longer occupied her brain. She could only think of Eva's voice spoken into her ear, mingled with the sound of the wind driving the sails and the water rushing past the sides of the ship as it slowly pitched up and down, a pendulum keeping time. Her breathing grew slower, deeper, and within minutes, she was asleep.

Mabel awoke the next day to a pale and purple sky, stiff but warm, covered in extra layers of sailcloth that she hadn't remembered using. Zane was standing over the ever-burning swords, dressed in black cloth and grilling fish. His face was shadowed by a short black beard, his cropped hair barely moving in the wind. The masts groaned, and Mabel knew that Eva was driving the ship at breakneck speed—to where, she didn't know, nor what they would do once they arrived. She rubbed her eyes and let out a long steamy breath. Her mind cleared, and the girl sat up straighter against the mast.

"Want something to eat?" said Zane in a subdued voice. His eyes were bloodshot, and Mabel could tell that he hadn't slept at all. "Fish again."

"Um, all right," said Mabel, hoping to sound indifferent. But her mouth watered.

He handed her a piece of the sizzling meat, speared on a dagger, and Mabel gave him the one that she had lodged in the deck beside her. For a while, neither of them spoke. Zane sat down and cleaned another fish as Mabel looked around, eating. There was J'san, manning the tiller beside a burning sword. Eva climbed out of a hatch in front of him and descended the steps that led to the deck. On the opposite side of the ship, Luther and Haden were working together on a broken line. Mercilus was sitting on the forecastle alone, wrapped in sailcloth and staring into the sea.

"We all had our dreams," said Zane, watching Eva as she headed in their direction. "Being frozen for seventeen years ended many of them." He looked back at Mabel. "Forgive our dismay, for not thanking you enough. We're forever in your debt."

Before Mabel could try to convince him that they were the ones who had saved her, Eva passed them, saying, "Come with me, Mabel." She did not break stride as she crossed to a deserted side of the ship. Mabel exchanged glances with Zane and shoved the rest of the fish into her mouth. She cast off the covers as she rose, drank two mouthfuls of rainwater from the barrel, and hurried after Eva.

Mabel joined her by the bulwark, the lady staring across the black waters of the Northern Sea. They stood shoulder to shoulder, identical in height, lost in a chorus of creaking wood, wind, and waves. Then came Eva's voice.

"I know nothing about you," she began, "only that you're a Reader and have chosen the Morning Star. You know, there are two worlds . . ."

Here the lady paused, stretched her arm over the rail, and clenched her fist. A golden light drizzled from her hand, into the sea, and drifted away. After a minute or so, Eva grasped Mabel's wrist.

"Here he comes," she said, and an iron-gray stark burst through the surface. The girl gave a little scream as its body left the sea, teeth bared, and plunged back into the water. The predator raced beside them, nearly invisible in the predawn waters.

"How can this be happening?" said Mabel anxiously, and the questions spilled from her mouth. "I mean, *here*, in our world? How can birds speak and Hadesha do magic and the ground open like that . . . and you command *everything*?"

"Not everything. Only creation in our world. The spiritual realm permeates the physical world in which we live. Like the sun, whose presence can be felt even though it exists outside of our world, so too the power of the Unseen. Hadesha gave herself to the stars, and they gave her their powers in return. Ours come from the Unseen as well—your ability to read the book, and our weapons of fire and light and my crown. All that we do is through the power of the Morning Star. See the shark?"

Mabel looked down and watched it following the ship, zigzagging beneath the surface.

"We and the fish exist together, yet in separate worlds. The surface of the water defines where his ends and ours begins. Dive through the surface and you will enter a world not your own. In the same way, when you pass through fire, you will leave our world for another. Angels that enter our world will burn, though their spirits remain, roaming, searching for bodies. The creatures that speak are those filled with spirits.

"But all humans will enter the Unseen when they die. Those of the Raptor are carried to Zaphon. Those who belong to any other god fall into Avaddon."

"Ava what?"

"The Underworld. A kingdom of Lavian, ruled by the Destroyer. When Hadesha was killed, the book fell with her body into the Unseen world below. There Lavian will find it and has found it already."

Once again, Eva cast light into the sea, and the shark swam away.

"Eva," said Mabel quietly, "why haven't I heard this before? I've heard about magic and everything, but never about the books . . . about Jezul and Lavian."

"The Darkness blinds men from the truth," said the lady. "If they don't believe they're dead, they'll see no reason to break the spell that holds them. Lavian deceives the rulers of Earth into believing they can become gods. Darkness is their power. Few know the truth, and even less will fight for it.

"Come," she said wearily and let go of Mabel's wrist. "We must meet with the others. You will give your story, and we will give ours. Then I will say what we must do."

The women joined the others who were sitting around J'san at the helm. Mabel sat down on the deck between Haden and the burning sword, Luther across from them, leaning against a barrel with a cloth tied around his head. Zane was perched on a hatch, feet dangling over a ladder that descended into the hold. Mercilus was the farthest away, peering through his windblown hair, his expression unreadable. Eva stood beside J'san and faced the rest.

"We know that we've been held under the spell for seventeen years," she said, "and little of this world to which we return. But the war still rages. We've seen the Darkness and know what it can do."

She stopped and a shadow crossed her face. No one made a sound as the wind droned in their ears. Eva took a deep breath, as if to marshal her thoughts, then looked at Mabel.

"Although I knew these men before, they don't know how I came under the magic of the blade, nor do I know how they were cursed. We will tell our stories." Eva nodded at the girl. "Then face the path we must take."

Mabel gazed at the horizon as the lady knelt beside her and told them how she was born in Rahmais during the second Plague of Lithom, how her parents died quickly thereafter, and how she was stolen away by her grandmother to Port Majoris.

"That's why," Mabel said, her voice quivering, "I never really had anyone to show me the way . . . in life, you know. My grandma did her best and everything . . ."

After a silence, the girl continued, telling them about her grandmother's death, how she had found the book and passed through the fire into the Unseen. She described every detail of Lavian in her mind, the war in the forest, what the angels had told her, and ended with her account of pulling the dagger from Eva's body.

"We jumped from the tower and flew into the courtyard," said Eva, continuing the story, "and the Titans came for Hadesha."

"Who are they?" said Mabel.

"Half-bloods," said J'san flatly, his eyes fixed upon the southern horizon. "Their fathers were angels, mothers, human."

No one spoke for a time. Mabel watched J'san, his mammoth arm glued to the tiller, his frame outlined against the sky, giving her more confidence than the ship itself.

At last, Eva's voice came again, telling the men how Mabel had struck the statue and set them free. But not in the way that Mabel remembered: Eva described the girl as fearless, slashing through the statue of Centrum Stella in the face of the Titans.

There was a murmur of thanks, the men giving Mabel grateful

looks. Even Mercilus caught her eye and nodded. Her face reddened for she had been terrified, but her heart swelled all the same.

"What news of Linden?" Haden asked Mabel.

"And Neo Padosta," said Luther. "Who won the War of Krusis?"

"The Alliance," said the girl, answering Luther first before facing Haden. "Not a lot, just uprisings. Ever since the king and queen left Avontris for Carnecia—"

"Enough!"

Eva had raised a fist. "We'll be sailing for a fortnight. There'll be plenty of time to learn of the past for any who cares."

She laid a hand on Mabel's knee. "Ours is a dark story," she said, her voice breaking as the ship smashed through a large wave. "I am the daughter of King Walker of Veldesh."

I knew it! thought Mabel, awestruck. *A princess.*

"About twenty years ago, our country was on the brink of war with Linden. While the rest of the world despised the smallest of the nations, my father feared its magic. To avoid bloodshed, he formed an alliance through marriage. Sören had already taken Hadesha as his wife, so I was given to the Lord of Sin Via."

"Sin Via!" Mabel blurted out. "The destroyed city?"

Eva tensed.

"Destroyed?" said Zane quietly. "When?"

"That's right," groaned Mabel. "You guys don't know. It was the year after the Ithycan Revolt when the Gates of Jupiter in Harren Sini—"

"We don't know any of this," said Haden bluntly.

"Right. About seven or eight . . . no, wait . . . nine years ago."

"What happened?" said Luther.

"That's the thing, no one really knows," said Mabel. "One day there was smoke rising from the city, and the gates wouldn't open. Some people climbed the cliffs for a look, but never came back."

Eva lowered her head, and her hand slid off Mabel's knee. "After I became his lady," she said slowly, "a prophetess called Abrís came to my lord one night and told him that Linden was held in darkness. And that a book could break it. She said marauders had destroyed Prince Macallo and his army, laid waste to his fortress, and found the book within. Abrís begged for my lord to attack them and retrieve it before they could give it to Lavian. But my husband wouldn't listen because he feared their power.

"That night, the Raptor came to me and showed me a valley where the people of Linden lay in death. There was a girl, standing in a whirlwind of light. Her face was hidden, but I saw that she was reading from a book. The light expanded and covered the valley. . . . The people rose and were alive. But the light vanished, and their faces fell into the grave.

"I cried for them, and Jezul came for me. He asked how the dead could be made alive. 'The girl,' I said. 'She can give them life.' He told me that it was not the girl, but the words of the book and that it was the very book my husband refused to deliver. He asked me who would take back the book that would raise Linden from the grave. I said that I would go.

"'You will,' he told me, 'but not alone.' Suddenly, I was standing in the dungeons with the fighters. Their master brought them before me, and I chose the ones with the Raptor's mark—the very men on this ship. Flames swirled around us and vanished, and we found ourselves amid the marauders on Mesheron Glacier. We cut them down and returned with the book to Sin Via, I to my lord, and the fighters to their master."

Mabel noticed the eyes that were darting between Eva and Haden, who was staring at his feet. The lady flexed her fingers.

"I did not tell my lord what I had done, though rumors spread. There was a shadow over the city, and the moon wouldn't rise. It was the Day of Xaill when my lord came to me, screaming that I had brought a curse upon us. The minions of Mesha and giants of Haubrion had laid siege to our city and called for the book outside our gates. My lord would not fight for me and said that I must give it to them alone.

"He threw me to the dogs. But the moment the gates locked behind me, Abrís emerged from a fire at my side. She took the book from me because my lord had despised it and said that it would be given to another. She placed a crown upon my head and told me that the Earth would be my sword. My enemies cried out for the book, but I gave the crown the death it desired. I smashed their bodies against the cliffs, and the river turned to blood."

"Oh!" Mabel breathed. "You're the Witch of—"

"I'm not a witch!"

"Sorry, I just meant that I've heard of you!"

The lady relented. She looked striking just sitting there, clothed in simplicity, her porcelain skin accented against the black cloth that fluttered in the wind.

"Abrís vanished through the fire, and I was alone," Eva resumed. "I hoped my life would return to what it was before, but my fame spread and I became greater than the king and queen in the eyes of the people. They said I could turn my enemies to dust and bowed to me, though I begged them not. Many coveted the crown, none more than Hadesha. She wanted to use it to expand our borders, past the Golkrom and Ur Sang, to the sea and what lie beyond. She would stop at nothing. But I refused to give it to her, and she plotted my demise.

"Jezul had known that men would seek the crown for their own. He blessed it so that whoever wears it will never die and laced it with a curse—the life that lifts it will be lost. It's a crown that can only be given and never taken."

Eva buried her face in her arms and clenched her hands.

"I had a baby girl . . ." Her voice was suddenly hoarse, and the men looked away. Mabel's heart was sinking, dreading what she was about to hear. "Hadesha turned my husband against me, and he took my baby while I slept. . . . In the morning, a vulture commanded me to come to Carnecia or my child would die. I went at once and found Hadesha in the courtyard. She told me that her power had risen and that I would never become greater than she. I groveled, swearing that I would never overthrow her, begging for my girl. Then my husband came to me and drove a dagger through my body. I couldn't move, horrible truths swirling in my mind.

"'This is the Betrayer's Blade,' said Hadesha, 'given to me by Lavian. It breaks your will by breaking your heart. See how the eyes in the handle glow? They glitter with the blood of the two closest you—one has been wounded, and the other wounded beyond repair.'

"I looked at my husband and saw the pain in his eyes. Yes, I saw his pain, but he stood before me nonetheless, so I knew my baby was dead."

Mabel stared at Eva, stunned, and Mercilus looked suddenly awake. There was a shuffling as Haden, Luther, and Zane stood, but the lady waved them off.

"I've drowned in sorrow," she whispered, lifting her head and wiping her eyes. "Weren't our minds awake all these years? Leave me. *Please.*"

They exchanged somber looks and sat back down.

"Hadesha was furious because the blade did not break my will, that I had enough strength to refuse her demands. That the crown stayed with me. It must stay with me," said Eva, speaking more to herself, "or it will be used to destroy the lives of many. And my pain will be theirs."

Eva covered her face again, her tears dripping on the floor and Mabel's with them. *I will never cry for myself again*, vowed the girl. *What's happened to me is nothing like this.* And her heart broke for the lady.

The eastern sky had turned to gold, but the sun had not yet risen. A slow time passed as J'san navigated the ship farther south, into emptiness.

"I can speak for us," said Zane finally, and he looked around at the men. "We all have our sins, which is why we were enslaved, doomed to the games with thieves and murderers. We had been brought to Sin Via for the Φfèimiga, when Jezul came to us in prison. He said that he knew our hearts, that we would fight for him. We were grasped in the talons of the Raptor, and the brands that marked us as slaves vanished from our skin. That night, our lady appeared to us, and we fought for her.

"Shortly after the Day of Xaill, soldiers took us to Carnecia. We were the last fighters alive, having destroyed everything in the arena. Every man. Every beast. We fought with steel, not with fire, afraid that our powers would be discovered. That we would be forced to fight for the king and destroyed if we refused. But we were taken nevertheless.

"They brought us to a garden where Hadesha was arguing with a prophet. 'I won't let her go!' she was saying. 'Not until I have the crown. How long will that be, gods only know. But I won't stay here, bowing to that statue every day!'

"The prophet told her to return to Avontris, but the queen wouldn't listen, saying it was too large to defend and that she had found a new god—a god of fortresses—but he wouldn't save her as long as she bowed to Centrum Stella.

"'They will not bow to any other god,' said the queen, pointing to us. 'Isn't that what you say? Aren't they indestructible? Let them rid the house of this stench!'

"The soldiers led us into a courtyard where Centrum Stella stood in a fountain. He thought we had been brought to worship him, but when he saw our scars, the scars of the Raptor, he fought us."

"Swords of fire," said Luther, sounding hypnotized. "Within seconds, we were through our chains. He was desperate as we closed in. I cut off his arm, remember him screamin' as he burned—"

"And Hadesha laughing like mad," said Haden in his own vague voice. "Shouting about 'how the fools turned themselves to stone.'"

"You could still *hear*?" said Mabel.

"At first," said Zane, "until we drifted into another world and lived only in our minds. Hadesha thought that we were dead. She didn't know the demon in Centrum Stella was still alive, holding us in stone."

"It trapped itself," said Eva musingly. "When a demon is killed, it falls into the Underworld," she added when Mabel looked confused. "It froze itself in stone rather than die in Avaddon."

The lady rose and seemed stronger now, her eyes clear once more. "The king and queen are dead, and the Titans will dominate Linden, killing any who stand in their way. We must break the Darkness, and when it's destroyed, the Titans will die with it. Lavian has the book though it fell into Avaddon, so there must be a wormhole—"

"Joins two worlds in the Unseen," Haden muttered to Mabel. Eva looked incensed as though she despised him talking to the girl.

"—that leads to Lavian's fortress in the middle heavens."

"The wormhole could be anywhere," said Zane. "How will we find it?"

"I believe—"

"In what?" said Mercilus, and there was a flash in Eva's eyes. "I believed in the Morning Star and fought for him, only to capture a book that's lost again."

A shudder that had nothing to do with the ship, smashing through a wave, passed through Mabel.

"I was the best fighter from Tulle, the best Octavius had ever seen, promised my freedom after the games in Sin Via. But look at us—seventeen years! Because of the book, I've lost my wife and son."

"At least they're alive," said Eva waspishly.

"How would you know?"

The others jumped to their feet as lightning flickered on the horizon. Mercilus stayed seated, a small funnel of wind swirling about him.

"Get up," Eva whispered.

Dry mouthed, Mabel grabbed Eva's arm who flinched, and a

distant expression flitted across her face. Mercilus watched them both through empty eyes. No one moved.

"The ship sails for the Island of Serenity," said Eva in a different voice, and she pushed Mabel's hand away. "There lies a pit that leads into Avaddon."

The wind left Mercilus as the lady turned to Mabel, whose heart was racing. "You'll return with the ship. I will command the seas, and they will carry you to Rell Mor."

"But where will I go?" said Mabel, more afraid of being alone than descending into Avaddon.

"You're the only one that can read the book. We can't risk losing you. Follow the winds when you arrive in Rell Mor, and they will lead you to the house of Abrís. She will keep you until I return."

The lady rounded on Mercilus. "Anyone else can return with her."

CHAPTER 11

THE LIGHT OF LIFE

E va walked down the steps onto the deck below and made for
the far end of the ship, the water boiling in the sea beside her.
"You'll get used to her," J'san said to Mabel, who was gazing
after the lady. And for a while, no one spoke, the wind rushing
through their minds.

"Mabel, how are things in Avontris?" said Zane at last.

"All right . . . I mean, the only thing I've heard was the murder
of the prophets of Niroc a few years ago."

"Any more games?"

Mabel shook her head.

"And Demarèv?" said Haden.

"Just the revolt. The Arinians were mad about getting paid in
maxima. They said it was worthless."

"Arinians!"

And the girl told them what she knew, realizing how little things
had changed. There had been extravagant weddings and funerals,
festivals and fights, but most of what she'd heard beyond the matters
of everyday life were rumors of killings, hauntings, and magic. She
had never traveled much herself and knew little of the outside world.
The men mostly asked about their respective towns, except Mercilus,
who Mabel suddenly realized was gone.

After a while, Zane and Haden turned to leave.

"How do you make the fire come out your arm?" said Mabel abruptly. "I know that I did it before, but don't know how."

"Easy," said Zane, who was grinning for the first time. "Think about a sword and make a fist." He raised his right arm, clenched his fingers, and a pillar of fire erupted in his hand. He relaxed his hand, and it was gone. "Want a shield?" He made another fist, and this time, there was a dazzling shield of light. "Think about a shield. The fire gives you what you need."

"If you want a weapon in your left hand," said Luther, "you can pass it off." He clenched his right hand and touched his wrists together. Flames spiraled from his scars, down his arm, and onto his left hand where a shield instantly appeared. He clenched his right hand again, and a sword burst in his fist. He opened both hands, and the weapons were gone.

"It reads your mind," said J'san, gesturing at the sword burning next to Mabel, "whether you want it to consume the wood or destroy your enemy."

Mabel raised her hand and made a fist. The scars opened beneath her sleeve, and a weightless flaming blade of light flashed in her hand. Something was stirring in her soul, a feeling that told her she was strong. One that intensified at the sound of Luther's voice.

"You look like a fighter."

That evening, Mabel finished recounting to Zane how Cuadra, king of the Highlands, had been cut down by his sons after he sacked Gathlenvame. They were alone at the helm, the others scattered across the ship, though Eva and Mercilus were nowhere to be seen. Mabel bade goodbye and left for the bow where she leaned over the rail and was lost in the setting sun. It looked like a moon now, sitting on the ocean, the sky a canvas of melted gold. But her heart stopped when Mercilus appeared out of nowhere and joined her. Their eyes met, and the girl looked away.

"I'm sorry I lost the book," she said. "And about your family . . ." She stopped, not knowing what to say. The words sounded empty to herself.

"And you . . . no family?" he said.

Mabel shook her head and couldn't resist glancing up at him. There was concern in his face, which made him all the more handsome. His eyes didn't feast upon her like those of other men, who had noticed her in the streets the older she became: whose looks were dark and bestial and made her feel ashamed.

He's probably used to girls staring at him. Say something! But Mabel could not find her voice.

"Then you're gonna have to fight for yourself. We have less than a month together, this voyage and the return to Rell Mor. Put your sleeves back." Mabel did as she was told, and Mercilus drew a dagger from behind his back. "Don't hold it like this," he said as he held out the blade. "Like this." He flipped the dagger in a reverse grip, the blade pointing toward his elbow, flush against his arm.

"You can't always fight with fire," said Mercilus, and he gave Mabel the dagger, the girl pressing the flat side of the blade against her arm. "It shows your location and makes you a target.

"I've never met anyone who could fight with a knife, but not a sword," he went on. "You're closer, so everything's faster. Keep your hands up"—he took Mabel by the wrists and positioned her hands away from her body, in front of her chest—"and feet apart. Bend your knees, left foot forward."

And the fighter from Tulle worked with the girl, showing her how to duck and move and shift from side to side. Mabel learned quickly, rarely making the same mistake twice and never a third. When Mercilus had seen her balance, he feigned a knife in his own hand and began teaching her blocks and counterstrikes. Mabel didn't know how long they practiced, only that the sun was sinking fast and that she had found something she loved to do.

"Come over the top," said Mercilus, pressing his wrist against hers, "then hook the hand."

He swept Mabel out of the way. Eva had whipped up the steps onto the bow and lunged at Mercilus. She threw a punch, but the fighter caught her arm and pinned her elbow against his body.

"Idiot!" Eva spat, wrenching her arm free and shoving Mercilus with both hands. "What are you doing?"

"What are *you* doing?" Mabel shot at her.

"Stay out of this," said Mercilus.

"She's a Reader—*brute!*—not a fighter," Eva stormed. "Don't put this filth in her mind. She'll think she can fight and get herself killed!"

Then Eva rounded on the girl. "Don't let me see you fight again! Not with a sword, a spoon—nothing!"

Mabel stared back defiantly, but kept her mouth shut as the lady turned to go. Her stomach dropped when Mercilus caught Eva by the arm and whirled her around, certain he would be thrown into the sea.

"Use your head, Eva!"

The sea began to churn, the lady frozen in rage, but the fighter plunged on. "You care about the girl? Good, then look at her! She's seventeen, gorgeous, and alone. What do you think's gonna happen to her? She's already a target. Lavian knows who she is, spirits will be searching for her, and you know the men he'll send."

Mercilus let her go, and Eva looked at Mabel with her mind somewhere far away. The waves subsided. The lady wavered where she stood, then turned, and was gone as suddenly as she had come.

"What's her problem?" said Mabel, offering back the knife.

"Keep it," said Mercilus, and the girl stowed it in her waistband behind her back. "Don't judge her, Mabel. The world is dark. It can make you into someone you don't want to be. Eva likes you, and she's . . ."

His voice trailed off, for he had seen a thin scar along Mabel's forearm. The girl was about to pull down her left sleeve when she looked up. He looked away.

"What?"

Mercilus said nothing.

"It's the scar, isn't it?" she said in a dull voice, pulling the sleeve to her wrist. "It happened when I was a girl before I could remember. Grandma said I fell on a stone."

"It wasn't an accident."

"You think I did it on purpose?" snapped Mabel and yanked down the other sleeve. "Wanna kill myself?"

"You were cut by steel," said Mercilus sharply and held out his arms. "Look at me." Scars like hers lined his skin, but they veered in every direction. "Yours is straight, but anyone defending himself would've jerked away. The cut would've pulled one way or the other. It was made when you were young, that I agree, when whoever did it could hold you still." And he looked into her eyes. "I can tell you're being honest, but so am I. What you were told was a lie."

The girl pulled back the sleeve and looked at the scar as though seeing it for the first time. Its perfect path, running along the inside of her forearm, had never felt like an accident, and the truth took hold of her heart.

"Listen," said Mercilus, over the hissing spray, "it wasn't your fault that we lost the book."

But Mabel barely heard. Gigi had lied to her.

The wind moaned into the night as Haden guided the ship, following Orion. Eva was sitting with Mabel behind the burning swords, the women reclining against the mast, sailcloth covering their legs.

"You want anything more?" said Eva softly.

"No thank you," said Mabel. She had barely eaten, her stomach writhing in torment, wondering if she knew anything about herself at all. If Gigi had lied to her about one thing, what about everything else? Every page in the record of Mabel's existence had been written by the words from her grandmother's lips: how old she was, where she was born, her parents . . . *If she even was my grandma* . . .

Mabel put back her head and closed her eyes, tired of acting like she was okay. They opened a second later.

"I'm sorry," said Eva, uttering the words as though they had never been used, "for how I spoke to you today."

Mabel looked over at her, a little surprised. Eva had been kind to her throughout the rest of the evening, going as far as to slow the winds so that Mabel could climb with her to the crow's nest. There they had watched the gathering night, black waters meshing with the twilight. The girl knew that Eva had been trying to make amends and had forgiven her in her heart.

"It's all right."

"These men, they don't think—" Eva stopped and began again. "You're innocent, Mabel. Not like us. I've seen things, things I don't want to see happen to you."

Mabel leaned her head against Eva's shoulder and suddenly felt tired.

"Eva," said Mabel, some minutes later, "what's your country like? Veldesh, I mean. Since it's free from Darkness."

"Out of darkness they came," sighed Eva and leaned back her head. "And into darkness they returned."

"But how? If the Darkness was destroyed?"

"The nation is free in the Unseen, that is true, and men are no longer slaves to darkness. But Lavian comes to humans after they have been set free and tempts them with power—to return to the lives they lived before. Only when he dies will evil be no more."

Mabel yawned and closed her eyes, her body wrapped in the heat of the flames. The ship creaked and groaned and smashed through the waves.

"I like you," said Mabel faintly, "because I know you won't lie. Kill someone, maybe, but I know you won't lie."

The lady gazed in silence then closed her eyes as though she were in pain. The girl fell asleep, and her mind entered the Unseen.

Mabel saw the ship melting into the sea, which had become a lake of fire. The sky descended and turned into stone, the stars falling into the fire and becoming the spirits of men. They were crying and meandering through flames as though they couldn't see, whispering for God, listening for an answer that would never come.

The spirits vanished, but Mabel's relief didn't last long. There were demons, writhing in white worms the size of serpents, a gruesome angel standing over them with his back to Mabel wearing a golden crown. Two yellow snakes hung from the back of his neck, and his wings were made of long, wispy bones that looked like withered reeds. A sea of worms slithered behind him.

The demons called him the Destroyer as they tried to flee. But they were chained, the angel thrashing them with the blades he had for fingers. Worms entered their bodies, and the demons screamed.

Suddenly, Mabel was flying down tunnels, trying to escape through the passages and corridors that opened before her. She zoomed into a cave and saw Lavian.

Mabel gasped and was suddenly awake in Eva's arms, panting as she looked into the lady's worried face. J'san and Zane were standing over them both.

"It's okay," said Eva as Zane dunked a linen in the barrel of water and placed it in her hand. Immediately, Eva began dabbing Mabel's brow and helped her sit up. "You're with us now."

Mabel said nothing, her heart still beating as though it would burst. She felt ashamed and looked down at her hands, wondering if they thought she was mad.

"What happened?" said Eva.

"It was a vision," Mabel murmured, her mind still reeling. "I have them sometimes. . . . The angels told me that I can see into their world."

"What did you see?" said J'san in his thick voice.

"Spirits of the dead," said Mabel. "I think it was Avaddon."
She paused and stared at the stars, suspended in their proper place,
then told them what she had seen. Her mind cleared, and her voice
became stronger.

"Then I was in a cave and saw Sören's head, the bodies of rulers
and a snake that disappeared through a mirror in the wall. There was
a flash, and I saw Lavian on a throne in the reflection—"

"The wormhole," said J'san. "Do you think you can find it?"

"She's not coming!" said Eva.

"But you'll never find it," said Mabel hopelessly. "It's a labyrinth.
There was something inside me, showing me the—"

"No!"

The women glared at each other.

"Was there anything else?" said Zane quietly.

"Not really," said Mabel. "Other than Lavian shouting over the
bodies. He came through the mirror and was searching for someone
who wasn't there, cursing a lord because he'd chosen the Morning
Star and didn't kill the girl—but I don't know what girl."

At this, Eva trembled.

"Did he say his name?"

"Yeah, Amanyára."

Eva dropped the cloth in her hand and got up, her lips quivering
as though she were trying to speak. For a moment, she stood frozen
then staggered into the night.

"What was it?" said Mabel as she got to her feet, but J'san and
Zane didn't answer.

"Come on! What'd I say?"

Mabel strained to hear Zane's voice amid the wind and the
waves. "Amanyára was her lord."

The sky was purple when Mabel rose the following morning.
Luther and Haden were sleeping on the other side of the swords,
wrapped in linens, and the pile of cloth that Eva had used lay

rumpled beside her. Mabel had tried staying awake, to wait for the lady to return. *But that fire . . .*

The girl turned her head and saw Eva sitting on the stern, next to a blazing sword, gazing to the north. Having no idea what she would say, the girl set off across the deck, climbed the stairs, and passed Zane at the helm, the fighter making her a slight bow as she edged by, and stood behind the lady. Eva looked around, her face haggard from a sleepless night, but there was a light in her eyes that Mabel hadn't seen before.

"Come," said Eva, sounding a little hoarse.

Mabel stepped forward as Eva rose and wrapped her arms around her. "You've given me hope that my baby's still alive," she said, and a warmth surged through the girl. "But what about you? Mercilus is right. No matter where you go, you'll face evil in this world. Should you go with us into Avaddon, you'll face an evil greater still."

"But I've already seen it," said Mabel quickly, who could sense that Eva was changing her mind. "I don't think you'll find the wormhole without me." The girl stepped back and looked Eva in the face. "And I want to stay with you."

For a moment, the lady didn't move, then a swell smashed the side of the ship and brought her to herself.

"Then you will lead us through Avaddon," she said in her commanding tones. "You will train day and night until you hate this ship. If you hate even me. But you must be ready for the fight that we face."

Mabel's love for fighting vanished by the end of the day. Mercilus had worked her over with knives, and the others fought her with swords of fire. But it was J'san who had killed her the most. He had found two swords of the raiders, blades that were forged in the fires of the sea and gave no reflection, and made the girl take one in each hand then hold them out like a cross. Her arms would shake and droop; J'san would command her to raise them higher. Haden had tried coming to her aid.

"C'mon, J'san, what's the point?" he had said, throwing up his hands.

"Pain."

"That's ridiculous!"

"She must feel it and learn to fight through it."

And feel it she did, gasping in agony when she awoke the next morning. But Eva seemed to have become as callous as J'san and gave no relief as Mabel grunted and groaned throughout each day: flattened by Mercilus who was demonstrating takedowns, her arms clubbed by Zane, teaching blocks, and shoved by Luther who showed her how to create space by pushing off an opponent.

But a change came over the lady at night, who sat with Mabel and spoke to her in that low voice, telling her of the epiphanies that she had seen in her mind those years she was held by Betrayer's Blade. The lady would fall silent, and Mabel would ask another question, not for the answer, but for the voice which gave it until sleep came and stole the voice away.

The water turned a brighter blue as the trip wore on, and the air grew steadily warmer. The pain in Mabel's muscles was fading now, replaced by the misery of sweating beneath her wintry clothes. One morning, the girl came to Mercilus, who was on the forecastle, drying fish for his return voyage to Rell Mor. She breathed in deeply and scanned the sky, unable to enjoy the dawn for the day of training ahead. Mabel drew her knife, flipped it deftly between her fingers, and pressed it against her forearm. Mercilus saw her walking toward him, picked what looked like metallic cloth off the deck, and got to his feet.

"For you," he said when Mabel arrived and held out a silver mail sleeve. "It was in the hull. Plunder from Tavar by the looks of it."

"It's beautiful," Mabel breathed. She touched the scaly links, and they shimmered like fish in the sea.

"Wear it on your left arm. Now you can change out of your cloak."

Mabel looked up, and her heart seemed to be melting. He had known she was hiding the scar on her arm, and his gaze was steady as he held out his hand. Mabel shook off her cloak and gave it to him, standing in a deep blue tunic that clung tightly to her frame.

"Arms out," he said, tossing the cloak on a barrel. Mabel did as she was told; and Mercilus cut off her sleeves at the shoulders, her skin sighing in relief as the wind streamed through one hole, licked her body, and escaped through the other. He slid the mail sleeve over her arm and fastened the leather strap around the opposite shoulder.

Silence came between them as they weighed each other.

"We're born fighters," he began presently, "and though we train, we must lean on our hearts and not our skill. There's going to be times when you can't run. Maybe there's nowhere to go or someone you love needs you. When the fight looks hopeless, I draw a circle around myself like this." He flashed a sword in his hand, pressed the tip into the deck, and paced around Mabel until she was standing in a ring of fire, flames rising to her knees. "If only in my mind. It's a message to myself that I can't be moved. There's no magic in the circle. You can still get hit and feel pain in the circle. But when I stand in the ring, I fight to the end.

"Be strong now, because that's what you are," he said, and Mabel suddenly felt her eyes stinging. "Don't let anybody move you. If you get knocked down, get back up. If you bleed, you bleed. But fight to the end."

Mabel nodded, her face hard. He opened his hand, and the fire disappeared, together with his sword.

"Hands up," Mercilus commanded, and Mabel raised her fists.

The days quickly passed, and the girl began to change. Her hair grew lighter from endless hours in the sun, and her skin became like bronze. Her arms were more defined from eating pounds of fish and wielding those wretched blades of steel. Eva summoned rain showers that would soak them all and then dry their bodies by turning the water into mist, except for Haden, whom she allowed to shiver in the wind. When Mabel mentioned him to the lady, thinking she'd forgotten, Eva threw her a look that froze the girl in place. Every night at dusk, Mabel descended into the hold where she would brush her hair with a golden mace, fashioned like a scepter. Something about Mercilus made her work the mess until every knot was gone—and made her hate herself.

The girl had been afraid the day would come when she would find a man who would enter her dreams. Mabel had believed that she was destined to eke out a living as a maid, would never marry into a respected family, and was expendable. As much as she had convinced herself that she would never meet her prince, she had found Mercilus, and there he was. He had eyes for his wife and no other and could never be tempted. Unlike the boys Mabel had known at school, who had wanted something from her, he had only given. He was strong and never intimidated. Confident, but not arrogant. Shame and anger simmered in her chest, Mabel realizing that she could never be with someone like him. She felt used, having slept with someone else in her quest for love.

The last evening of the voyage had arrived. Mabel gazed over the port side rail, the sun setting behind her. She was alone, that weight pressing upon her, wanting someone to talk to. The others were scattered around the ship, and she looked over her shoulder. Eva was standing with her back against the mast, silhouetted by a fiery horizon.

God no, thought Mabel. The lady was a lot of things, but definitely no huss. The girl glanced to her left and saw Luther leaning over the rail some ten yards away. He seemed to have gathered the longing in Mabel's face and moved along the bulwark to her side.

"How ya doing?" he said with a smile.

"Good."

"I thought you were still mad at me."

Mabel laughed, though her eyes were still troubled. Knowing

that it was their last day, Luther had pushed her harder than ever. She had snapped halfway through their training session, her curses louder than the wind as she threw three or four wild punches at him, Mercilus shouting her down: *"Lose your head like that and you're gonna get killed!"*

"You might hate me," said Luther, drawing nearer so that he didn't have to shout over the wind, "but I'm gonna push you past your limits because I know there's more."

"I don't hate you," said Mabel, but her smile faltered. "Luther, can I ask you something?"

"Go on."

"It's about this guy I like."

His smile returning, Luther propped an elbow on the railing and leaned sideways to listen. "Tell me about him."

"He's from back home," she lied and did her best not to look in Mercilus's direction, the fighter seated in his usual place on the bow. "Older than me. I don't really know him, but I feel this connection with him like we're the same somehow. He's beautiful, and it's like he always knows what to do. I feel safe with him."

Luther said nothing, waiting, his brown eyes dissolving a wall inside her—a wall she wanted to come down. Mabel hesitated and pulled the strands of windblown hair from her mouth.

I can't ask him.

"Do you think he'd want someone like me?" she said, getting closer to it now. "I don't have anything to give. He'll never get a dowry or land or anything. I don't have any position."

"That's why he's gonna want you." Luther's gaze was intense, and he straightened up as Mabel squinted in confusion. "I'm telling you, as a man, that you're the girl I'd want *because* you got nothing to fall back on. I know you're gonna be all into me—not your friends, not your money, not your family, but me. 'Cause I'm all you got. . . . What's wrong?"

Luther paused as a tear trickled down Mabel's face.

"But I'm not a virgin," she said chilly. "I can't give him all of me, can I?"

And the weight lifted off Mabel's chest. Someone else knew, someone who could carry the burden with her. It was worth the shame, and she braced herself for the answer.

"A real man doesn't want your body," said Luther. "He wants your heart. Love is about the other person, not yourself. It's about pouring yourself into someone else, to fill their emptiness, to make them whole. There're things in him that he can't fix without you, not without money, but without *you*. It's like a fight—I fight for the ones next to me. What matters to me is sacrifice for them, for the bigger goal, which is *us*. There's something special about you, Mabel, something that you can never give away. If he doesn't take you, he's missing out on the greatest thing in his life."

Mabel threw her arms around Luther and stifled a sob; his words had cleansed her soul like a rainstorm, leaving her clean and pure.

"Who is this joker anyway?" said Luther, smiling as Mabel stepped away. The girl half choked, half laughed as she wiped her sparkling eyes. "I'm gonna have to meet him when this is over."

Neither Eva nor Mabel spoke that night by the burning swords, the girl struggling to fall asleep. Her eyes twitched beneath her closed lids. Scenes of tucking children into bed before lying down with Mercilus were cropping up in her mind. *But he's married*, she told herself. *At least he was*, another voice battled inside her head. *But what if he can't find her . . . what if his wife is with someone else?*

"What's wrong?" Eva said at length, brushing her fingers across Mabel's wrinkled brow.

"It's the tunnels," she said, her eyes still closed. This was not wholly untrue, the girl fearing that she would not be able to find the wormhole. "I don't know how I knew the way. It was just this feeling like you've been down a road a hundred times and know where to go. But what if it doesn't come back? I mean, I won't remember."

"It doesn't matter," said Eva. "Our bodies don't need food in the

Unseen, and we won't grow tired. We'll find it, as long as it takes. Just stay close to me."

And for the first time, Eva leaned her head against Mabel's. The swords seemed to burn brighter, and the wind was wailing softer. The women fell asleep, each dreaming of the other.

"Land in sight!"

Haden's voice sounded from the crow's nest the following day. Mabel leaned over the rail and squinted to the south. What she had thought was a cloud hovering on the horizon was in fact an island. Her stomach tightened. The glare of the afternoon sun sparkled on the water as Serenity took form, its low, tree-covered ridges rolling gently to the east, becoming larger, darker, and more concrete. No one spoke as they lined the bow. J'san, Luther, Haden, and Zane were wearing their shoulder guards, arms bare, midsections exposed. The women were standing with them, Mabel's arm still covered in mail, the hilt of her dagger rising from her waistband. Eva stared ahead with radiant eyes.

Mabel turned around to face the stern where Mercilus manned the tiller, his head swaying with the waves, and her heart constricted. She couldn't endure the thought of never seeing him again and made her way toward the helm.

"Mercilus," said Mabel, when she had reached the top of the steps. He seemed diminished, his face empty of the fierce expression that he normally wore as he faced the horizon. "I . . . I just wanted to say goodbye. And thank you for everything." The girl waited a moment or two before adding, "You know after you find your family and everything, I'll be in Port Majoris when this is over. I'm not going back to school. . . . I'll be working for Dr. Huseau," she invented quickly. True, he had always been friends with Gigi but had never offered Mabel a job. The girl would beg to be his maid and lick the floors clean if it meant seeing Mercilus again. "You can ask anyone in town, they all know where he lives."

If you can't find your wife, you can start a new life with me. Mabel stood a few seconds longer and turned to leave when a hand caught her by the wrist.

"The angels," said Mercilus, gazing into her face. "They showed you the darkness over Linden?"

"Yeah."

"They showed me the darkness in my heart."

He let go and stepped away from the tiller, saying, "Take the ship."

Mabel started and seized the bar with both hands. The ship careened slightly, and the others spun around, watching Mercilus rip a sword from the statue of Chrom by the helm. The fighter walked toward the rail, twirling the blade before throwing it into the sea. He stared at the place where it splashed, the water returning to normal, as though the sword had never been, then turned and flashed seven fingers at Eva.

CHAPTER 12

AVADDON

Mercilus guided the ship through the turquoise waters, past two rock formations that rose like victorious fists from the sea. Mabel stood with the others on the bow, trying to see what lay beyond the white sandy beach, but her view was blocked by the rainforest.

They skimmed over a coral reef and barreled down the center of a bay, the beach growing larger, the trees swaying beneath the howling winds. It looked as though the ship was going to smash onto the shore, and Mabel glanced nervously at Eva who said, "Vetra mái halle cy ramerra cy regovin, deya yeul tevanu cy viri ela!"*

The winds ceased, the ship sinking into the water as it slowed, and the palms grew still beyond the beach. About a minute later, the hull struck the sandy bottom, thirty yards from the beach, and the vessel rolled port side as it settled into the sand.

"Let's go," said Eva, and a staircase of water rose from the sea and congealed in front of her. Mercilus left the stern and joined the rest as they walked down the frozen steps onto a pathway of ice that led to the beach. The seven walked across the surface and arrived on the sands of Serenity. The staircase instantly melted and crashed into the surf, rocking the ship as the ice path dissolved.

---

* Winds that lash and rage and reign, end your current and refrain!

Without looking back, Eva trudged across the beach and entered the trees, J'san and Luther at her heels. Mercilus nodded at Mabel, the next to disappear into the forest, and Haden and Zane followed. They waded single file through a sea of ferns as beautiful as the waters they left behind and climbed a jagged ridge where they glimpsed the ocean before descending into a ravine with shallow pools—some clear, others covered with algae so bright that it hurt their eyes. The canopy was pierced by wide rays of the sun that hung like shining curtains. There was no wind, no birds, nor the sound of birds.

Mabel couldn't remember when the distant drumming of the waves had been erased and knew that she should be terrified as they made their way toward the pit, the demons, and the dead. But how could they lie in a place like this? They climbed another hill, the sweat running down her skin as though she had taken a bath. Eva stopped an hour later, and the company gathered by a break in the trees where they stared miserably across a valley of ferns to the east.

"Why's this place called Serenity?" said Mercilus.

"Because there's nothing to fear," said Eva shortly. The sweat poured from her body, and Mabel could tell that she was hungry; her own stomach growled. The lady summoned seven tiny clouds that hung over their party, just below the canopy, drizzled thin trails of water into their mouths and rained over their bodies. Then they were gone.

"I know you're hungry," Eva said to Mabel, with a sudden softness in her eyes. "But when we enter the Unseen, you'll feel hunger no more." She looked off into the valley and pointed to what looked like an enormous shadow beneath two peaks on the horizon. "There it lies."

"Two more hours at least," muttered Haden, as J'san wrung out his hair with both hands so that his arms flexed, appearing as thick as the tree beside him.

Eva turned and descended into the valley.

The afternoon wore on, and the heat intensified as the leaf cover dwindled and the ferns died away. The tiny rainclouds returned, and this time never left, shadowing the company and releasing a cool, continuous mist. Mabel wondered why Eva had not simply blanketed the sky with clouds, but the lady glanced forlornly at the sun as though she might never see it again.

They reached the bottom of a ravine, and Mabel was grateful for the even ground, her legs aching from the steady descent. Dead trees began to appear like skeletons among the living. The sky dimmed as the sun sank lower, and Eva sent the rainclouds away. Soon, all the trees were warped and bony until they gave way and there was nothing left but large dark rocks that forced the seven to slip their way between them. The ground cleared ahead, and they approached the edge of the pit, which spanned two hundred feet in diameter. Giant cavities dotted the black rock walls that descended no more than forty feet into the Earth before disappearing into a massive pool of darkness. Mabel went numb; she could feel the spirits of the damned. The silence spoke of their existence.

Mabel stood with Eva as the men crept along the perimeter, gazing into the dreary hole with tight faces and darting eyes. "We've seen the Darkness before," said Eva, looking straight ahead. "Night, darker than the grave, that held us for seventeen years. But it could not break us. We've seen the demons that prey on mortals and spirits that plagued our minds. Now we go to them, and there will be nothing between them and our wrath."

Eva pulled off the cloth around her head, and the light of the crown destroyed the blackness of the pit. She removed the crown in the other hand, turned her head, and spoke so softly that Mabel could not hear the words. The crown spun and cut Eva's fingers, her blood spilling onto the glorious band that opened and released its light.

"Eva!" cried Mabel, who watched in horror as the light mingled with her blood.

"Be still," said Eva, and she held out the crown. The blood

glowed like lava as it streamed through her fingers and poured onto the ground. A fire ignited on the rocks and rushed around the rim of the pit, spiking into a wall of flames that beckoned them to pass. The crown dimmed as though it were dying, and Eva pressed the tips together. It united and burned as brightly as before.

She placed the crown on her head and opened her hand toward Mabel; her fingers had been cut to the bone. Mabel tore off the cloth around her own head, but the wounds were healed before she could wrap Eva's hand.

"The light that opens the Unseen can only be found in two places on Earth," said Eva, as Mabel dropped the cloth in awe. "The book and the crown."

The lady tied her cloth around her head, hiding the crown once more, locked eyes with J'san, and nodded. The fighter dove through the fire, into the pit, and vanished.

"He just *jumped*?" Mabel gasped.

"He'll fly," said Haden, who was the closest on her right. "You had wings with the Raptor, right?"

"Yeah, but . . . How do you know we're gonna have them now?"

"We're given what we need," said Eva. She waved brusquely for Haden to go, and Mabel saw the contemptuous, almost malevolent look that flickered on her face.

"Because I opened the fire, it will vanish with me when I pass," she said. Zane leaped through the flames after Haden. Eva stepped back as Mercilus and Luther positioned themselves on either side of Mabel. "You must go first. I'll be right behind you."

Mabel nodded mechanically and stared into the fire. Scenes of falling forever flashed through her mind.

"We got you, Mabe," said Mercilus. He took her left hand, and Luther held her right. The knot in her stomach loosened and then clenched as she was catapulted forward, the men jumping with her through the flames.

They were falling into darkness. Luther and Mercilus extended their arms to keep Mabel from somersaulting through the air, their skin glowing like the moon and eyes shining like the dawn. Wings burst from their backs, spreading through the same holes in Mabel's clothes from before and piercing the armor of the men as though it were cloth. They let go of each other, wings fully expanded, Mercilus diving below Mabel as Luther glided to his right, giving her room to spread her wings.

Mabel felt a gusher of relief as the freefall ended and she began soaring around the oval walls. She glanced down and saw the others gliding in wide circles as they descended into the abyss then over her shoulder and smiled at Eva who trailed closely behind. J'san flashed a sword that filled the chasm with light, but the bottom could not be seen.

On and on they flew, and Mabel's attention was drawn to the changes in the walls, whose tones transitioned from black to reddish orange. Strange markings appeared in the rock, marred by gashes that looked as though they had been formed by the claws of a dragon. There were images of beasts, some with fiendish grins as if they knew the future and were delighted at its coming. Others were tearing their victims to shreds. Mabel's blood ran cold at the sight of people with outstretched arms, begging for mercy in the face of death.

"ANIMALS!"

The voices were many, some low and wheezing, others screeching, but they rang as one.

Mabel froze and collided with the wall. Her wing crumpled, and a rock sliced through the strap around her shoulder, the mail sleeve sliding off her arm.

"Catch her!"

Eva dove after Mabel who had plummeted past a startled Mercilus, but the girl leveled off after a nifty flip and spread her wings, too shaken to notice the burning sensation in her arm. Swords erupted in the hands of Haden and Zane as the company halted their descent, Mercilus and Eva flanking Mabel, a glittering stream of blood running down her arm. Eva yanked off the crown and placed it on the girl who felt it fuse to her head—her body had the feeling that it was standing under a waterfall, and the bleeding stopped at once.

"We know who you are, animals of light!" The eyes of the beasts were shining in the walls like fallen stars. Their mouths opened and issued black vapors that swirled above and beneath the floating figures.

"Let us pass!" Eva shouted at the vapors below. The men looked ready to fight, their heads snapping this way and that, but were confused all the same. How could they battle an enemy little more than air?

The vapors beneath them congealed to form what looked like a mirrored floor. The voices came again, speaking slowly, as though a thought had suddenly occurred to them. "You say, 'Let us pass,' but why? Wretches! Why have you come?"

"You know my god," said Eva. "Then know me! I am Eva, daughter of the Morning Star, Lady of Sin Via, who has come to break the darkness over Linden!"

Laughter rang out then trailed away as the vapors over their heads thickened like billowing clouds and turned to stone. The eyes on the walls went cold.

"Live with the dead, daughter of the Morning Star," they whispered. "How then will you break the spell?"

Mercilus flew downward, making a sweeping pass around the perimeter of the pit, and landed on the floor. Seeing that nothing horrifying had happened, the others exchanged glances and touched down beside him. Mabel looked around at the foreboding shadows, dancing on the wall from the light of the swords, and knew they all had the same sinking feeling.

Mabel reached for the crown, gripped the burning band, and felt it let go.

"Keep it," said Eva quietly, and Mabel lowered her hand. The crown fused to her head once more.

"Released after seventeen years," Haden sighed bitterly, "only to be trapped again."

"Shut up, Haden," murmured Mercilus as he stared intently into the floor. He seemed unfazed as he flashed a sword and waved it over the surface. It trembled. Mabel could see what looked like large shadowy fish flitting beneath it.

"We seek a path to Lavian, to come for the book and break the Darkness," Mercilus was saying to the shadows. "Then comes the day of your torment."

"Open the gates to Avaddon," said Eva darkly, who saw where he was going and flashed a sword in her hand. "Or it begins now." She pressed the tip of the blade into the stone. The surface sizzled and burned like withered husks. Stabbing screams echoed around the seven until they couldn't think. J'san fell to his knees and plunged his sword through the floor, driving the blade until his hands struck the surface; flames spewed across the floor in all directions, the chamber quaking so violently that the others dropped to their knees. Mabel clenched her fist and did the same, followed by the swords of Eva and the rest. Within seconds, the room was filled with fire. The floor convulsed, and the tremors ceased.

"Enough!" The whispers mingled with the hissing flames.

"Open the gate!" bellowed Eva. "And we will end your pain!"

There was silence as the seven rose, their swords burning on the floor, flames up to their shoulders. A streak of emerald light appeared in the wall ahead and trickled up from the inferno. At least a dozen beams fell from the ceiling on its right and left, forming what seemed to be the bars to a set of gates. A lone vapor spiraled high overhead, dove through the gate, and the lights were gone. Mabel stared through the narrow gaps that were left in the rock, into a mammoth hall, filled with luminous bodies that stumbled through deep red flames. A wave of desolate cries greeted her ears as the gates swung inward without a sound, lying before Eva and the men what Mabel had seen in her mind.

"Come," said Eva, who seemed to be pulling herself together.

The lady walked forward, flanked by J'san and Zane, the rest at their heels. Their eyes darted back and forth like rats in a maze. The spirits did not seem to notice the opened gates, and Eva paused over the threshold and looked back with Mabel and the men. Each extinguished his sword in his mind, and the fire in the pit vanished. They passed through the gates, not bothering to watch the vapors rising from the floor behind them, and the doors closed with a crash. The flames of Avaddon cowered, as though allowing the sound to travel, unimpeded, across the cavern and down the tunnels on the other side. Suddenly, the sea of worms rolled back like a wave across the floor, slithering through the fires.

Mabel caught Eva's wrist.

"He knows we're here."

"The spirits don't seem to see us," said Zane.

"Not *them*—the Destroyer!"

CHAPTER 13

THE RACE TO THE WORMHOLE'S WALL

How d'you know?" said J'san, as the others gathered around Mabel.

"I can tell by the worms," said Mabel. "How they moved."

"Who cares how she knows!" said Haden. "Do you really wanna stand here and watch this? Let's get moving."

Luther murmured his assent, glancing around to make sure the spirits were kept at bay.

"Mabel, do you remember the way?" said Mercilus.

She looked at the tunnels bored into the opposite wall and shook her head.

"I never saw which one. I was flying and had this feeling . . . everything was opening in front of me."

"But they're chained, right?" said Zane. "The demons."

"It won't matter if we fly into them," said Mercilus.

"The Destroyer wasn't—"

A whisper seeped into their ears. *What was it?* The flames flattened further along the floor, the room grew cold, and the spirits tore their hair from their bodies. Their cries dropped to muted whimpers. It came again, stronger now, thrilling shrieks from somewhere in the tunnels.

"Let's go!" said Eva.

"I don't know which tunnel!"

"Just pick one!" Eva pressed her forehead against Mabel's. "Look at me, you have the crown and your life is safe. But don't use it. It speaks to your mind," she added quickly before Mabel could interrupt. "You can't release its power, especially in the tunnels. It'll bring the house down if you don't know what you're doing. We'll fight for you."

Her men exchanged nervous looks.

"You sure you want her—"

"Mercilus!"

Eva looked back at Mabel, her eyes burning. "I'm right behind you."

Mabel gave a quick nod, flashed a sword in her hand, and rose into the air. The spirits became a blur as the arches rushed toward her. The girl looked around and saw Eva and the fighters trailing in tight formation and was about to plunge through an opening ahead when her heart pulled left. Mabel gritted her teeth and banked hard, the air pressing against her wings and throwing her across three tunnels before she flipped in the opposite direction and vanished through a looming arch.

The girl reached tremendous speed and zoomed down the tunnel like a comet, her body bathed in sword light. The passage was cramped and gave her wings little room to maneuver, the light driving back the darkness just enough for her to see around the bends that came with increasing speed. The figures zipped and zagged as Mabel relived her dream, the passage splitting and splitting again.

Silvery-white streaks began to appear in the walls, and the cries of the spirits could be heard no more. Mabel's heart thundered as though it was determined to break through her chest. *He knows where you're going,* said a voice in her head. *Gotta get there before he does.*

Mabel had no idea how much time had elapsed since they left the fires of Avaddon. Her head was aching, the walls a streaming blur, dips and turns coming so fast that she couldn't think of anything else. There was a growing roar, a dull and vacillating hum. Two more switchbacks and a pink light played along the walls. It was a second longer before Mabel realized that she had led them to the demons, by which time she'd zoomed out into an open gorge, the air vibrating with the buzz of a thousand wings.

"*Umph!*"

Eva slammed into Mabel's back as the girl pulled up, the fighters swerving to avoid them. The seven hovered over the black bottomless ravine, eyes fixed on the wall before them. Lines of glowing pink passages were stacked on top of each other like a honeycomb.

"Where are they?" said J'san. Mabel looked up, nauseated. A massive chain spanned the ceiling, to which thousands of demons were shackled in the middle, forming what looked like a giant beehive. They began communicating with clicks and pops that gave her the urge to dive into the Abyss.

"Which one?" Zane shouted over the droning noise. They were all looking at Mabel who was looking at Eva. For the first time, she saw fear in the lady's face.

"I don't know," Mabel yelled and pointed at the honeycomb wall. "I have to get closer!"

"No way!" shouted Haden. "It's loaded with demons!"

He pivoted in the air and faced the direction from which they had come, but the rock melted over the tunnels and hardened.

"Leave him!" said Eva, and Mabel instantly felt better. The lady's fury had returned.

"Come on, boy!" said Luther. He grabbed Haden by the armor and jerked him toward the opposite wall. "You scared?"

"Let's go!" said Mabel and led the way as they soared under the hive, her skin crawling at the symphony of clicks.

There! The entrance to a dark tunnel, shaped like an oblong mouth with downturned lips, caught her eye in the wall below. The girl had no sooner dived than a swarm of demons burst through the combs like rabid dogs into the gorge.

Mabel tried to reach the tunnel before her team was cut off, but the surrounding demons had enough length in their chains to leave their combs. A large number was suspended in front of the entrance, eyes as black as the Abyss, saliva dripping from icicle-looking teeth.

Breaking in midair, the seven backed away from the demon-infested wall when the bone-white body of the Destroyer, that Angel of the Abyss, rose from the chasm beneath them. He came with long, flowing strokes from his bonelike wings, rising like a stingray from the floor of the sea. His head was shaved, with eyes that burned beneath a golden crown, black lips, and yellow fangs.

Mabel was the first to see him. A waterfall was cascading inside her, a glorious light welling in her hands. The demons grew silent apart from their whirring wings. *Defy the Destroyer*, said a voice in Mabel's mind, her arms aching now, *and death will be his demise.*

"Give me the crown!" shouted Eva, even as the angel kept his distance.

Mabel seized the crown and nearly slammed it on Eva's head, unable to control her shaking hand. The lady floated toward him as her men surrounded Mabel, the angel rising above them and extending his arm. The demons retreated into the wall, and the tunnel was clear.

"Why are they letting us pass?" said J'san. They all looked at Mabel again, who didn't know what to say.

"That can't be the way," said Luther.

"Go wherever she leads!" Eva snapped over her shoulder.

"Eva!" said Haden, who was almost shouting as he pointed his sword at the Destroyer. "D'you think *he's* gonna help us? I'm not flying anywhere he wants us to go!"

The Destroyer made an airy hiss that seemed to come from everywhere at once, the hiss of one not used to being defied. The pink glows dimmed in the tunnels, and a spear of toxic green flame flared in his hand. Eva drifted in front of Mabel and conjured a shield of light.

The Destroyer flew higher, twirling the spear like a baton through the jointed blades that rose from his hand. He glanced over his shoulder, drifted to his left, and threw the flaming missile at Eva, which exploded against her shield. Mabel shrieked as the sparks rained. Eva drew back her arm, and Mercilus yelled for her to stop. The lady told him later that she hadn't heard his voice, but a sensation that she hadn't felt for seventeen years had risen within: that of a mother defending her child. Something about Mabel— vulnerable and counting on her to survive—made Eva want to send the Destroyer to the bottom of hell.

She fired a light wave that missed the angel, twisting his body, and blew apart the giant chain. The blast echoed as the hive swung across the chasm, still anchored on one end of the ceiling, and smashed against the opposite wall, snapping the demons' chains and spewing the monsters like vomit.

Eva gaped in horror; it was the most gruesome sight that Mabel had ever seen. Pink blood oozed down the wall from the shattered exoskeletons, screams filling the air from those with crushed wings that plummeted into the Abyss. But hundreds were free, shaken, and flying in circles as they regained their senses. The sound of the drunken swarm filled the gorge, their patterns becoming crisper, their heads turning toward the seven. The Destroyer drifted further away, and his message could not have been clearer: fly into the tunnel or die with the demons.

"We can't fight them all!" shouted Zane and drifted toward the dark and frowning arch. "Let's go!"

A demon broke away from the rest and sped across the chasm. Mercilus threw his sword and cut the creature in half, flashing another as five more followed.

"*Go!*"

He grabbed Mabel's wing, spun the girl around, and forced

her into a dive. Mabel raced toward the tunnel as Eva showered the demons with light waves that disintegrated their bodies then turned and plunged after her through the opening. The fighters swung their swords and sent thin trails of fire through the air like whips. The tongues coiled themselves around several demons, who fell burning into the Abyss, but the swarm was relentless.

"*Let's go, let's go!*" yelled Mercilus. He and his fellows pulled their wings against their bodies and dove into the tunnel, followed by a river of pink lights.

The tunnel brightened, and Mabel wanted to make sure that everyone was there, but couldn't look back as the turns came quickly again. Grisly deaths—dragons and walls of swords waiting to impale their bodies like pigs—filled Mabel's brain. Why else would the Destroyer have sent them down this path? Her stomach tightened around every bend until it hurt. They were trapped in a nightmare, fearing what lay ahead and fleeing what came behind.

"Ow!"

Distracted, Mabel had misjudged a turn and brushed her wing against the wall, slowing just enough for Eva to fly into her feet.

"You okay?" Eva grabbed Mabel's ankles and threw her forward.

"Yeah!" said Mabel and gave herself a mental lashing. *C'mon, stupid . . . Focus!*

And the girl pressed on, somewhere far beneath the Earth in an Unseen realm. She couldn't hear the sound of her own beating wings, only the high-pitched, whining noise of their pursuers and the jingle of their chains. Mabel snaked through two splits in the corridor, keeping left both times, whipped around a bend, and plunged down a tunnel beneath a series of caves. A brief straightaway gave her a second to glance over her shoulder—a pink glow appeared along the walls behind them and was getting stronger.

"Mabel!" called Eva. "How much farther?"

"Dunno!"

"*What do these things want?*" came Luther's voice.

"They're comin' for the wormhole!" yelled Mercilus, as Mabel led them around a harrowing turn that broke out over an ocean of fire and wailing spirits. They angled right, hugged the inner wall, and disappeared down another dark tunnel. Mabel knew he was right: the demons wanted nothing more than to escape, and were following them to the wormhole. What the beasts would do once they arrived, she dared not think.

"Go on!"

Gliding lower, Eva allowed her men to pass overhead, flipped on her back, and sent two light waves at the ceiling behind her. There was a deafening explosion, and it collapsed in an avalanche of glittering black earth that filled the tunnel, but the aftershocks continued. Eva rolled facedown and caught up with the others, trails of dirt trickling from the fissures that spread down the ceiling as fast as they could fly.

A column of earth poured from the ceiling in front of Mabel, who swerved left, grazing the wall before completing a barrel roll that brought her back to the center. The others flattened themselves along the wall as they zoomed past the torrent and hurtled down the tunnel, which straightened to reveal a gaping cave ahead.

"We made it!" Mabel shouted. She flew through two stalactites that hung from the mouth and landed inside.

A scene of beauty and horror met her eyes. Skulls littered the room, some tucked in crevices while others dangled from stalagmites like hats. Jewels, armor, weapons, and coins were strewn across the ground and glittering in the flames, glaring as six more swords entered the cave.

No one spoke as they scanned the room; each of them could tell these were the prized mounts of Lavian. Mabel looked at the only complete skeleton, lying in a recess, and nearly fainted when she realized that it was Hadesha. There were muted chimes as the ground began to tremble, and a head fell from the wall.

"They dug through!" said Eva as they spun around.

"You control the Earth," said J'san. "Swallow them!"

"I can't! The crown only rules creation in the Seen."

"Just find the wormhole!" barked Mercilus, the pinkish light in the tunnel glowing brighter by the second. There was an outbreak of shrieks and clicks as the creatures realized the sword light was no longer moving away. "J'san, Luther, Haden—stay with me!"

"It looks like a mirror," Mabel called to Eva and Zane as the group split, the three of them scrambling around rock formations and jumping over the breastplates, shields, and relics that lined their way. "Somewhere in the wall."

They spread out, though Eva seemed to be more worried about keeping Mabel in sight than searching for the wormhole. The cave was much deeper than it appeared; there were gloomy recesses that looked like tunnels but immediately led to dead ends, cluttered with body parts and weapons. The darting figures bobbed in and out like shadows, racing, each fearing for Mercilus and the others who would fight the demons any second. But the sounds of the beasts ceased. There was a muffled crash and silence.

Mabel stopped dead, and her shining eyes found Zane's through a gap in the stalactites.

"Keep going!" said Eva, her voice echoing in the stillness. They moved on, ears ringing from being confined in the tunnels with the demons. Another minute had passed when they came to a large shallow pool streaked with blood. Zane spread his wings and flew over the water, Mabel and Eva soaring behind him, and the three of them landed on the other side.

It was as though they had arrived in a different cave: pearl sand covered the floor like the beaches of Serenity, the walls were white, marred by nasty yellow stains, and the voids in the rock were filled with thousands of clear stalactites that hung like icicles. One of the cavities reached to the floor, with narrow winding paths etched in the sand beneath it. Zane cast a look at Eva and ducked through the low-hanging arch, snapping a stalactite with his wing, and was gone.

More light was cast onto the walls, and the women turned their heads to see Mercilus, Luther, Haden, and J'san gliding across the water.

"What happened?" said Mabel, as the figures touched down beside them.

Mercilus looked down, opened his hand, and watched his sword vanish. "The cave closed just before the demons arrived." He lifted his head. "The Destroyer is king in this place and let us pass. He sealed us here, away from them."

After a silence, Haden said what they all were thinking. "Lavian wants us alive."

The truth echoed coldly on the walls, and Mabel could tell that Eva was avoiding her gaze. The girl felt lightheaded. They had sailed halfway across the ocean, faced the Destroyer, and raced like rats through Avaddon, only to come to the very place the Snake wanted them to be. If he knew they were coming for the book, why didn't he have them killed? What did he want with them, and what would he do to her?

"I found it!"

Zane's head popped out from under the arch when no one came. "What's wrong?"

Eva shook her head.

"Nothing. Cave's closed."

The lady walked toward Zane, Mabel, and the others right behind her, extinguished her sword, and crawled after him through the void. Five more figures squeezed themselves through the gap and stood in a vast chamber on the other side. Lightning flickered along the fissures in the ceiling so that those carrying swords put them out.

Zane led the way to the opposite wall, covered with more of the icy stalactites. There was a space in the center between two thin pillars, no more than four feet apart, that descended to the floor. The fighter flashed a sword, whose glare exposed a shimmering substance that covered the space like a liquid spiderweb.

"That's it," said Mabel, nodding. "The snake passed through it."

"Then so shall we," said Eva. She stepped up to the wormhole, her image reflected in its surface.

"I'll go," said Zane in low tones. His sword vanished as he threw out his arm and held Eva back.

"It must be me. He knows we're here and will be waiting on the other side."

But Zane gave a faint smile. "All the more reason that I should go, my lady."

Eva's mouth quivered as she held his gaze and then stood aside.

Luther walked over and clapped Zane on his steel-covered shoulder. "Right behind you."

And without another word, Zane stepped through the wormhole. Mabel watched in surprise as the delicate substance didn't pop as she had expected, but stretched like a curtain of honey, drizzled over his head, and covered his body. Zane faded, became like a shadow, and was gone. The liquid filled the wormhole and tightened like glass once more. The rest of the men filed slowly through the opening until Eva and Mabel were alone.

"Stay with me," said the lady, her voice weak as though she doubted her ability to save. She took Mabel by the hand and led her to the gap in the rocks, the girl trying not to think about Lavian and his angels. Mabel entered first, but Eva slid an arm around her waist and pulled herself close so the two could pass as one. The girl held her breath and closed her eyes, the warm liquid trickling over her body, filling her insides. Her lungs were suddenly breathing again though her mouth was closed. She felt weightless and knew her body would soon be carried away, but something about Eva's arm around her waist—her head, pressed against her shoulder—had already taken Mabel to another world.

CHAPTER 14

ESCAPE FROM THE MIDDLE HEAVENS

M abel was rising through a current of pale shadows that felt like it would throw her to the moon. There were mad cackles and distant screams. The girl shouted as something grabbed her arm, but the cry fell on her ears alone. Eva glided out from behind her and moved just ahead of Mabel. The current began to wane, the cries were silenced, and the two of them were pushed gently into the throne room of Lavian.

The women stepped away from the black stone wall and joined the men, staring around at what looked like a cathedral. Sunbeams passed through slits in the walls, rays so thick that Mabel felt as though she could grip them in her hand. And in front of them, raised on a dais of skulls, was the throne with the engraving 𝔄 𝔦𝔩𝔭𝔰 𝔥𝔢𝔟𝔦𝔠 𝔪𝔬𝔧 𝔱𝔯𝔬𝔫𝔞𝔠 𝔞𝔨𝔥𝔞𝔫𝔬 𝔇𝔢𝔬𝔰 𝔭𝔢̂𝔩𝔩𝔢* upon its back.

The room had no doors.

Mabel's eyes widened as the floor pitched slightly, and she remembered they were floating somewhere over the Earth.

"This is it," Eva told them. Her low voice mixed with the wind that passed through the windows. "Find the book. I'll blow a hole

---

* I will raise my throne above the stars of God.

through the wall, and we'll fly back to Earth." She looked at Mabel and gestured toward the row of violet flames. "Don't pass through the fires."

The sound of popping ice echoed in the room. They turned to discover that the wormhole was frozen.

"We couldn't have returned anyway."

"That's not the point," said Mercilus tersely. "It means they know we're here."

"Just find it!" Eva spat.

"It's not gonna be here!" said Haden. "He's way ahead of us."

"*Shh!*" Luther raised his arm. Distant sounds were coming from the flames.

"Hide!"

Mercilus grabbed Mabel's arm and ran with her to a column that supported the vaulted ceiling. He pinned her back against a pillar and then sprinted to the one on her right as the rest scattered behind columns and the statues of demons. The sounds were growing louder and took the form of voices.

Without warning, Lavian burst through a column of flame, gashes marring his fleshlike body. His lightning bolt vanished as he moved toward the center of the room, followed by no fewer than twenty Dark Angels who poured through the violet flames. The creatures were wounded, blood spattering on the floor as they surrounded their god.

Mabel's heart was hammering so madly that she was sure the angels must hear it. She dared only to move her eyes and saw Eva standing behind the column on her left. The lady shook her head with a look that said, *Stay where you are no matter what.*

"We failed," said the tall and thin angel, Balim, as he neared Lavian.

"We had Aurèle," fumed another, "but his angels—"

Lavian's hand shot to the angel's face, his fingers plunging through the mouth and sockets.

"Blasphemous imp!" screamed Lavian and lifted the angel off his feet. "I warred against a legion! You only had to escape with the star!"

"We needed its light!" said Balim, his sunken face contorting with hate. "Now we cannot release the spirit!"

The Snake hissed, a blue vapor escaping his mouth and infiltrating the nostrils of the angel in his hand. His body became like stone, and the green light of his soul flashed and then disappeared through the floor. Lavian set the figure on the ground, drifted back, and smashed the angel with his tail, showering the floor with his remains. The others remained silent, eloquent with rage.

"We must kill Estelle," said an angel at last. He appeared the most intimidating of his fellows, with a gaunt face, deep-set sockets, and a salt-colored body covered with markings that resembled spiders from afar. "Until then, the Raptor's own will come for the book."

The Serpent stiffened and looked over his shoulder, the slits in his eyes narrowing.

"The Raptor's own will come soon enough," said Lavian in his swarming voice. *"Yessss, even now, they are here."*

Mabel felt the blood draining from her face. Her eyes flashed to Eva, and the girl screamed in her mind. The lady had squared her shoulders and stepped out from behind the pillar, into the open.

What are you doing!

"Lavian!" said Eva in a carrying voice. She strode past a column of flame and stood before his throne. "We have come for the book."

Mabel shimmied just enough to peer around the pillar, through a column of flame, expecting Lavian to strike. But the Snake signaled for his angels to stand back and turned toward Eva, his mammoth tail unwinding as it lifted him into the air. Mabel's eyes darted to Mercilus—his place behind the pillar was empty—then back to Eva, where the blond-haired fighter had appeared at her side as though by magic. The other fighters emerged, looking as large as the angels with their wings and armor, and the lady was flanked by five burning swords.

The angels, save Lavian, turned to obsidian. No one moved.

"Eva," said Lavian in a low voice. "It is as I've seen, as the spirits have told me." He began slithering among the angels who stood like statues, peering over their heads at the lady. "Jezul has given you the crown, but I too can give you life." He paused as though his mind had wandered for a moment then continued, "Has the crown saved your life? True, it protects your body, but it cannot save your heart. Are you alive, daughter of men, if your heart is already dead?"

Lavian was no longer moving and looked squarely into Eva's eyes. "*Yessss*, the Serpent will restore your heart. Eva, take your daughter, for the girl that is with you is not Mabel, but Chloe."

Eva trembled, unable to keep her eyes away from the pillar behind which Mabel stood. Zane drew near to her as though to keep her from falling, and Mabel crept further around the column, staring at Eva, possessed by the feelings a girl had always wanted but never known. Ancient secrets that whispered she had finally found herself.

"Are you so dull?" said Lavian, making his way toward the crystal ring in the middle of the room. "Did you not feel your heart burn while the girl was with you, from the first time that you looked into her eyes? She's created in your image, seventeen, and came to you in Carnecia . . . to set you free. You wondered, but would not hope, that she is the one returned to you.

"I sent the Betrayer's Blade to Hadesha," Lavian pressed on, now staring at the mediums of magic scattered on the floor. Some glittered, but others looked faint and seemed to be neither solid nor gas, as though they weren't really there. The tip of his tail coiled around a glittering object. Mabel felt an infinite chill as he lifted the blade that she had pulled from Eva's body off the floor. The eyes were still glowing in the golden hilt. "The weapon with the power to break your heart, which breaks your will. *Yessss*, it was my plan to break your will so that you would give the crown to Hadesha, and that she would pass it to me."

"The blade did nothing!" said Eva, trying to sound defiant rather than anguished. "Even in bondage, I could think and feel. Even then, you could not break me!"

Lavian looked back at Eva, and his flickering tongue froze. He looked as though he would have liked nothing better than to swallow her whole.

"You know nothing, daughter of dust, save what your god has told you. Listen and learn the secrets of the Dragon. The blood of the two closest to a human soul must fall on the blade to waken its magic—the blood of pain and the blood of death. This is what Hadesha told you. This is true, but not wholly true, and therefore is a lie. For the power of the blade to be complete, it must taste the blood of death . . . of the one *closest* to you. *Yessss*, the one closest to you must die. And who is closer to a mother than her only daughter?

"But why did the queen use Amanyára to wound and kill and drive the blade through your body? Why not Hadesha herself? Because the power of betrayal is made greater by the one who betrays. *Yessss*, are not my words true? Is that not what has haunted you for seventeen years?"

At this, the angels let out noises that might have been low and hissing laughs. They shifted ever so slightly, the scales over their eyes glittering in the sunlight.

"Hadesha lured Amanyára with power and gave him the blade. He was to wound himself so the blade would taste pain—then kill your child, giving the blade the taste of death.

"But your husband turned against me," said Lavian, hatred in his voice. "He came for your daughter to kill her, but spirits tormented his mind. Spirits of pride and power, spirits who crucified his heart, mocking him as a black widow father. But came too the cry of the Raptor. He knew not what to do—wretch!—and drove the blade through his arm, falling at your daughter's side. He let the blood flow until the wound was beyond repair . . . *yessss* . . . he struck himself with a fatal blow.

"But with the lifeblood still in his veins, Jezul appeared to him and whispered to Amanyára the deep secrets of the blade—for the Morning Star knows the secrets of darkness as I know the secrets of light—that only someone whose blood has fallen on the blade can remove it. He told Amanyára that Hadesha would betray me, that she would seek to keep the crown for herself and refuse to deliver you to me. And so the crown would protect your life, Eva, princess of men. You would lie in a dream until your daughter would come for you one day . . . *someday* . . . to pull the blade from your body.

"Amanyára then wounded your daughter with the blade. Have you not seen the scar on her arm? Or has the child hidden it from you?"

Mabel lowered her eyes, staring at the cut in her forearm, and a strange feeling overtook her. Tears ran down Eva's face, her arms hanging lifelessly at her side.

"Your lord covered his arm to hide the wound," said Lavian, "and Jezul left with your baby, given to another, hidden from the Serpent.

"Amanyára came to Hadesha with the blade, but she did not know that his life was short. No sooner had Amanyára driven the blade into your body than he died. Hadesha raged, knowing she had been deceived, for you would not heed her command—you would not give her the crown. The Betrayer's Blade had only wounded your heart, not broken it, for the one closest to you—your daughter—was still alive."

At these words, the fortress rocked, lifted by a gust of wind that whistled through the windows. Eva staggered into Luther. The room swayed twice more and was still.

"Hadesha did not know the deep secrets of the blade . . . *tsssss* . . . but kept you, Eva, hoping to wear your crown. When the girl was sent to Carnecia, I knew then that she was Chloe, the one who could set you free. My lying spirit spoke through the vulture and told Hadesha the girl had the power to pull the blade. *Yessss*, this was

true, but not wholly true, and therefore was a lie. My spirit made
her believe the power was given to her by the angels. Hadesha did
not know that the girl was your daughter, and the power came from
her blood.

"Am I a lie?" Lavian said quietly, and the lady trembled as
though he had read her mind.

Lavian slithered through the ring, halted on the other side, and
threw the blade across the room. He reached out to an altar beside
him, apparently retrieving something that no one else could see. A
green fire erupted in his hand and then vanished to reveal the book
in his grasp.

"I have warred with you, this is true, but it profits me nothing
to kill Chloe."

For a split second, Mabel wondered to whom he was referring,
then almost sank to her knees. Her legs quivered as though it was
she and not the pillar beside her that bore the weight of the vault.
She was the girl, the daughter of Lord Amanyára—a lost treasure,
risen from the waves of the past. She was the orphan no more, the
light of Eva's life restored.

"If she dies, Jezul will choose another, and if she dies, you will
never give me the crown for your hatred will consume you. Yet,"
Lavian rasped, "if you leave without the book, the power of darkness
will reign over Linden. Even now, the Titans are destroying your
country, slaying all who lie in their path. The more blood they drink,
the more they will thirst. But if the Darkness were broken, their
power would be no more."

He held out the book to Eva and whispered, "Place your crown
on my head, and I will give you the book. After I have the crown,
you and your daughter will leave this place together."

"If you wear the crown, you will live forever," said Eva, and she
sounded vacant. "The prophecy against you will fail."

"What is that to you?" said Lavian wickedly, rising on his tail
as lightning flashed in his fist. "Forget the Morning Star! Who is

he that you should be his slave? Give me the crown and go your worthless way!"

"Liar!" shouted Eva. Her voice was clear now, as though there were no feelings, mists, and echoes in her mind. "You will destroy us when I give you the crown. Who are you that I should be your whore?"

The lady fired at Lavian, who blocked the wave with a shield of black energy, then threw a jet of light in Mabel's direction, which nearly clipped the pillar before it blew an opening in the wall behind her. Mabel glanced back at the deep blue sky. It could not have been clearer that Eva wanted her to flee.

But the girl faced the fight and knew that it wouldn't last long. She took no notice of the men—the fighters unleashing streams of fire at the angels, some of whom were hit and burned while others flew out of the way with lightning in their hands—her eyes glued to Eva, dueling with Lavian.

A loud roaring filled Mabel's brain, and the room swam before her eyes. They locked on the book in Lavian's hand. *If I get the book, they'll leave them and come for me.* And before she knew what she was doing, Mabel sidestepped out from behind the pillar and ran at Lavian.

In two strides, she was soaring as eight or nine angels drifted toward the hole, their backs to the wall. They didn't see Mabel until she had slipped between two of them, then past another who threw a backhanded fist. Mabel flashed a sword and severed his arm, rolling like a barrel as a bolt sailed over her head, never slowing down as she leveled her wings and flew on. More angels turned in her direction, two swords whizzed past her face, and two angels shattered into a million pieces. There was a flash of light—Mabel couldn't see—and Eva screamed.

Mabel's sight returned a split second later. Nothing was standing between her and Lavian, his eyes fixed upon Eva. Mabel had seconds.

The book was in Lavian's outside hand and lightning in the other. The girl zoomed ahead.

No way I'm gonna get the book . . .

Lavian rose higher on his tail, unsteady as he dodged a stream of fire, then opened his wings, and drew back his arm.

But Mabel speared him before he could strike. The girl plowed her shoulder into his side, using her body as a missile, wrapped her arms around his waist, and drove her wings once more. Mabel shouted, feeling as though she had just hit a tree, but the tree fell and together their bodies went crashing to the floor.

Lavian opened both hands as he hit the surface, the book went sprawling, and his bolt vanished. Mabel let go and rolled, jumped to her feet, and scooped the book in her hand. She fled as Lavian flung his tail from the floor. The tip coiled around her knee, and the girl spun like a top. But Mabel planted her right foot and drove forward with her wings. The next second, she was free, running from the Snake as Eva fired a light wave that blasted a hole in the wall ahead. There were explosions, shouts, and wildly thrown bolts that zipped past Mabel and pelted the wall. But the girl never looked back as she spread her wings and flew through the smoking breach.

Mabel hurtled through the sky, the fortress descending like a wedding cake beneath her. She was able to look past the outer wall at the Earth below, a gleaming bed of jewels that cheered for her to come. *Gotta get down!* she thought as she hurtled past a tower, narrowly missing a low-hanging arch, folded her wings, and dove toward the wall. The wind was roaring in her ears, but her heart was beating slower and the mind becoming clearer. The girl careened this way and that, buzzing structures on the way down, zooming under buttresses like a fly and gaining speed until they passed in a long, continuous blur.

Mabel banked hard around a watchtower. The black shape of Lavian shot around from the other side, and the two nearly collided as they crisscrossed in midair. Their bodies glided apart, Lavian banking to his left in a wide sweeping turn, coming back for the girl who looked left, Dark Angels pelting toward her, and swerved right, anchoring the book in one arm while flashing a shield in the other. The Snake threw a lightning bolt that never reached the girl, the missile crushed in a rainstorm of sparks by a brilliant wave of light. He flashed a shield and blocked a second wave that exploded and sent him spiraling through a tower.

Mabel glanced over her shoulder, and her spirits soared. Six shining figures were weaving among the spires, diving toward her. Tongues of fire jetted through the air and wrapped five angels in burning coils. The screaming creatures veered and crashed into the spires and columns around them as a series of light waves pulverized four more. And the next moment, the six became seven.

"Yeah, girl!" shouted Mercilus, who pulled alongside Mabel with blazing eyes. "You okay?"

"Yeah!"

"Let's go, baby!" said Luther's voice from above.

Mabel felt something tug her wing—Eva, threads of gold streaming from her eyes—and her own vision blurred.

Dozens of angels rose from the wall and flew toward the fleeing party. Eva and her men pulled in front of Mabel, issuing light waves and jets of fire. Dark Angels fell, and a hole opened in their ranks. Mabel shielded her face as the two lines closed at a frightening speed. . . . The girl shouted, and the angels roared. Lightning zipped for her head, and there was one giant blast.

Mabel's shield exploded, taking three bolts at once, and she felt like her arm had been shattered with it. Sparks burned her skin, her ears must be bleeding. Stunned, Mabel's wings contracted involuntarily, and her arms froze around the book. The girl was falling, but her mind suddenly cleared, her wings opening once more. A woozy smile crossed her face. They had crossed the wall and were plunging toward Earth, and the Earth was rushing up to greet them.

Mabel was beginning to see rivers, silver threads snaking between sapphire mountains when the four winds screamed across the heavens and converged beneath them. A milky layer expanded in all directions, and the Earth was lost to view.

"He's freezing the sky!" cried Zane.

They pulled up and threw out their hands, except for Mabel who hugged the book to her chest, vowing never to lose it again, struck the ice, and slid on their bellies like penguins. Haden hooked one of Mabel's arms, flashed a sword, and drove the blade into the ice. The others did the same, and the forces of fire and ice battled with each other, the swords consuming the latter so that Mabel thought they would never stop. But their bodies slowed, and they came to a rest, leaving long and burning trails in the ice.

They slipped and slid as they scrambled to their feet, but the angels that had landed to the west walked steadily toward them, as though the ice were on their side. Lavian fell out of nowhere and crashed like a meteor before his angels, spraying fragments of ice as dull popping sounds reverberated throughout the sky. Hordes of Dark Angels were landing to the north, south, and east and formed a distant ring around the seven glowing figures, their backs to one another, Mabel in the middle.

"Eva!" shouted Lavian. He opened his rock-solid arms, and his angels stopped. "The crown will save your life, but not theirs!" At this, he leveled a lightning bolt at their number. "Give me the crown or watch them—"

Lavian broke off as trails of golden light rose from the book. The first entered Mabel's mouth, and the second spiraled around her arm before snaking through her nose. Brilliant letters appeared on her arm, burning so brightly they could not be deciphered through the glare. And the dreamer spoke in a language not her own. The girl stood slightly taller now, as though she were in control.

Eva glanced back at her.

"Wha—"

Mabel had flung the book at Lavian, which smacked as it hit the ice. The cover flew open, and the book spun, its pages fluttering until it bumped against Lavian's tail. The Serpent hissed because the pages were blank.

The girl held out her arms, light streaming from the writing on her left, scars on her right, down onto her hands. She made three rapid twirls, and the light flew from her fingers and followed her through the air, golden wisps that looked like threads around her body. Mabel dug her toes into the ice, stopped spinning, and faced Lavian. But the light continued to whirl. The voice fed the light, and the light fed the funnel, moaning, daring any to come. The girl flicked her wrists, and the funnel opened to surround Eva and the men and spiked into a cyclone.

An angel fired a bolt of lightning. Mercilus flashed a shield behind Mabel, which shattered the bolt as soon as it passed through the wall. The cyclone flared again and more lightning came, but this time, the bolts were consumed by the light. Mabel could hardly see Lavian through the rushing wall. He rocked from side to side, and she had the foreboding feeling that he knew something about her, something that she didn't know herself. But the feeling slipped away; the Light told her there was nothing to fear.

The cyclone bored through the surface, and the ice inside the light gave way. Mabel and her team fell through the hole and were diving toward Earth once more.

Lavian slithered toward the cyclone, Balim walking at his side, and the angels closed in until they were standing several feet from the light. The funnel began to die as though it longed for the voice of the girl.

Mabel soared over a sapphire mountain, its peak covered in a sea of pearls that cascaded down its sides into the mouths of a dozen rivers. She couldn't think, didn't know what she would do once they landed. Her vision blurred once more, and she felt a warm liquid running down her cheeks. But a power guided her from within. She never heard the emeralds that crunched beneath her feet when she landed in the foothills, never saw Eva reach for the crown to release its light, to cross into the Seen. The lady dropped her arm as Mabel held out her own and said, "Keem yú vä medella e cuyan, yú ilys ihlo mares."[*]

A thin stream of fire issued from her hand and ignited the ground ahead. A wall of fire towered before them. Mabel lowered her arm, not looking at the stunned faces as the men passed through the fire. A hand took her own, and Mabel walked through the flames.

She was standing on the other side, back in the world of men—dark eyes, fair-skinned, and wingless. Mabel turned toward Eva, backing away, wanting to see the light that had been taken from her and thrown away in time. To see Eva for who she truly was, the mother that she craved. But Mabel could only make out her quivering shape through a wall of tears. The lady stumbled forward and threw her arms around the girl, who pinned her face against Eva's neck, and together they fell to the ground.

---

[*] When you walk through the fire, you will not be burned.

CHAPTER 15

WHEN THE GIRL DIES

The cyclone was sighing now, and a minute later, the light was gone. Lavian, Balim, and a host of angels moved forward and stood on the edge of a steaming hole. They peered through the mist at the Earth below.

"The girl holds the light of Zaphon," sighed a hypnotic voice. An angel sifted his way toward Lavian, his skin thawing from obsidian to flesh, but his eyes remained as scales armored against the sun. 𝕯𝖊𝖈𝖊𝖎𝖛𝖊𝖗 was written under his right socket, and 𝕮𝖞𝖈𝖆 carved beneath the left. "What does it mean?"

"You know nothing, Cyca," said Lavian. His tones were low and acid. "None of you. I alone stand between you and the Lake of Fire. If it were not for me, even now you would be tormented day and night."

A shiver ran through the angels that were close enough to hear. The Serpent held his gaze, his body frozen as though his soul had flown away and left an empty shell behind.

"The prophecy of the Morning Star has been fulfilled," said Lavian, and the winds carried his voice to the masses. "'A ilys tæjah moj Raima sai bahen saidra cy erevenu aiya von bahen correles.'* Jezul has taken the words from the book and written them on her

---
* I will put my Word within them and write it on their hearts.

heart. *Yessss*, the light of Zaphon courses through her veins, her heart burns with the light of his words, for I have seen it."

The angels pressed closer.

"If the words are written on her heart," said Cyca darkly, "it is to our avail. The book could not be destroyed, but the girl—"

"Can be overcome," said Lavian. "And when she dies, the words die with her."

"Kill her now!" shouted an angel from the horde.

"It's too late!" Balim snapped in the direction of the voice. "We should have ended her life in Carnecia. Now Eva will give her the crown."

Lavian shouted him down.

"Have I not told you, *fiend*, that I have my plans for her? It was my design that Eva know her daughter is alive. She will give the crown to her daughter, *yesss*, but the girl is closer to death than before!"

Lavian turned away and stared into the mist. "I have sown joy in the girl's heart—joy that will grow, only to be thrown down to the grave. It will not be enough for the crown to keep her alive. Even if she lives, she will die, for I will kill her from within."

"My father," said Cyca in his spellbinding voice, "if you take my life and send my soul to the Lake, so be it. But hear the words of the deceiver, the one who is the same as you—foul devil of foul devil, night of true night."

Lavian said nothing.

"Who can know your ways, my god, as you are higher than we? But the plot of the Serpent—that infallible, mysterious design—will take time, and only one prophecy must fail. The Morning Star has stumbled and written the words on her heart. Take her life now, let the words die with her. The darkness over Linden will never be broken. Only one prophecy must fail."

"*Yessss*," hissed Lavian. "But which one? Shall the dragon kill the dreamer or the Serpent weave his lies?"

The eyes around him sparkled with a light that had nothing to do with the sun, thirsting for the blood that would end their demise.

Lavian rose on his tail and looked to the north. "The Titans will do my will, for my curse flows through their veins. I will send them to hunt Eva in the Seen."

The angels hissed and jeered.

"The half-bloods are worthless!" said Balim. "Eva broke them in Carnecia and will break them again."

"Enough!"

Balim shrank back as though he wanted nothing more than to dissolve into the bodies behind him. The angels shoved him away. "Eva will give her daughter the crown," said Lavian, "and lose her ability to fight with the light . . . *tssss* . . . for her power comes from the crown."

And the Serpent lowered his voice. "I will strike terror in the heart of Eva and the girl, terror that one will live and the other will die. For there is one crown, but two lives. I will summon every abominable spirit—every sprite, goblin, and wraith, every phantom of our race—to make Eva afraid to lie down at night, afraid of forests, where predators lie in wait; afraid to stay in villages where witches, destroyers, and villains do my will. Fear will drive Eva into the Unseen, to set Linden free—for when Linden falls, all that is vile falls with it. Then, and only then, will she find peace with the girl.

"But I will go down to Earth . . . *yessss* . . . and wait for them in the Unseen. I will find the girl before she can break the Darkness, for I know where she will lie. When she's alone, I will spill her blood."

"And if she wears the crown?" said Cyca.

"Don't I know the heart of the girl? She loves the lives of others more than her own. But the girl is easy to play. Draw Eva's blood, and she will give the crown away."

The angels erupted, and the winds screamed in celebration. Lavian waited until the frenzy reached a state of madness before he opened his arms.

"Send every spirit to Veldesh!" he shouted, and the pandemonium died away. "Send them to the womb of the Trethinian rivers, roam from the ruins of Aram Eræcen, and back again. The girl's time is short, and ours draws nigh!"

With that, the Serpent rose into the air, folded his wings, and dove through the misty hole. The ice suddenly became a layer of clouds through which the angels fell, the creatures screaming toward the Earth. Midway through Lavian's descent, there was a flash of lightning, a shock wave that ripped the heavens, and the Serpent was gone.

———•◦•———

A cold gray sky threatened dawn over Novecca. The coastal city had not yet awakened, nor ever would. Blood filled its wandering streets, and the gutters were dammed with bodies. There were no cries of animals or screams of children, only the sound of crackling fires that rose from the decimated city, strange fires that melted rock and iron, devoured timber, and left no ashes. The Titans convened outside the mangled gates.

"We should be in Zoridia by now," grumbled a Titan with a wolflike skull. "We've become like vampires. Look at us!" The beast named Hydro-Vor pointed at several Titans lapping the blood that trickled through the gates.

"What are we to do?" growled Andromede. "The thirst consumes us."

"But it grows by the day," breathed another. "Soon we'll do nothing more than hunt for blood."

"And rule nothing!" said Hydro-Vor. "We're groveling leeches!"

"We should have never returned to his world," said a Titan whose voice whistled as it passed through his bearlike fangs. "It would have been better to stay in Magatha."

At these words, yelps and muted whimpers mingled with the

popping flames. Andromede held his gaze, jaw quivering. For a fleeting moment, he looked like an insect against the burning ruins.

"I see. . . . If anyone prefers the chains of the Unseen, come now." Andromede turned absently and faced the one who had spoken. "*You*, Mosca?"

The albino backed away.

"Even if we rule, we kill," said Andromede, his voice growing stronger. "So what if we must live on their blood?" He gestured toward the burning city. "There's no shortage of men. I took the power once and would take it again. No one can stand against us."

"Have you forgotten Carnecia?" said Hydro-Vor scathingly. "Those with flaming swords and the witch that rules them?"

"We will see her again," rasped Andromede. "Her magic comes from the crown, but I'll cut off her head and make the power mine."

The words had scarcely expired when a sunbeam pierced the sky, thrown from beyond the eastern hills, and Hydro-Vor erupted into flames. His body burned with a vengeance, and the Titans watched as the wind swept his ashes away.

"The curse!" said Mosca feverishly. "We're still under the curse!"

"But we delivered the book!" came another voice, and humming sounds could be heard as lightning flashed in the hands of the pack.

"You defy me?" howled Andromede, unfazed by the calculating eyes upon him. He raised his own bolt of lightning. "Let's bleed the curse from our veins!"

"*Vermin . . .*"

The half-bloods looked toward the shore in the direction of the voice. A torrent of water stormed onto the barren fields and surged like a river for the gates of Novecca. The pack split as the water flowed into its midst, still connected to the ocean as though it were an enormous umbilical cord. It ebbed slightly and rose like a gusher.

"Kneel," said the voice again, nearly drowned by the spraying water from which it came.

"Who are you?" snarled a Titan with charred and shriveled skin. "We've done the will of the—"

The blue light of his mouth flickered, and his jaws froze. The beast struggled to breathe as a stream of water broke away from the gusher, covered his feet, and froze him to the spot. A thin trail rose like a serpent for his skull, slithered through his left earhole, and out of the other. The Titan collapsed.

The others fell to their knees and pressed their skulls to the ground.

"One of your number has fallen," said the voice, "and even now dies in Avaddon. He dies because of the curse."

"We gave the book to the Serpent," said Andromede, grinding his teeth and refusing to lift his face. "It fell into Avaddon."

"But the words are no longer on its pages. They have been written on the heart of the girl. Wound the life of her mother, and you will live. Kill her, and you will die."

"We will shed her blood, but spare her life."

"Then look into my water."

The Titans lifted their heads. The column opened, much as a cobra spreads its hood, and froze. Eva's image appeared on the ice.

"The witch from Carnecia!" said Mosca, and a venomous laugh almost drowned the crackling fires.

"If it were not for my god, the Dragon, I would sever your empty skulls!" said the voice. "The mother is no witch, but the Raptor's own."

"What difference does it make?" growled Andromede. "Give us time. Lift the curse, and we shall not fail."

"I give no time. . . . But my god will open the mind of one of your number, to see what can't be seen. *The beast with earth instead of eyes, shall see the mother where she lies.*

"Come, and I will take you to Veldesh, near the place where the mother rides."

The warped column of ice became gushing water once more.

Andromede stood and led the pack through the water, which returned to the sea once they had vanished.

Two thousand miles away, the Titans rose beneath the surface of a wide, slow-moving river deep within Phantom Forest. There was no sound, save the sloshing water as they waded to shore and fanned out among the moonlocks, the figures hidden beneath an unending spiderweb of tangled branches.

"Who has the eyes of earth?" called Andromede, his voice muffled by the trees. A murmur rose as a Titan forced his way to the front of the pack. His body was covered in thin, fishlike scales that darkened as shadows moved across the ground and rested on his frame. But the scales over his eyes were gone, mud drizzling from the sockets.

"Domena, can you see her?"

The creature knelt as though he hadn't heard and raked three wasted fingers back and forth in the ground. He scattered leaves across over the earth, and the shadows swept them away.

"Yes," he answered slowly, in the voice of a dozen whispers. "I see seven through the eye of the falcon, and the witch is one. They ride through Val Ingradis. We'll slay them by sundown tomorrow."

"Tomorrow!" seethed Andromede.

"Another will fall," said Mosca. His pale frame slid through the Titans and stood over Domena. "The witch, does she wear the crown?"

Domena sank his fangs through his arm; his blood streamed down his elbow and spattered on the ground. The Titan stared into the pool of blood as a cluster of leaves swirled around it, though no wind blew, and rose moments later.

"No, Mosca. The spirit of the falcon has spoken. The witch rides with the girl, and the girl rides with the crown."

"We will hunt all day and through the night," said Andromede, peering at the sky through the tiny gaps in the branches, "then hide when the first light rises."

"They are seven," repeated Domena, "and the thirst will return before the morrow. Few cannot satisfy many."

"Fate has brought us together," said Andromede, now gazing at the Titans who stood as motionless as the thin bronze-colored trees around them. "We bleed the witch and break the curse, then kill the girl and take her crown. I will use it to bring down the nations. They will pour their blood at our feet."

The Titans stood on the western slope of Mount Dravenghedi, livid from having hunted like dogs throughout the night, only to learn from Domena that the falcon had been destroyed. Their prey was last seen moving north, and the pack would have to run another day to head them off in the valley—unless another spirit could find them before. What was more, the thirst for blood had returned, flooding their brains so that it became difficult to think. Needles pricked every inch of their skin, and the feeling grew by the hour. Andromede knew they should be stalking the next sacrificial city, but the curse must be broken. Until then, more Titans would die, and he would need them all to take the crown. The half-bloods moved around. It was torture standing there with the thirst screaming in their veins, but they mustn't leave the shadow of the mountain.

"Wait for the sun!" said Andromede in a voice that pulsed with fury.

Minutes later, the sun rose somewhere in the east, and a Titan burst into flame. Those nearest him jumped back as Andromede threw a lightning bolt that shattered the burning body, spewing embers as thunder rolled across the valley. He gazed at the bloodred coals, issuing vapors that created a mirage, and licked his skull; it was as though he were lapping from a pool, if only in his mind.

"We cannot hide from the curse," said Mosca loathingly. "Its power comes not from the light."

"What was his number?" called Andromede, who had returned to the world around him.

"297!"

"The curse moves from the greatest to the least," he said coldly. "Hydro-Vor wore *300*, and Nightblade was next. Witch of Carnecia! Because of her, we are few. The curse will move quickly. . . . *Who's next?*"

There were snarls and growls before a voice shouted, "Domena! His number is *294*. Tomorrow, he falls!"

The Titans grumbled even louder, swearing and hissing at Andromede. Only Domena could see, and without him, they were lost.

"Save Domena!" shouted another, and the Titans began chanting for the seer. The alpha raised an arm, and the throng grew still.

"Raine bore 1," cried Andromede, "and *2* is the number that I carry. Bring me the one who wears the next lowest number. I will cut it from his body and give it to Domena!"

They roared again, this time with shrieks of affirmation.

"*Inax!*" bellowed one of the Titans. "Inax wears *5*!"

Inax killed the first who grabbed him, but his arms were severed by two more Titans that threw him to the ground and dragged him to Andromede. The leader dropped to his knees, ripped the number from Inax's belly, and leaped to his feet, olive worms pouring out from the wound. The captive moved no more.

Silence overtook the pack. More tongues flickered as if the Titans envied the worms that wallowed in his blood.

"There's no escape!" said Mosca.

"Place the number in me first," said the whispers from Domena's mouth, "then take mine."

Andromede gashed Domena's chest, and the seer shrieked, blood streaming as Andromede drove the number *5* into the wound. The number froze in his skin, and the bleeding ceased.

"Now take the higher number," said Mosca impatiently, and Andromede tore away the flesh with *294*.

The Titans were motionless, their skulled faces unreadable. The seer did not fall.

"He lives!"

"Only for the moment," said Andromede wretchedly. "His days are still numbered, as the days of us all."

CHAPTER 16

INGRADIS

Night loomed as seven figures rode through Val Ingradis, their faces frozen and bodies soaked in sweat beneath their furs. The manes of their horses streamed like tattered banners, hammering hooves muffled by a thin layer of snow. Five men flanked Eva and Chloe, who had decreed that she would never be known as Mabel again.

The girl had hated being an orphan and having no hope, able to envision the future of others and never her own. There had been moments when she was angry with her parents for not staying alive, for leaving her. But her father had died in her place, and her mother was at her side. Chloe stared across the frozen plains, no longer afraid of tomorrow because she knew who she was, the daughter of Lord Amanyára, the granddaughter of the King of Veldesh.

She was Eva's. The girl had a mother and a defender, one whose love she would never have to work for or worry about losing. Her life had become a dream that she feared would be vanquished by the morning, but it had been two days since they had escaped from Lavian's fortress, and the dream lived on. The sound of "Chloe" falling from the lips of those around her would not let it die.

The rumbling grew louder as a herd of fifteen horses came out of nowhere and pulled alongside them. The party slowed, the new arrivals growing tame in the presence of the crown.

"Bring them," said Eva. The men dismounted, looking like commoners without their shoulder guards, covered in cloaks from Tsaulks they had met along the way. They placed halters on the new horses and tied them quickly to their own. Within minutes, they were riding again.

Eva had decided they would travel three days before returning to the Unseen (Lavian knew where the lady and her party had entered the world of men, in her former country of Veldesh, but could not see them as long as they moved in the Seen) then fly to the center of Linden and break the Darkness. But even in their own world, the company was on edge. Just that morning, Chloe had blasted a falcon out of the sky, certain that it was possessed. Eva was afraid to use creation to hasten their pace, that any phenomenon would draw the attention of spirits, and so they rode.

"Listen," said the lady, as they trotted toward the city of Ingradis, lurking against the Tristis Mountains. "I don't want anyone to know that we're from Linden. Don't use Xersian. I'm the only one that speaks Bàleol, so stick with me. If anyone talks to you—"

"Are you serious?" said Haden, dumbfounded.

"What?" said Eva hotly. Her eyes narrowed beneath a silver fur hat. She had been at Haden's throat over the last two days, hating the nicknames he had given Chloe for sacking Lavian—the Rahmais Assassin and Venom Stalker—that resurrected the horror of seeing her daughter in the arms of the Snake. But Chloe loved them, though outwardly she deflected the praise; they made her feel like she belonged.

"Eva, they're looking for seven." Haden waved an arm at them all. "We need to split up."

"We're going through the Northern Gate. We'll look like horse traders."

"I don't care if we go through a sheep gate, they're looking for
seven."

"They don't know that!"

"Come on, we can't ride faster than spirits fly. Someone in
there's gotta know . . ." He looked around for support then plunged
on when no one spoke. "We're not that hard to see—two girls, five
goons . . ."

"I agree," said Zane in low and steady tones. "I can ride through
the Valley Gate with—"

"I stay with Chloe!" said Eva, who avoided his disarming eyes
and looked at Haden. "And everyone else stays with me!"

There was not another word.

Chloe knew that Eva dreaded the city, yet had deemed it safer
than sleeping in the wild where any owl could see them, where a
spider, serpent, or beast could strike them where they lie. The lady
wasn't afraid for Chloe's life—the girl wore the crown—but for her
own: if she died, her daughter would wander the world alone. They
had been sleeping in villages, but tonight would be bound within the
walls of Ingradis. J'san had expressed concern about being trapped.
Eva spat that she would level the city.

The silence thickened as the city grew larger, roofs climbing at
the same perilous angles as the frozen peaks behind them, jutting
over sand-colored walls that were veiled in shadows. The company
passed the Valley Gate on their way to the northern wall, half closed
and hanging like a set of fangs. Cult prostitutes were seated outside
by open fires, wrapped from head to toe. Five minutes later, they
turned the corner and rode along the northern wall, Haden glaring
at the back of Eva's head before lifting his eyes, as though asking
God for patience as they passed under the archers overhead. Soon,
the bleating, barking, and neighing of animals greeted their ears.

"Pəsəmir!" bellowed a short, fat man, who emerged from the
gate waving a stubby arm that barely reached over his fox-skin hat.

Chloe could tell that he wanted them to hurry and pushed her horse as the gate began to close. "Pəsəmir vuyslan!"

"Kotşofıl es!" Eva shouted back then dropped her voice as she looked over her shoulder. "Let's go!"

But the riders and their trailing horses were forced to wait, two scrawny boys and their dogs funneling dozens of goats through the low archway ahead.

"Imgani tasabor çaqıfk!" the man yelled at the boys, who scowled in return. He kicked one of the goats, turned toward Eva, and beckoned frenziedly with an instant smile on his face, staring at the horses. "Bəy! Bəy!"

He shouted something to the gatekeeper that might have been a plea to hold the door a little longer, and at last they were through, trotting past the armored guards as the gate slammed closed behind them.

The rays of the sun no longer cleared the mountains, outlined in a heavenly glow. Chloe looked around and saw they were in some sort of market, shopkeepers closing their stores and hanging lanterns beneath the windows. The squat, purple-faced man strode quickly to Eva's side and whistled in the direction of the stables. Seconds later, three men wearing sheepskin and riding leathers came jogging out to meet them.

Eva slid off her horse and spoke to the man that Chloe guessed to be a dealer. After a few words, she signaled for the others to dismount. The dealer barked at the weathered men, who guided the barebacks toward a corral and helped Eva lead the saddled horses into the stable.

"Look at this," Haden muttered to Luther as he pointed at the deserted square. "No one in the streets. We're gonna stick out like elephants." The steely fighter said nothing; J'san and Zane both looked unsettled.

Chloe moved past them to join Mercilus, who was standing alone beside a battered carriage. Sometimes she thought that he knew. His blue eyes would catch her glances, and she would feel as though every part of her had been laid bare. He watched the horses galloping to the opposite side of the corral, his brow wrinkled, where a man filled a trough with some hay.

Was he thinking about his wife? And Chloe couldn't suppress a rising hope that he would never see her again. He blinked and turned his head. The girl was caught again. *He can't see me blush*, she thought, thankful for her frozen face. Mercilus slid up to her, their shoulders nearly touching.

"How are you feeling, Mabe?"

"Chloe."

There was a playful gleam in her eyes. He gave a slight smile.

"One more day and this will all be over," he said in a subdued voice. "You're with Eva now. She'll look after you. . . ."

Chloe's heart was racing; his eyes were close and she wanted them closer.

"We can go with you," she said quietly, "as far as Tulle."

He looked long into her face, and it was a few moments before his voice came again. "The only thing I know is fighting. I couldn't settle down. . . . I tried once, but went back to the life I lived before. That is why I was arrested and taken from my wife. She's with someone else now, someone who loves her enough to come home every night, someone that she doesn't have to worry about losing. I want to see her one more time to tell her that I'm sorry and find my son. She's better off without me. You as well."

Chloe struggled to hold his gaze, suddenly ashamed. How this girl must have loved him, to have been with him and given him a son. To lie awake with the boy in her arms and hope that one day Mercilus would return . . . and have the hope slowly die.

"You're a good girl, Chloe."

"No." She shook her head.

His lips parted. He gazed at her a moment longer, then glanced in the direction of the stable. Eva emerged, pocketing a pouch and muttering under her breath.

"Filthy cheat!" said the lady before catching herself and finishing in Bàleol. "Jaş bəhəmnir krəll!"

"One more day and it'll be over," Chloe echoed softly. "I'll miss you."

Before Mercilus could reply, Eva took Chloe by the arm and set off with her down the street, lined with vanilla stone buildings, walking quickly toward the square. The seven assumed their usual formation, with Chloe in between Zane and Eva, Mercilus lagging behind with J'san, Luther and Haden hanging as far back as possible. The spacing had worked well the nights before, the company allowing the faces of the crowd to pass among them and disguise their number.

But tonight was different. They had arrived too late; the crowds were gone, and the city was shutting down. Although they staggered themselves, it was obvious they were traveling together, the occasional drunk and beggar doing nothing to mask them in the empty lanes. Judging by the way Eva navigated the city, Chloe knew that she had been there before. The girl peered beneath her hood at a castle rising to the west and wondered if her mother had ever stayed there in her former life when she was the princess of Veldesh. Eva turned her head in the same direction and back again.

They walked for half an hour, the sky growing darker until the outline of the mountains melted into the night. Chloe shivered. Her body was no longer sweating, and her clothes were as frozen as the air around them. They descended a narrow, sloping street, passed under a wide archway, and came to a two-story building on the other side. Laughter was seeping through a metal door with wafts of food that made Chloe's stomach cramp. Although Eva was the only one that could read the dingy sign over the door, there was no doubt that they had reached the inn.

"Same drill," Eva whispered and looked over her shoulder. The trailing figures were gone. Eva took Chloe by the hand and pushed her way through the door, Zane at their heels.

Chloe always felt bad about the drill, which began with Eva asking for a mug of water for her daughter and the three of them following an innkeeper to a room that overlooked the street. Chloe would stand next to the door as Eva complained about the room until the innkeeper got so animated that he didn't notice the words Chloe muttered or the water that rose from her mug, entered the lock, and froze an instant later. Eva would then stride past him, through the door, and demand to see another room—at which point, the innkeeper found that he couldn't lock the door behind them as they left. After a few vain attempts, he would give up and show the next room, precisely the same as the one before. Eva would accept.

Tonight went exactly as it had the two nights before. Chloe, Zane, and Eva had no sooner entered the second room than the lady nodded her approval. The innkeeper, a hunchbacked man, thrust his lamp into the lady's hands, marched out of the door, and closed it sharply behind him.

They listened as the sound of his footsteps grew softer.

"He's gone," Zane said presently.

"Olo dên weur," said Chloe, and the ice evaporated in the lock next door.

"If you need us . . ."

Zane bowed as Eva set the lamp on a wooden table and went back to the first room. Eva and Chloe embraced each other as soon as he was gone, barely noticing the muffled grunts as the rest of their men scaled the wall and wriggled through the window into his room. Neither knew how long they stood there and let go only when a soft knock came at the door. Eva answered to find a small girl holding a bag under a tray of food with two jars of water. The lady passed the tray to Chloe, took the bag, and watched the girl skip down the hall, gray rags fluttering behind her.

Eva opened the bag and glanced down at the bread, smoked meats, and cheeses; accepted a jar from Chloe; and then slipped next door where she knocked and left the food and water. The lady came back to her room and cast her hat on the bed and shook her hair; it was fading to its natural amber color and made her resemble Chloe even more. The girl removed her own to reveal the crown, wrapped tightly underneath, her hair almost blond. The women shrugged off their coats and stared at the writing etched in Chloe's arm, golden letters that ran along her bicep and disappeared into her shoulder. 𝕮 𝖘𝖔𝖓𝖏 𝖈𝖈 𝖆𝖐𝖍𝖆𝖓𝖔𝖐𝖆𝖒.* They sparkled like diamonds in the lamplight.

"Let's eat," said Eva softly.

Chloe drew her dagger and plunged the blade into the table beside the lamp. She hated not knowing what to say to Eva. Her mother. The two of them had no time alone during the day, what with the brutal pace, the freezing cold, and pounding hooves that made talking impossible. It seemed the nights would come without warning and they would suddenly be alone. Eva looked vulnerable now, which made Chloe feel insecure. The silence was deafening.

They sat down together on the floor, shoulder to shoulder, backs against the wall with the wooden tray straddled across their laps. Eva split a black loaf, stuffed it with cheese, and gave it to Chloe.

"Here . . ."

"Thank you." Chloe could hardly wait for Eva to fix a loaf for herself before shoving hers in her mouth. A minute later, it was gone.

"Ma . . ." Eva's hands froze for a second. She put down her loaf and picked up another for her daughter. "What was it like, living in a palace?"

"I prefer this," said Eva, her voice barely above a whisper. "Living where no one knows who you are. In the palace, there are black

---

* The one who overcomes.

hearts, eyes that lust for power, and tongues that lie. Not openly, but using love as a lie."

"What was your father like?" said Chloe, wanting really to ask about her own but was too afraid.

"Like all kings, worried about war and power. He looked at me as an asset. . . . I was his daughter, born of the queen and not a concubine. I was a pawn to be given in marriage, to secure peace and trade."

Eva offered nothing of her mother. Silence.

"Do you miss school?"

"No."

"Why?"

"They thought I was crazy." Chloe told her of the times she had been found lying on the ground, how some said that she only wanted attention, while others believed her a witch. "My only friends were Jay and Issy. After what happened, you know, the last time we were together . . . They won't wanna see me again."

Another silence.

"Why don't you like Haden?" Chloe didn't know what made her say it, only that it popped into her mind and she wanted the silence to end.

Eva's windburned face became white. Her mouth opened slightly, and she set the plate on the floor, got to her feet, and took a step forward. Chloe jumped up behind her.

"Ma . . ."

Eva moved farther away, pressing her fist against the wall in front of her face and then her forehead against her fist. Chloe followed and put her arms around her mother. "What is it?"

But she wouldn't answer, rolling her head from side to side.

"You can tell me."

Eva was motionless. Chloe waited for a time, unable to tell whether her mother would unlock the pathway to the past, but had no sooner rested her head on Eva's shoulder than came the shadow of her voice.

"Haden was angry with me . . . for not setting them free. The fighters. After they helped me take back the book from the marauders. But it was not my decision to make!" Eva straightened up and pounded her fist against the wall, then gritted her teeth. "His blood was spilled in the arena . . . one day after I had the crown. I ran to where he was, where they had dragged his dying body and gave it to him. He was healed but refused to give it back, saying he would use it to set himself free. I read his face. I saw power in the eyes of the wrong man."

"What did you do?"

"I told him that I would kill his family." Tears gathered in Eva's eyes, cold and empty. "I told him that if he didn't give me the crown, I would kill them all."

"But you wouldn't . . . you didn't, *right?*"

She shook her head. "No," she said hoarsely. "He too could read my face. They were already dead in my heart. He gave it back."

"Then I don't get it," said Chloe. "Nothing happened."

Eva looked up, anger flashing on her face. "Mabe—*Chloe!* Nothing just happens. Nothing! Don't you see? What I threatened to do to him was done to me. Hadesha killed my family for the crown. You reap what you sow! Everything that's happened to you . . . to your father . . . was because of my filthy life." She let out two gut-wrenching sobs and fell to the ground.

"It's not your fault!"

But Eva wouldn't listen and pushed the girl away.

"No!" she cried, covering her face with her hands.

"Get up! *Get . . . up!*" Chloe nearly shouted as she pulled her mother violently to her feet and spun her around; the girl seized Eva's wrists and forced her hands away from her face, staring fiercely into the tear-stained eyes.

"It's not your fault!" Her voice broke as Eva tried wrenching herself away, but Chloe pinned her against the wall. "Listen! I don't know what to say, okay? I don't know anything, only that you're like God to me. I don't wanna be with you . . . I wanna *be* you!"

She let go, and they flung their arms around each other.

"I can't believe that you're mine," whispered Chloe, and Eva shook her head and sobbed even harder. "I never thought my ma would be like you."

It was late in the night before Eva extinguished the lamp and got into bed, taking Chloe in her arms. The girl had already fallen asleep with the crown murmuring its secrets: how to stir the monsters of the deep and conquer mountains, cry with wolves, cast an army to its grave.

But the low, enchanting voice of another entered her mind. "You're perfect," it said. "I'm not going to let you become like me. Tomorrow, we'll break the Darkness and go somewhere safe. I'll protect you all the days of your life."

"Chloe."

The girl groaned, and her eyes fluttered open, her body aching from endless hours in the saddle. Being thrown down a mountain could not have felt any worse. Eva sat fully dressed on the bed beside her.

Can't be time already, Chloe thought.

"It's time."

The girl groaned once more and slid out of bed, loathing the thought of returning to the cold.

"The men will be here in a minute," said Eva. The softness in her voice was gone, and war was in her eyes. "We're going to pass into the Unseen and fly to Mount Nin then return to our world and use the crown to carry us to Mayko."

"Why don't we stay in the Unseen"—Chloe yawned as she pulled on her coat—"and fly the whole way?"

Eva shook her head. "Linden's in darkness, and our bodies glow.

Lavian will see us coming miles away. Mount Nin is the farthest we can fly while staying in the light."

"Mayko," said Chloe musingly. "Wait . . . you don't mean . . ."

The look on Eva's face was a little too prepared.

"We're going to the Temple of Death!"

When Eva didn't flinch, legends swam through Chloe's brain of a temple built by witchslayers and war worshippers for death itself, the devourer within its tomb, and how King Ley had sent an army to destroy it during the Belshayan Rebellion, only to be seen no more. And she remembered the words of Aurèle: *They laid stones in the center of their countries, and built temples upon them. And the people of Earth worshipped Lavian.*

"So it's true then?" said Chloe, looking shocked. "It's the temple of Lavian? I mean, I knew I had to speak in the middle of Linden, but I didn't think the temple . . . *that* temple . . . It still stands?"

"For a thousand years," said Eva quietly. "Lavian knows where you must speak and will blanket the area—angels in the Unseen, an army in the Seen. . . ."

Her thought trailed away, and the lady furrowed her brow.

"What?"

"I won't make you kill. Give me the crown in Mayko, and I will destroy whoever he sends. Then I'll give it back to you. We'll enter the temple, and you'll speak the words on your heart."

The lady cupped her hands around Chloe's face and stared into her eyes. "Whatever happens, do not give me the crown before I tell you. They'll try to hurt me so that you give me the crown and then kill you. Promise me you won't take it from your head."

"No," said Chloe defiantly. "I'm not gonna lie. I will if I have to. You think I'm gonna let something happen to you?"

Eva's mouth tightened, her fingers pressing Chloe's skull. When she spoke again, her voice was low and cold. "Chloe, I swear to God . . . *Promise me.*"

But the girl wouldn't budge, and her eyes burned. A light rap came at the door.

"My lady."

Eva turned away when Chloe continued to say nothing and opened the door. Five fighters filled the tiny room so that it became difficult to move.

Mercilus's eyes flickered between the women.

"Still fighting?" Chloe's mouth went dry; they had heard everything she shouted the night before. "You really are mother and daughter."

Eva glared.

Luther stepped toward Chloe, and the others formed a crescent behind him.

"Today's your day," he said to the girl. "There's no yesterday, and forget about tomorrow. It's about *right now*. Refuse to be defeated. Refuse it!" Luther struggled to keep his voice down as he smacked his hands together. "Don't believe what you see, believe what you *can't* see. The fire in you is greater than the darkness in them. Do what you do. We got your back."

"You're chosen for a reason," said J'san. "No one can break you."

Chloe nodded back at them both as Zane placed a hand on her shoulder.

"Don't worry about your mother," he said, and Eva's lips quivered. "We've always been at her side. We'll protect her, with or without the crown."

"You're a queen worth more than gold," said Mercilus. Eva's eyes shot to his face, but he didn't seem to care. "I knew it from the first time I saw you."

Chloe was shaken by a glorious feeling as she listened to the words of a father she never had. She knew what they said was true: she was born to fight and made to be great. They believed in her, and she would not let them down.

The silence strained as everyone waited for Haden, who addressed Eva instead.

"I'm sorry about what happened"—the lady's expression was glacial, as though she would slit his throat at the first wrong word— "to you and Amanyára . . ." He broke off and must have realized there was nothing he could say. Chloe saw the imploring look on his face.

"Let's go," said Eva and turned away, Haden gazing blankly ahead as the other men moved toward the back wall. Zane parted the curtains and opened the window. Chloe avoided Haden's eyes as she slipped past him and yanked her dagger from the table. She wanted to tell him how much she respected what he said, but the air was electric.

Outside, the sky was ocean blue; and although the sun had not yet cleared the eastern ridge, the city was coming alive. A rooster crowed in the distance as a tottering man led two mules past the inn below. As soon as the coast was clear, J'san, Mercilus, Luther, and Haden squeezed through the window and dropped to the street. Zane closed the window, Chloe and Eva snatched up their hats, and the three of them left for the common room.

They ate breakfast, crammed in a corner, waiting for more people to fill the streets. The lady caught the innkeeper and paid for another bag of food, the man snatching the silver out of her hand, and then signaled it was time to leave when the bag was thrown at her feet.

Chloe squinted as they stepped outside; the yellowish buildings turned to gold in the early light. The atmosphere rang with the sound of barking dogs, shouts, and clopping hooves, but the air was still.

Eva dropped the bag on the ground, waited for a cart to pass, and was about to cross the street when pigeons took off from the roof above. They watched the flock out of sight and exchanged uneasy looks before continuing to the other side, passing a tavern and turning down the first alley into the sun. Mercilus emerged from an archway. J'san, a step behind, scooped up the bag and followed, failing to notice the black hawk that landed on a balcony beyond the tavern. Haden and Luther came into view as Mercilus took a handful of biscuits from the bag before J'san tossed it on the ground. Haden bent forward to pick it up, but not before he spied the hawk, wings cracking as it rose into the air.

Eva guided Chloe and Zane around another corner and moved down a crowded alley, dominated by the smell of roasting meats, voices, and clinking coins. The lady took Chloe's hand as they snaked through casks of wine and tables laden with everything from weapons to produce, the merchants bellowing after them. It was not until they had reached a cobbled road that Chloe looked over her shoulder and spotted Mercilus, peering at her beneath a silver hood. She breathed easier at the sight of J'san at his side.

"C'mon," hissed Eva, tugging Chloe's arm and turning up the road. If the alleys had been crowded, this was a sea chock-full of human fish. People swarmed from one side to the other, horses barely moving, and anyone foolish enough to have brought a cart into the fray was at a standstill. Zane took the lead and kept to his left, shouldering people out of the way as Eva fell to the rear. The road began to rise, and their pace slowed as they filed past the Temple of Dethos. Fifteen minutes later, they reached a crest where the road fell away, and Chloe gazed over the bobbing heads at the Valley Gate ahead.

Zane beckoned Eva, who squeezed past Chloe to his side.

"Horses?"

"There's a stable at the gate—" Eva looked back in time to see J'san shove a horse out of his way. A wild-looking man stood up in the cart behind it, yelling and brandishing a club. "We gotta get out of here," she said sharply, "before these idiots start a riot."

But the crowd roared behind them as soon as they set off. Twenty soldiers on stallions poured from adjacent alleys onto the road, their black crests like razors, as wicked as the tips of their spears. The soldiers formed several lines the width of the street, not far beyond Luther and Haden, and began riding toward the gate. People shouted, unable to move fast enough to avoid the mammoth beasts. The soldiers hastened their pace and trampled those in their way.

"They're coming for us!" yelled Eva. She and Zane grabbed Chloe by the coat and plunged toward the gates, screams filling the air as people clambered over each other and dove through doors, giving the soldiers room to press harder.

"Wait for them!" shouted Chloe, looking over her shoulder at Mercilus and wrenching herself free as they stumbled past a well. The girl was no longer thinking, only feeling the waterfall that stormed through her veins.

"Don't worry about them!" cried Eva, and the gate closed with a boom. Pigeons began circling above them, even as more soldiers stormed up the road from the gate. Arrows were fired from the wall in the direction of the birds. Two men collapsed next to Zane.

Flames streamed through the air that wrapped themselves around four or five soldiers and melted their armor. But the firelight revealed Mercilus, J'san, Haden, and Luther. Arrows were unleashed their way; the men flashed shields, errant shots killing the people around them. Zane and Eva smashed two oncoming spears as Chloe faced the Northern Wall and threw her hand away from her body. The earth rose, splitting the wall as though it were clay, then sank and carried the archers to their grave. The soldiers reined their horses as an earthquake shook the city, but the crown thirsted for their blood.

"Unim mocce akhánoflöns te!"* shouted Chloe, raising her right arm. The water in the well shot like a gusher into the sky, spraying tongues that froze like a thousand arrows. "Megaar deres skyá, lur deres sâgan!"† Chloe spun her body and drove her fist toward the

---

* Give me the depths of the flood!
† Kill their shadow, spill their blood!

ground. A cyclone whipped the ice through the air and severed the soldiers' necks.

The girl stood with clenched hands as Eva threw her arms around her neck. The tremors ceased. A hawk landed on a fallen soldier behind them.

Mercilus sprinted toward Zane and the women, followed by his fellows, dust from the ruined wall creeping like fog into the city. Everything was still, save the cries of those cradling the dead.

"We gotta cross now!" said Mercilus. "Every spirit's gonna be here!"

Eva let go of Chloe and watched through misty eyes as her daughter opened a wall of fire. J'san, Mercilus, and Luther hurried through. A shape rose in the billowing dust behind Eva, a hawk on its shoulder and a spear in its hand. Zane vanished through the flames.

Haden was feet from the fire, Eva right behind him, when a screech rang through the mourning voices. He whipped around, caught Eva around the waist, and continued to spin so that his back was to the temple. A spear pierced his spine a second later, the tip passing through his chest and breaking Eva's sternum. He fell forward, and Eva stumbled through the fire.

Chloe threw a light wave that annihilated the shadowy figure, the second missing the hawk as it flew away, and shouted as she dragged Haden through the flames.

CHAPTER 17

LAVIAN STRIKES

G ive him the crown!" said Eva. She dropped to her knees as Zane took Haden away from Chloe and Luther pulled the spear out of his back. They laid him on the diamond-covered earth, Eva taking him in her arms as Chloe threw off her hat, seized the covered band, and placed it on his head. She removed her hands, but the crown fell to the ground.

"Try again!"

Chloe snatched it up and held it once more on Haden's head, Eva lifting it higher. The girl let go, and there was a soft thunk as the band hit the ground. She realized he was dead. A brilliant thread of light spun around his head and corkscrewed down his body, and he was gone.

Eva bowed her head. Stunned, Chloe looked at the fighters but could not fathom the meaning on their faces.

No one paid attention to the city that sparkled like glass around them or the wrecked wall that gave a glacial light. There were no voices, no men or women, beast or bird. They were all staring at the bloodied spear, alone in the Unseen and seven no more.

"You have to pick it up, Chloe," said Eva defeatedly. "The crown's not given until it's been received. It still belongs to you."

Chloe picked up the crown as her mother rose and was about to place it on her head when she saw the blood that had soaked through Eva's clothes.

"You're hurt!" said Chloe, holding out the crown.

"No!"

Eva knocked the arm away.

"What d'you mean *no*?"

"Don't you see? You can't turn your back for a second! Keep the crown and never take it off. Never! You blink in this world and you're dead!"

"But there's no one here!"

"There will be!" said Eva, and she looked around at the men. "Let's go!"

But Chloe wouldn't listen. She stepped toward her mother and raised her arm again, but Eva shoved her away.

"*I said no!*"

Chloe swung the crown at Eva, who ducked as it whistled over her head. The girl lunged forward and swung again, Eva jumping back into the arms of Mercilus, who caught her and wouldn't let her go. J'san grabbed Chloe.

"*Put it on!*" screamed Chloe.

"Don't tell me what to do!"

"Stop!" said Zane and Luther together, leaping between them.

"Listen!" hissed Mercilus in Eva's ear. The lady was breathing hard, furious, but said nothing. "Angels are going to be here any second. You can wear the crown so we can leave, or we'll wait until you pass out and put it on your head. What's it gonna be?"

A moment later, Eva relaxed and the fighter released her. Chloe ran out of J'san's arms and placed the crown on her mother's head. Her eyes brightened, and the bleeding stopped.

"Quickly!" Eva drew her dagger and looked anxiously at the sky. Mercilus turned around as she cut the fur away from his wings, which allowed him to shed his coat. Chloe took her own knife and slashed the back of J'san's furs then handed him the blade as he cut her own coat free. Within seconds, the garments were lying at the feet of figures in black tunics, with bare arms, and wolfskin leggings.

Eva rose into the air, and the others followed, racing toward the eastern ridge. They had just passed Mount Orren when thunder broke the silence. Chloe looked around and saw lightning over Ingradis then dove after Eva behind the next peak where they flew over an onyx forest and fled to the sea.

Chloe stared aimlessly ahead. Despair was mauling her heart, not for the lives she had taken, but for the one that was given. Over and over she played Haden's death in her mind. It was her fault that he was gone. She had been too slow to react or not ruthless enough when she had. How had the soldier risen? *I should have ripped every limb from his body.*

It felt like they had been flying for hours when the sea finally appeared and the land gave way beneath them. The figures turned north as they soared over the water, water barely thicker than air that did nothing to mask the golden sand beneath the surface. An eon passed. Chloe could see the Darkness now hanging over Linden like a curtain from space. They were zooming straight for its heart until Eva dove toward a lone island, which grew larger and larger as they circled like birds before landing on the crystal peak of Mount Nin.

Chloe jogged a few steps after she touched down, folded her wings, and then walked past Eva toward the eastern face.

"Chloe."

The girl turned around, and the men lowered their gaze. Eva was standing as tall as ever but looked overcome.

"I'm sorry."

"Me too," said Chloe in empty tones. She could tell that Eva wanted to give her the crown, but the lady held back, afraid of starting another fight.

"What happened wasn't your fault. And the men you killed . . ." Eva stopped and quickly began again. "Those that fell, forget them. You did what you had to do." She stepped forward and froze when her daughter didn't move. For some reason, Chloe could only think about the way her mother had treated Haden.

"I just want to be alone," Chloe said abruptly, and Eva looked like she'd been struck by a spear all over again.

The girl turned and made her way to the edge of a cliff, where she felt as though she were standing on another planet, the sea spreading endlessly in all directions, except to the north where darkness reigned. There was something about the golden sand glittering beneath the surface that calmed her spirit. *I just wanna stand by the sea.* The thought grew stronger until Chloe believed that touching the water, and the water alone, would give her peace.

A strange feeling overcame the girl, as though her heart had been hooked by something outside of herself, tugging so strongly that it would be pulled from her chest if she didn't go with it. Chloe tried resisting . . . or did she? A weight pressed upon her mind, her feelings clear and confused, knowing what she wanted but not knowing why. *I won't be long.* . . . The impulse pulled once more, and she dove from the cliff.

Chloe glided down the precipice and landed on the beach a short time later, the waves barely making a sound as they lapped the metallic sand. About to enter the water, she spotted an archway in a rock wall that jutted away from the mountain. Her heart burned.

The water began flowing away from her, through the arch, and the girl's expression became vacant as she followed the waters along the beach.

"Chloe!"

Her mother's voice called from another world.

A minute longer . . .

Reaching the crude archway, she entered the warm water, waded through the gap, and found herself in a small cove, surrounded by walls that encircled the beach and fused into the mountain on her right. Chloe had ventured out of the water and into the middle

when a cold wind snapped through the arch behind her. She came
to herself, not realizing where she was, and turned around.

Lavian emerged, slithering through the gap.

Terror flooded the girl, who pleaded with herself to believe that
it was someone else.

The Serpent moved slowly around the perimeter of the cove, his
left fist held in front of his navel, his right forearm tucked behind
his back. As soon as his tail cleared the entrance, a wave smashed
through the archway and froze. Chloe wanted to flee, but his eyes
rooted her in place.

Lavian appeared calm as though he had already won. His tongue
glided out, the sky turned to ash, a chill went down Chloe's spine,
and her wings were gone.

"You are trapped in a shadow comb," breathed Lavian. "A world
within a world, like a dream within a dream. . . . Sealed with me,
away from Eva. She will search for you and not find you. She will
hear the twilight of our voices and the echoes of your scream."

The girl began to retreat as Lavian moved toward the back of
the cove, the blood pounding in her ears.

"I know your thoughts," said the Snake. "Moj Deo, în mocce
ihlo derrujën . . . vur ivela id proximal cy noenn id tero dên mogite."*
Chloe's eyes widened, and the Serpent hissed, incensed by the look
on her face. "*Yessss,* I too know the words written on your heart,
for they existed long before they were given to you, from the days I
lived with your god—the one who has promised to stand with you
but is not here.

"Today you will fall, for I am a god and you are dust."

Lavian stopped and faced the girl, his tail coiling beneath him.
He took his right arm out from behind his back, the Betrayer's Blade
in his fist. Lightning flashed in the other.

Chloe retreated further, but there was no means of escape. She

---

* My God, do not be far from me . . . for trouble is near and there is no one
to help.

stopped, trembling, and gasped, "A leen cy di noi Åneprans sevak."* Fear owned her voice, but light flashed from the writing on her arm. The girl swung the opposite arm around her body, releasing a stream of fire that burned a circle in the sand.

"Fira ihlo, vur A id gyle yú; în ihlo jendum, vur A gyle yeul Deo. A ilys balacer yú. A ilys mogite yú . . ."†

Her voice became stronger with every syllable that she uttered. The writing burned brighter; the winds howled somewhere in the sky. Her breathing slowed.

Hatred dripped from Lavian's eyes, though not because Chloe no longer backed away. He saw that she believed the words of the book and the god who wrote them.

"Moj Deo id enå tarsinis cuyon . . ."‡

Lavian launched himself through the air; he was faster than Chloe could have imagined. The girl miraculously spun out of the way, swinging a right hand that hit Lavian's shoulder as the Snake went streaking by.

There was a flash of golden light and a sonic boom, and Lavian reeled sideways into the wall. He shrieked as he straightened up, crossed his arms over his head, and snapped them forward. Chloe blocked the violet ray, inches from her body, with a cry of her own. Fissures split the walls from the explosions, and stones rained from the cliffs. Lavian flung his tail at Chloe, who completed a backflip as it sailed under her body. No sooner had she landed than Lavian threw a black wave of light, forcing the girl to flash a shield that destroyed the wave with an explosion that knocked her to the ground.

Chloe flipped onto her stomach and jumped up, ears ringing as she flashed her hands over her head, not feeling the blood that

---

* I live and die by the sword of the Spirit.
† Do not fear, for I am with you; do not be afraid, for I am your God. I will strengthen you. I will help you.
‡ My God is a consuming fire.

flowed from the gash in her cheek, and leveled a stream of fire at the Snake. Lavian dropped to the ground, narrowly avoiding the blaze that flew over his body and scorched the wall.

Lavian snaked to his right then to his left, dodging two more streams of fire before drawing himself up to his full height, blood like pitch streaming from his wings.

"Your blood falls!" he shouted. "How long will you believe?"

Chloe stared at Lavian and pounded her chest.

"Come on!"

Rocked by her defiance, Lavian looked toward the heavens and screamed, "By *my* might and *my* power!"

And he called the winds from the corners of the Earth. Dark clouds swirled over the cove as they arrived, howling with voices of their own. He snapped his body forward and drove his fists into the sand. The winds fell from heaven and hit the floor of the cove with such force that they split the ground, forcing Lavian into the air as Chloe toppled over. A vortex formed in front of the girl who leaped up, flung an arm behind her back, and spun three times. A burning whirlwind rose around her.

Lavian hurled his cyclone toward Chloe, but she threw an arm forward and unleashed her own. The two forces met, wind and fire, and battled each other until they screamed as one.

The walls of the cyclone opened, passing over the Serpent who shrieked as the flames scorched his body and flung Chloe to the sand. The girl crawled forward, out of the raging winds, and had no sooner risen than Lavian sprang forward and drove the blade through her arm. The girl spun away, unleashing a flurry of light waves that Lavian blocked with his own, slithering backward as he fought.

Blood poured from the Snake as he struck the earth with his fist once more. A violet light flashed in all directions, and the girl collapsed.

Moaning, Chloe sat up, grasped the dagger, and wrenched it

from her arm. She slumped and dropped the Betrayer's Blade, the world spinning around her. Lavian was lying facedown, gasping, arms extended as he held his chest off the ground.

Chloe lifted her eyes and saw the circle burning in the sand just feet away. Pain ravaged her body, and she couldn't think, save her resolve to return to the ring.

Lying on her stomach, she dug into the sand with her right elbow and pulled it toward her chest, inching her body across the ground. She dug in with her left and crept forward again. Soon the girl dragged herself back into the circle and cried out as she struggled up from the ground. Her hair was matted in blood, a pool forming beneath her—blood streaming down her arm, mixing with the light as it passed over the letters in her skin.

"Pisa hvi stejke mocce dámin . . ."*

Chloe stepped toward Lavian, lifted her knee high, and pointed toward heaven.

"A ilys beshe sai eyam."†

A wave of light arced over her knee as she drove her foot into the ground. The wave shot across the cove and smashed the Serpent, who somersaulted backward against the cliffs.

She sank to her knees, and the shock wave roared. The cliffs parted and the sky pulsed with the colors of the rainbow, stars like diamonds falling from heaven as the Snake lay motionless on the ground. Chloe thought she could hear demons scream. The earth shook, and darkness filled her mind. The girl knew that she was slipping away, but didn't care whether she lived or died. She had fought Lavian and won.

---

* Though he slay me.
† Yet I will trust in him.

CHAPTER 18

THE BLOOD AND THE BLADE

L avian lay on an altar beside the crystal ring in his throne room.
A number of angels stood sentry around their god who made
no move, his eyes staring lifelessly ahead. Darkness poured in
through the windows like smoke and filled the room until its purple
fires were lost to view, the essence separating into long, thin tongues
that wrapped their coils around Lavian's charred body. He seemed to
breathe easier now, as though the darkness were keeping him alive.

Thunder rolled somewhere in the heavens and the Serpent
stirred.

"Bring me . . ."

The angels looked at each other as if they had imagined the
utterance, but the blue light that escaped Lavian's mouth proved
otherwise. They strained their ears, but it was an hour before the
voice came again, stronger than before. "Bring me the blade . . . that
struck the girl . . ."

"Our father," said Cyca, who bowed and strode toward the
dais of skulls, unimpeded by the darkness, where lay a thin object
wrapped in animal skins. The angel lifted the bundle and brought
it to the Serpent. The darkness disentangled itself from Lavian and
retreated against the walls.

"The blade," breathed Cyca. He bent over the altar so that his ear was inches from Lavian's mouth.

The Serpent took three rasping breaths before saying, "The blood of the girl . . . will open the gates of Sin Via." At these words, thunder cracked with a mighty roar that shook the fortress; then silence took its place. "Give the blade to the Titans, for they have the blood of men and can pass through the fire. . . . Command them to open the gates and summon the Osprey. My strength returns. . . . Soon I will rise. . . ."

He paused; the angels could feel the weight of his presence as it grew and pressed upon them. "Bring me the Osprey," said Lavian, his head rolling slightly. Two more breaths and the Snake went on. "In seven days, I will slay Estelle, and the Earth will return to emptiness."

The angels nodded in the darkness, hissing.

"Silence!" spat Balim, and all was still.

"As you desire," said Cyca, who rose and was turning away when Lavian caught him by the arm.

"And bring me the chalice."

"My god," said the angel. Lavian let go and touched the ring.

"Valporgahen . . . Ingradis."

The crystal ignited through which the angel passed, and he vanished with the flame.

Darkness returned from the recesses of the room and enveloped the altar, and a black drizzle fell over Lavian. After a while, the bleeding stopped, the raindrops becoming dragonflies that swarmed his body and mended his wounds.

"The witch is not here," said Domena.

The Titans had drunk the blood of the slain and were standing along the ruined wall of Ingradis. The sun hung like a jewel over the mountains, casting beams that made the crimson streets glisten. Not a door or window opened, no animal moved—every heart knew that death walked before it. The Titans could think clearly now, and their minds returned to the hunt.

"She crossed into the Unseen," said the seer, pointing to a charred line on the cobblestones.

"Where is she?" said Mosca menacingly.

Domena walked over to the well and gazed into its depths. Mud dripped from his sockets, into the pit, and his body shook a short time later. "I see a girl," said the seer, now speaking with whispers not his own. "She has been struck down, but not destroyed. The mother lies with the girl until she walks again."

"Where?"

"Linden."

"Linden!" roared Andromede. "Back to where we began! How many days? How many of us will fall?"

Shrieks and howls split the atmosphere. Two particularly gruesome Titans lashed out at the rest and fought their way toward Andromede.

"Curse Domena!" said the first. He had deep purple scales, with blood-soaked fur that covered his arms and legs. Etched on his skin was 288. "Domena wears the number 5 and has no fear of the curse! He *sees* but brings us too late. Give him my number! If we do not find the witch, let him die!"

"I'm with Lemus!" boomed the one behind him. He was unlike the rest with ultraviolet eyes. "The seer led us astray. . . . Let him fall!"

The pack moved forward, Andromede shouting for order, but would not relent until he threw a lightning bolt into the throng. A Titan fell with a smoking hole in his head.

"Enough!"

The pack halted.

"Xoar," said Andromede to the Titan with ultraviolet eyes, "you

stand with Lemus, only because you wear 287 and will soon fall."
He flashed another bolt and faced Lemus. "Die now, beast, or by
the sun tomorrow, but Domena lives."

Lemus made no move, and the alpha snarled before calling out
to the rest. "Only Domena sees! He will lead us to the witch, and we
will find her. The girl has been struck down and cannot move—"

"The angel comes soon," said Domena, "to carry us away."

The Titans wavered for a minute, and the madness seemed to
fade. Their swollen veins deflated slightly, and those with lightning
relaxed their fists. One by one, the blades vanished. Seeing that the
pack had sided with Andromede, Lemus stretched out his hand and
plunged a bolt of lightning through Domena's chest.

"Beast!" shrieked Andromede as the seer collapsed.

Mosca struck Lemus across the skull. "We only know the witch
is in Linden, but don't know where!"

"He led us astray!" howled Lemus, standing his ground. "Give
me his number!"

Andromede and Mosca faced off with Lemus, the three of them
circling each other. Xoar watched closely as Lemus edged by and
then lowered his gaze to Domena's fallen body. His own number
would allow him to live only one more day, and who knew how
long it would take to find their prey? Until then, he with the lowest
number would live the longest.

An instant later, Xoar seized Lemus by the neck. Voltage flashed
from his eyes, down his arm, and consumed the Titan. He let go,
and Lemus crumpled to the ground. "Domena's number is mine!"

Xoar cut the number from the body then screamed as he tore a
hole in his flesh and placed the number 5 in the wound. He ripped
away 287 and threw it on the ground.

The Titans stood in silence, their miserable state sinking in.
Without Domena, they were nothing but wanderers, scouring the
Earth for someone they may never find; death would come for them
by the number assigned.

The wind stirred as they glanced mechanically from one to another. Those with the highest numbers had become predators, the beasts with the lowest, the prey. Lightning flashed in their fists as the pack split, the hunted retreating toward Andromede, the stalkers breaking off and circling around them.

There was a blinding volley of electricity, peals of thunder that ricocheted throughout the city, shrieks, light shields, and lightning as the beasts fought wildly. Andromede and his flock would soon be overcome.

"With me!" he shouted and slashed his way through the attackers with Mosca and Xoar. They sprinted toward the crumbled wall with their band running closely behind, and the predators gave chase. Several fleeing Titans took bolts to the head, but not before Andromede and most of his party had reached the ruins, wending their way through chunks of the wall, and bounded across the snowy field.

They had just turned toward a series of boulders strewn across the valley when a wall of flame erupted before them. They ran through the fire and were gone.

"Where are they?" cried a voice, the predators slowing to a halt.

"The gods . . . have taken them," panted another, hunched over with his hands on his knees. He had the stripes of a tiger and a raised bone that ran down his skull like the crest of a helm. His number was 143. He straightened up, only to have his head split by a Titan wearing 245. The attacker bent forward to cut the number from the fallen body, but a figure with ghost-white shoulders killed him from behind. Two more fought over the same number, another fight broke out, and several others were killed. The Titans realized they would be dead in minutes and scattered, their cries growing fainter and fainter as they fled throughout the valley.

Andromede and his Titans stood stock-still. They had seen a violet flash and felt as though every fiber of their being had been torn in two and instantly sewn together. The mountains were gone. There was no light or darkness, only giant steel fangs that were spread far and wide, rising from a sandy red floor. The beasts had been breathing heavily seconds before but were now breathing with ease. Their bodies looked more dark and hideous.

"The gods are near," murmured Mosca.

"Too true," came a cryptic voice, and the Titans gnashed their teeth as Cyca stepped out from behind a fang. The angel approached the half-bloods, his feet making sickening crunches as he strode on what might have been human remains. A shadow flickered around one of the curling fangs, tore away from the ground, slithered up Cyca's body, and entered the tombs of his eyes. Though he was no larger than they, the Titans fell back; they sensed a force they could not overcome, one emanating from the object in his hand.

"You have passed through the fire of the Dragon," said the angel, "into the wilderness that lies between Seen and Unseen worlds."

The Titans shifted but said nothing as he continued.

"My god is the Serpent, greater than the fallen stars, any demon or king of demons. More powerful than the waters that gave you the curse. I will show you his power and take the numbers from your bodies."

Lift the torment through my verse,
Of the woe that came by curse—
Through the wrath of waters at night—
From the Titans in my sight.

No sooner had Cyca finished than the ground shook, releasing the cries of the dead. The scales fell from the Titans' eyes, and their hands flew to their throats as serpents came out of their skulls. The bloodsnakes fell to the ground, thrashing as the numbers vanished from the Titans. The half-bloods leaped back and destroyed the snakes with lightning, the iron fangs reflecting the flashes but consuming the thunder. Seconds passed. Everything was still.

"You are miserable," said Cyca in hollow tones. "Though you became stronger, your number is less, and soon you will die—unless you give the Serpent that which he desires. He has sent me to go with you, that you should not fail."

"The curse has been lifted," said Andromede. He flipped a lightning bolt and caught it with the opposite hand. Another flared in his right. "You control us no more."

Low growls fluttered in the Titans' throats as they rallied behind him.

"The curse has been lifted," mocked Cyca, "but where will you go? The only one way to leave this place is through the fire of the Dragon. Of course," added the angel malevolently, "if you prefer to wander, your lives will be stripped away until your brains can no longer discern whether you're dead or alive. Until your bodies fall at last, and your souls are bound in Avaddon. There you will be tormented, day and night, and given bodies of wrath. Bodies that will only feel pain—torn apart, lash by lash, and filled with worms that ravish your skulls. They will terrorize you from within. The Destroyer will crush you from without.

"Magatha," sighed Cyca. "You will beg for Magatha."

The fangs nearest the half-bloods curled forward, the razor-sharp tips hanging inches from their heads. The Titans looked helpless and ancient; if it were possible, the arrogance was gone.

"How can we pass?" said Xoar faintly, as though his voice had already been annihilated.

"Walk with me for seven days," said Cyca in low and clouded tones. "Here, in this place. On the seventh day, I will open the mouth of the Dragon. We will pass through the fire and stand together in the Seen."

"And what more?" said Andromede dully, a shadow suddenly

appearing at the base of the fang beside him. The dark wisp flickered up his body and entered his eyes. His mouth opened and then closed. The Titan rocked in a trance.

"Worms, do you not know? I've come to save us all. . . ."

There was a pause while more shadows filled the Titans' skulls; then Cyca pressed his advantage, his voice growing more narcotic. "Power is locked behind the gates of Sin Via, power that will make you greater than me—"

"But the city is cursed," murmured Andromede.

"And I have the key to unlock its gates." Here, the angel held out the wad of skins. "Drive it between the gates of Sin Via, and they will open for you. For us."

Reflections of the Titans flickered in the steel around them, and they gazed at their images. They looked invincible.

"Why do you need us?" said Mosca, swaying softly to and fro.

"The gates can only be opened from without," said Cyca, as Andromede came forward and took the bundle. "From the Seen, a world in which my body cannot pass."

"We open the gates, and nothing more?"

"No, devils, you must give me the spirit of the Osprey within."

"Give us the power first," said Andromede, now retreating to the pack.

"Yes," said Cyca. A thin smile spread across his blackened lips. "Open the gates, and I will give you power. Then deliver me the Osprey."

"How will we summon the spirit?" said Mosca.

"I will show you what to do. Though my body burns, my spirit will come to you in the form of another. In Vice Valley, it will come to you, before the Iron Peak that rules the Twelve Mountains. There you will find Sin Via."

There was another pause, and a loathing, yet victorious expression flitted across Cyca's face. The lightning vanished as the Titans opened their hands and touched their reflections in the silvery fangs.

"Why must we wait?" asked a Titan. "Take the spirit now."

"We must wait for the sons of God," said Cyca, staring into the distance. "They must fight us and be defeated. We must kill them from within."

CHAPTER 19

THE ANGEL OF THE SUN

E va sat on the bed where her daughter lay, the girl wrapped in a blanket by a melancholy fire. The lady's face was gaunt, blue veins standing out on her forehead, her emerald robes clinging loosely to her body. Chloe's face was full, her hair pearly white. Peace resonated throughout her frame for she wore the crown. Though her wounds had healed, the girl had not yet woken; and so Eva sat spellbound, watching her daughter's chest slowly rise and fall.

Hoping that its unharnessed light would arouse her, Eva had uncovered the crown but to no avail. Despite its light, vivid and alive, the room felt dreary. Mercilus was on a stool by the fire, stirring coals with a poker, Zane leaning against the wall behind him in between two shuttered windows, staring at the flames. Luther sat against the opposite wall, a bowl of stew in his hands, chewing absentmindedly.

An old woman entered the room and approached the bed, parting the sea of red hair around her face and looking imploringly at Eva. She was Abrís.

"My lady, please eat."

"Thank you," whispered Eva, her eyes fixed on Chloe. She reached down and traced the outline of her face. "But not until she rises."

"You're killing yourself!" said Abrís desperately and laid a hand on Eva's arm. "Long ago I mourned for you, only to have you return. And for what? To die before me?"

"So what if I do."

Abrís bit her finger and exchanged glances with J'san, who was standing beside a heavy wooden door, listening for an alarm. Although the day was wearing away, few people moved in the streets of Rell Mor. The dread of the Titans had fallen upon them like a suffocating fog, seeping into their lungs and torturing their souls. The destruction of Hevethod and Antalioth—Eran Dethens and Novecca—had made everyone believe the gods walked among them. But what made the terror unbearable was that no one knew where the Titans had gone. Each feared that he would be next.

Luther set down his bowl, rose, and came to Eva's side. He said nothing as he embraced her at the shoulders and drew her close. The wasted lady looked like a girl in his arms.

"It's my fault," she murmured for the hundredth time. "These girls, they think they know everything. I was afraid to push her away. I wanted her to love me. But I know better. . . ."

Eva rose, pushed away from Luther, and paced toward the fire and back again. "This will never happen again. . . . Never! I'll rule this girl with an iron fist, I swear it! I don't care if she hates me. At least she'll be safe."

The others glanced listlessly in their direction, as though watching a play they'd seen a thousand times before. Luther came forward, right on cue, and caught Eva as she buried her face in her hands. "I wasn't there for her," she choked, and the lady began to cry.

"There was nothin' you could do," said Luther emphatically. "It was her time. She was led to the fight, taken to a place that you, me, none of us could go. We all have our day. We all gotta face the enemy for ourselves so that we know when God is for us, no one can stand against us."

"I know," said Eva weakly, lifting her head and wiping her eyes.

"It's just . . . to see her like this. . . ." She stepped away, leaned over the girl, and lowered her voice. "Twice I've failed you, but never again."

The others drew near her. "You can't blame yourself," said Mercilus. "None of this is your fault. Not now, not then."

Eva rose and turned away, too tired to fight; but Mercilus pressed on, tired of holding back.

"She saved your life, Eva. She'll come back, but how can she move forward when she finds you like this? Be strong for her. She will rise."

Tears streamed down Eva's face, and her hands trembled. "How do you know? It's been days, the crown never takes this long. Will God take her from me? Aren't the dead the first to rise?"

The only answer was the crackling fire and a shutter caught in the wind, rapping lightly against the wall outside. They found themselves staring at Chloe, entranced, as though they could see the crown at work. The color had returned to her cheeks, and warm, radiant energy played around the edges of her eyes and mouth. It seemed the slightest sound would awaken the girl from her sleep. The shutter cracked, but Chloe didn't move.

"You have to believe," said J'san flatly. His face was no more giving than a mask, but his eyes penetrated Eva's heart.

"And eat," said Luther.

Eva hesitated then gave a feeble nod that sent Abrís bustling through the same door she had come. The prophetess returned a short while later and found Eva settled in the only armchair in the room, resting beside Chloe. Abrís handed her a bowl of venison stew, which Eva began to guzzle, and set a heaping plate of bread, cheese, and dates at her feet. The next minute, Abrís took away the empty bowl and gave Eva the plate, but she was already full. The lady picked at a few dates and set it back on the floor. Her eyes grew heavy.

"Abrís," said Eva, sinking back in the chair, "what happened to Sin Via?"

"Why, my lady? Why add to your torment?"

"Tell me. Sleep will come all the same. . . . There's something over my heart."

"What is it?"

Eva heaved a sigh, shifted in her seat, and wedged a pillow between the side of the chair and her head. "We overheard Lavian and his angels talking about a spirit they wanted to release. One trapped in Sin Via." The lady closed her eyes. "I'm afraid, Abrís . . . that Sin Via will haunt me again."

"Peace, Lady Eva. Sin Via's been destroyed."

"Tell me how."

A cold draft suddenly came down the chimney and swept through the room. The flames dimmed on the hearth, and everyone glanced around. Mercilus gazed warily at the windows. They still didn't know how they had come to the house of Abrís. They had found Chloe when Mount Nin split, opening the cove and the shadow comb with it. The sea retreated as Dark Angels came for the body of Lavian; a chasm had opened between the Serpent and the girl, revealing the foundation of the world and worlds beyond, like an endless hall of mirrors. A wall of fire had risen between Chloe and Lavian. Mercilus and Eva lifted the girl and carried her toward it, a quivering stream of images flickering in the flames. Suddenly, Abrís wavered before them. Eva had shouted, and they passed through the fire and arrived in the house of the prophetess.

"No one knows we're here," said Zane, but his words did little to calm their nerves. Eva no longer commanded creation, and they had no way of passing into the Unseen. If they were discovered, they would have to fight. Even with fire and light shields, six could not withstand an army.

It began to rain. Mercilus held his gaze, contemplating the change in weather, then laid the poker on the hearth, pulled over his stool, and sat next to Eva. Abrís took a seat on the edge of the bed, and Luther drew closer to Zane. J'san held his position by the door.

"I told you that I gave the book to another," Abrís began, "to the one Jezul commanded. What became of him, I do not know. What I didn't tell you"—she cleared her throat and looked down at her hands—"was that after you disappeared, Hadesha said that you were a witch. That you killed your daughter and lord."

"*Witch!*" snapped Eva, her eyes burning hotter than the fire. "So everyone thinks I murdered my family?"

"They used to," said Abrís. "Hadesha didn't want anyone searching for you . . . for your crown. So she killed another and said that it was you."

"Who?"

Abrís bowed her head. "I knew it couldn't be you. I knew the one with the crown would never die. Nevertheless, I went to see for myself, for the queen had hung a girl's body at the gates of Sin Via. For a moment, I despaired—she looked like you—but then I saw she didn't have the scars of the Raptor."

Eva closed her eyes. "Ocie."

"You knew her?"

"One of Hadesha's maids. Had to be. Everyone thought we were sisters."

There was a silence. Mercilus traded places with J'san, whose muscle-bound arm rocked Eva's chair as he dropped onto the stool.

"Go on," sighed Eva.

And the voice of the prophetess came again. "While many believed you were dead, there were those who searched for your crown. Years passed until even they believed that you were legend and that the crown never existed. Meanwhile, Ives and his lady, Pheriche, became the rulers of Sin Via.

"Ives gave himself to the Serpent and received a chalice in return. He wore it on a chain around his neck, eating with it, sleeping with it, riding into battle with the chalice. He used its magic to prey upon the sons of men. He opened the city to demons and offered sacrifices, even children, to the stars and himself.

"Spirits came to him, and he used the chalice to give them divine bodies—spiders that could not be crushed, rats that would never drown. But he loved his birds the most—spirits clothed with feathers that could fly like angels. They passed through Linden, unimpeded, into the warchambers and bedchambers of his enemies. They were his eyes and ears, and his knowledge became unmatched. But everything ended the night hell came for Sin Via."

"It was destroyed by gods?" said Zane.

Abrís nodded. "The magic of the chalice was great, so much so that Ives learned how to create the fire of the Serpent. The fool entered the Unseen, followed demons to Magatha, and released the Titans. He brought them into our world, thinking they would do his will, but they killed Ives—he and his lady—the moment they stepped into Sin Via. The earth opened to receive their bodies, and the fires of Avaddon burst through the earth and flooded the palace. The Titans withstood the flames, but the Destroyer rose, standing in the fire, killing many before the rest fled in terror."

"How do know you this?" said Mercilus.

"I saw it in a dream. A deep sleep had overtaken everyone in Sin Via until the scream of the Destroyer woke us. Some of us. We rose and ran through the gates. . . . I was among the last to leave. Fire engulfed the streets and slammed the doors closed. We watched in horror as the flames shot into the air, weaving like ghosts as they rose above the cliffs and consumed the spirits that tried to escape."

There was another silence. Eva reached over and placed her palm on Chloe's forehead, the men staring at the floor.

"D'you know anything about the spirit?" said Luther. "The one that Lavian wants."

"No," said Abrís. "There were so many. What scares me is *why* he wants it. There are legions that roam free in our world. Why this one? Did he say anything else?"

"Yeah," said Luther. "Somethin' about killing Estelle."

"Who's that?"

"The Angel of the Sun," said a voice, ringing like a sword. "The one who carries time in his hands."

Everyone leaped to their feet and stood back as the fire spread onto the floor. Eva and the men had no sooner surrounded Chloe than flaming trails sifted through the air and entered their noses. Peace overcame them. Seconds later, the flames streamed out from their mouths and rejoined the fire, which rose and swirled before the mantel. The flames licked the ceiling, but the ceiling wouldn't burn.

"I am Lunen, angel of the Raptor and brother of Estelle," said the voice. A blurred face appeared in the middle of the fire, wavering through the flames with white and shining eyes. "I have been sent to reveal the Serpent's plot and save the faces of men. Be not afraid.

"Estelle carries time in his hands," said Lunen, as the figures in the room leaned forward. "If he dies, the Earth will return to emptiness—to what it was before time began, when there were no separations, when the land was fused to the sea, and the sea married to the sky. When light was joined to darkness, and time with eternity. When the Seen and Unseen were one."

"What good would that do to Lavian?" said Abrís, her voice quivering.

"The Serpent's doom has been written in time. Every morning that Estelle steps into the heavens, he brings Lavian closer to his day."

"What day?" asked J'san.

"The day that he dies. Like Sören who fell into ruin, so too the Serpent. And do not think his day comes by chance. The book foretells his destruction, but time brings the destruction into existence."

Eva and Mercilus looked at each other.

"So if Estelle were no more . . ."

"Lavian's day would never come."

"Not only his day, but all days," said Lunen. "All men on Earth will die."

The angel went on before anyone could speak, an unlikely prospect judging by the blank faces staring back at him.

"When Jezul created the Earth, he tore time away from eternity, divided the land from the sea and the sky from the same. Light was separated from darkness, and after angels were banished from your world, the Seen was severed from the Unseen. If Estelle dies, the separations will be lost. The Earth will become formless and void.

"Jezul knew that Lavian would come for my brother and gave Estelle a veil that covers his body. No weapon can break it. But there's a spirit of darkness that is clothed in light, given the body of an Osprey by Lord Ives, which draws its power from the chalice. It can pass through the veil. If Lavian retrieves the spirit, he will use it to kill Estelle."

"I saw it!" exclaimed Abrís. "Lord Ives loved the Osprey. It sat over his throne, gleaming like the sun, but there was something about it, something chilling . . ." She caught herself and gasped, "But the Osprey is no more! It burned in Sin Via."

"Its body burned," said Lunen, "but the spirit remains."

"They can't release it," Mercilus argued. "We heard the angels saying something about a star—"

"They failed to take the star fastened to Aurèle," said Lunen, and his eyes rested on Chloe. She looked like a goddess, bathed in the light of the crown. "But Lavian has found another way, the blood of the girl."

"What do you mean?" said Eva fearfully.

"The gates of Sin Via are locked by hell, and only the light of Zaphon can release them. The blood of your daughter carries that light. When she fought Lavian, her blood covered his blade and the light with it. Lavian has given it to the Titans to raise the Osprey."

"You can't stop them, can you?"

"No, daughter. Sin Via can only be entered through its gates in the Seen, a world in which no angel can stand. The city sank beneath the fires of Avaddon, burned to its very foundations, both in your world and in ours. In the Unseen, Sin Via exists only in Oblivion, a world we cannot find."

"We'll go," said Mercilus, shooting determined looks at Luther, Zane, and J'san. "We'll take the blade before they can open the gates."

"Destroy them," said Lunen. The men pulled off the woolens that hung over their shoulders and stepped toward the fire. "You will not fight alone. Angels are scattered throughout Linden, calling those who belong to Jezul. They will join you at Sin Via."

"How many of them?" said Eva. "The Titans."

"Forty."

"Then we all go," said the lady, shrugging off her tattered coat and looking anxiously at Chloe.

"You crazy?" said Mercilus, and he grabbed her by the arm. "Stay here."

"I can't!" said Eva, wrenching herself free. "If Estelle dies, we all die. I'll never see her again."

Mercilus stepped aside as she leaned over Chloe and wrapped her arms around her neck.

"Walk through the fire," said Lunen's voice, "and you will arrive at the gates. The spirit must not leave Sin Via."

J'san looked at Eva and the girl then strode through the flame. Luther and Mercilus followed.

Eva kissed Chloe's forehead, and a shudder ran through her frame. "I love you. . . ."

Zane took Eva's hand, and together they left the girl's side. The fighter stopped three feet from the fire, and Eva gazed into his face, partly hidden behind that shadowy beard. He looked in control.

"You'll see her again, I promise."

Eva's eyes glittered as Zane let her go, turned, and walked through the fire.

"Eva, you who are treasured by God," said Lunen. "He has given me the bread of angels. When you walk through the fire, your strength will return."

"Thank you."

"I will stay with your daughter. Soon she will rise."

The lady drew a long breath, as though an enormous weight had been lifted from her chest.

"I won't leave her," said Abrís, standing by the bed.

But Eva didn't look back as she stepped toward the flames.

"Eva."

The lady stopped inches from the angel's eyes.

"Be strong. You will face your demons of old." She stood a moment longer and walked through the fire.

CHAPTER 20

SPIRIT OF SIN VIA

A curtain of violet flame erupted in Vice Valley, and the Titans emerged between two mountains whose slopes were covered in shattered rocks. The weathered peaks were invading a murky sky that the sun itself could not break. Confused winds snapped this way and that, and a line of clouds marched from the south, threatening snow.

"Where is he?" said Mosca in a vague and airy voice.

No one answered. They had walked for days in shadows and reflections, days spent drowning in Cyca's voice. They looked helpless as they watched the angel suddenly pass through the flames. A shriek escaped his mouth, like the black mist that slipped through his nose, and the angel burned. The vapor hovered, glided downward, and entered the body of a tarantula that had fallen from Mosca's mane. The spider froze as tiny forks of lightning flickered over its body, then gathered itself, and darted toward Andromede still holding the bundle of skins, scaled the Titan, and stretched itself across the earhole of his skull.

Andromede's head twitched as though he was listening to the creature. He walked forward several paces, turned, and faced the pack. "There's the Iron Peak," he said, stretching an arm toward the highest summit that jutted into the sky like a twisted spire. "The gates of Sin Via lie beneath. *Come!*"

They walked up the trenchlike valley and reached a decayed road, covered in gravel, that ran along a dry riverbed. The figures moved like zombies, realizing they had left one wilderness for another: the slopes were gray, the mountains were gray. They trudged on and on, up the terrain as though ascending into the heavens whose sky was gray.

Three hours later, the valley leveled off, and the company traversed around the Iron Peak toward the west. The valley narrowed and became a gorge that was barely wider than the road on which they traveled. The Titans snaked through one switchback, then another, to find themselves facing the gates of Sin Via. The behemoth structure was built so seamlessly into the cliffs that its frame seemed to be growing out of the walls on either side. The She-Wolf was carved in the black iron doors, looming with empty eyes. Archers' nests and lions' heads were cut into the cliffs, suspended over tunnels filled with ice.

The pack stopped, and the spider twitched on Andromede's skull. The Titan reached into the bundle and pulled out the Betrayer's Blade. A fantastic light radiated from the bloodstained dagger and filled the gorge with the glow of the setting sun.

"Snakehive!" called Andromede, who dropped the skins and threw an arm over his eyes to shield them from the light. A yellow-scaled Titan came forward, long braids swinging as he stumbled. He covered his face with one hand and took the blade from Andromede in the other.

"Drive it through the gates, but do not pass through the fire."

Snakehive pinned the blade behind his back and staggered toward the gates, where he swung the dagger like a hammer and lodged it between the doors with a hollow ring. He stood back as the golden-white light streamed upward from the blade, flowing along the groove between the doors, split across the top of the frame, and traveled around the perimeter.

The dagger hit the ground as the gates suddenly fell inward, grating on their hinges, the blood and light no longer on its blade. The doors swung slowly at first, and then with increasing speed until they opened wide. Howling, the beasts threw their arms across their sockets as the light exploded and filled the gate with fire.

Andromede shouted for the pack to follow, but no one moved. The spider sank its legs into the Titan's skull and he spoke again, but this time in the spellbinding voice of the angel. "*Walk with me. . . .*"

The Titans swayed like the grass of the Laudican Plains and edged toward the gates, never lifting their faces, feeling their way by walking toward the pain. Andromede reached the gate and flashed lightning through Snakehive's chest. He glanced up as the Titan fell and crossed through the fire.

Once inside, the half-bloods uncovered their faces and kept the fire to their backs. They gazed into the fallen city, the Unseen, and the judgment that ruled it: Darkness reigned in a starless sky, firelight dancing over buildings whose walls and pillars were warped as if they had been melted. The cliffs widened like a funnel before them, away from the gates. Columns of smoke gave the impression of a recent demise, though blackened skeletons told of a time long ago.

"Xoar and Mosca will come with me," said Andromede. "The rest of you, guard the gates! They are the only way to leave. We stand in judgment—the farther you fly away, the farther you fly into Oblivion. The sons of God will be here soon to close the gates and trap us within."

"We do nothing!" snarled Xoar. "Not until you give us the power in this place!"

"Yes," said Andromede darkly. "You are weak for the battle that we face." The Titan stepped forward, opened his arms, and shouted,

From this haunt I call on legions,
Lending bodies unto demons—
Down-cast spirits, your eyes are restless,
For these vessels are not endless;
Seize them!—condemned prisoners that bleed—
And leave for me the Andromede.

Syn-de Sig! come swiftly thirty-nine,
And yield the Serpent his design;
Syn-de Sig! and tear your shackles,
Loathsome spirits, prey like jackals—
Hunt with lusts that dost profane;
Come, thirty-nine! let the rest remain.

For a moment, everything was still; then screams filled the atmosphere as trails of smoke flew toward the Titans, weaving through the air before diving down their throats.

The Titans buckled as they were transformed by the demons within. Xoar shrieked, his skin giving way and scales turning into stone. Iron claws burst from his hands, and fleshlike wings erupted from his back, his cries ceasing as blood streamed from his mouth and formed a pool on the ground. Mosca lay three feet away, gasping, rib cage breaking apart with horrifying cracks; it tore through his skin and formed an exoskeleton of stone. His tongue split down the center, thrashing as two more arms ruptured from his abdomen. The wings of an insect rose from his spine. His fingers smoldered and became blades of steel.

The shrieks subsided and the figures rose, dressed in stone and steel, poised to fly on the wings of insects and dragons. A glowing red liquid drooled from their mouths, and scales covered their eyes. The Demons reigned in their bodies, and the Titans were no more.

"My brothers, keep them open until I return!" cried Andromede, gesturing toward the gates. The Demons turned and faced the light unimpeded. "Today we free the Osprey! Succeed, and you will leave this place and rule the Earth. Fail, devils, and the Serpent will devour you—in this life and the next!"

"Vur draaken cy hvis angeli!"*

Andromede, Xoar, and Mosca headed into the ruins, walking over the dead that were scattered amid gold and jewels—plunder left by a destroyer that had not come for riches. The cliffs spread farther apart and laid before them a city that had died and was dying still. Whispers came from the billows, voices that became screams and faded to whispers again. The sound of beating wings echoed against the walls, but no birds could be seen.

Darkness thickened as the ground fell away, the light from the gates unable to reach the bottom of the gorge. They had just passed a cluster of tombs when the gloom parted a hundred yards away, showing two stars that hung low over the city. Their blue and silver bodies shone dimly, illuminating nothing in the valley but the gilded pyramid beneath them.

"The castle mount," said Andromede. He ran toward the structure with stairs on every side that led to a flat top where a building had once stood. "Hurry!"

Soon they were clambering up the contorted steps and reached the top a minute later, which was covered in ashes. They paused and beheld the city below, their eyes cutting through the darkness and billows that rose as though they were trying to escape. Mosca pointed at the riverbed; fire had consumed its waters and left what looked like a scorched serpent snaking through the ruins.

"Tannin," he said in vacant tones. It was no longer the Titan who spoke, but the voice of the demon within. His hand moved to the north, following what appeared to be a line of black rocks, equally spaced, in the middle of the bed. The procession culminated in a smooth boulder that rested beneath a dead waterfall.

---

* For the Dragon and his angels!

"He will rise," said Cyca, speaking through Andromede. "Find the chalice and the dragon flies."

And without warning, the spider dropped from Andromede's skull and disappeared into the ashes. It was some time before the creature scurried back and climbed the Titan's frame, returning to its perch. "Come with me!" he breathed.

The figures walked toward the southern side of the mount where Andromede halted fifteen feet from the edge and raised a hand. "Here it lies!"

The Demons spread out, knelt down, and dug frantically through the debris. Mosca had barely scattered a few charms before his bladed fingers struck an object with a soft, indefinite chime. He yanked a golden cup from the ashes, which Andromede snatched from his hand. The others stood as he sliced his arm and held the chalice to the wound. Having filled it with blood, he drank from the cup, and the pair of stars descended upon them.

The orbs transformed to reveal the gods. There was Malströn, black and twisted horns rising from his skull, his body made from the bones of animals, bound in sallow skin. Ishva hovered close beside him, her dark frame looking emaciated, her eyes glimmering like scarlet moons, legs chained together.

"Why have you come?" said Malströn in a hollow voice. He hovered over Andromede and looked down at the spider through the halos that floated around his head. A maniacal smile was fixed like a chasm on his face. "I am god in this place. Those within belong to me."

"Yes," said Ishva. Her voice murmured like water, though it seemed her body had never tasted rain. "I was too weak to save this city, for it once belonged to me. It has been given to another." She turned slightly, and her body snapped as though it were glass. A flurry of ashes fluttered over Xoar.

A hiss came from the spider that spoke through Andromede. "We have come for the Osprey," it said. "The one who was, is not, and yet will come. Give it to me!"

Cries echoed in the distance, haunting cries that seemed to come from everywhere . . . and from nowhere.

"And what will you do for us?" said Ishva.

"What will I do for you?" shrieked Andromede. "It's no wonder that you're worthless and unable to save! You despise this place? Good! For our doom will be far worse than this! Prepare to burn— loathsome soul!—in the Lake of Fire if we do not end the prophecy!"

The angel stormed on, blinded by his hate. "I'm Cyca, angel of the Dragon—one of the Fallen that seeks to end our demise. I've lost my body to come to this place, forever I'll roam from beast to beast, all to spare my doom and yours. Now my god calls for the Osprey. Give it to me, or suffer the wrath of Lavian!"

The bodies of the gods dimmed. Ishva shrank back toward the ruins, the shadows, and the sighs; there were no screams, nor the spirits' dismal cries.

"As the Snake desires," said Malström. He lifted his head and called over the city, *"Sin Via!"* Empty and evil was his voice.

You lie cursed in silence,
Drenched by the blood of your defiance!
Awaken from the fallen,
And again your will be done;
For beneath the billows of corruption,
And the ashes of destruction,
Lies one your doom will carry,
Through the Angel of the Sun;
On whose wings death shall pass—
And his covering succumb—
Who was, is not, and yet will come.

From the demons of your ruins,
A loathsome spirit we now beckon,
Dressed in light, bathed in death,
From the Dragon to the phantom,

Speaking truth that is a lie,
Deceiving sons that they may die—
This vessel once enchanted—
Lo! amid the stars once sung;
Release the Osprey from the fallen,
He that makes the world undone—
Who was, is not, and yet will come.

Emptiness will the Earth abhor,
Yet prophecies shall endure no more,
For by vengeance the veil shall fall
From the Angel of the Sun.
We shall make the world aghast,
A retribution of our wrath;
Now breathe power in the wings
Of he that makes the world undone;
And give to us the spirit—
He that heeds the Serpent's tongue—
Who was, is not, and yet will come.

No sooner had Malströn finished than an eerie, distant screech reverberated from somewhere in the billows. A black vapor broke away from the ruins and drifted toward the northern face of the pyramid. It flattened as it came, the edges rising and falling, mimicking the wings of a bird as it floated toward the gods.

The spider pulled its legs out of Andromede's skull, darted across his face, and opened the Titan's jaws. Andromede was about to rip the creature from his mouth when Malströn threw two halos that smashed against his head. Onyx particles showered the Titan, wisps of yellow dust entering his nose. He went rigid as the birdlike vapor bored into his mouth, then toppled and sent the spider cartwheeling into the ashes.

The seconds waned. Little white flames began rising through the Titan's scales, dancing like a thousand candles. The scales melted and flames flattened, congealing in the shape of feathers. Andromede's head shrank and became that of a bird, his arms widening into wings, legs shriveling and feet withering into talons. The half-blood transfigured until he no longer existed, the Osprey lying in his place, white like the sun. But its eyes were empty.

The bird stood, wings open, and rose into the air. Within seconds, it was streaking over the city and released an evil cry, a creature as lifeless as the ruins from which it came. The Osprey let out another screech, circled back to the pyramid, and landed on Xoar's shoulder.

The spider climbed Xoar's body and latched onto his skull. His jaw moved, but it was Cyca's voice that spoke. "Raise the dragon!"

The gods were silent as the figures strode out from beneath them, leaped from the top of the pyramid, and glided into the ruins below. The Osprey let go and zoomed toward the riverbed, Xoar and Mosca at its tail, flying over the extinct waterfall where Xoar dumped the contents of the chalice. The line of rocks shifted in the bed, tremors crumbling the nearby ruins as Xoar and Mosca landed at the foot of the pyramid.

But the Osprey continued to circle as the dragon rose. The charred stones along the river were in fact its spine, and the boulder beneath the waterfall its skull. Gigantic wings were surfacing as it struggled up from the ground. More tremors tipped the arches of a wasted bridge behind it. Within minutes, the dragon was free, standing more than thirty feet in height, bones smoldering as it scanned the ruins. The monster folded its skeletal wings and dove into the earth as though it were water, a smoking hole in its wake.

"Where is it?" said Mosca, the earth trembling as he scanned the city.

"He will come, for I have given him breath," said Xoar. "He will do my will."

The ground exploded before them, and the dragon emerged transformed. Whether the beast had passed through the hands of time or the magic of the Underworld mattered little now. It had returned to what it was before. Midnight scales covered its body, and its eyes shone like the moon. It shook itself violently, and the ground spilled from its back like rain.

Tannin screamed, showing rows of bloodstained teeth, and the demons came. The dragon inhaled the endless trails of smoke and was filled with the spirits of Sin Via. The Osprey landed on its head, sank its talons through its skull, and took control of the dragon.

CHAPTER 21

THE BATTLE AT THE GATES

he Destroyer! Chloe struggled to get free but was wrapped in a tomb with no light or darkness, land or sea. Her heart was pounding as the angel sped toward her, shrouded in a dismal haze, eyes glowing like the embers of a fire.

She couldn't run and couldn't fly, though it wouldn't matter. *I'll fight him.* . . . But the girl could not lift her hands.

The figure flashed and became a bird that passed inches over her head, shining like a star. Chloe twisted her neck and watched the creature as it hurtled toward the faces of men. They were crying for the girl.

She opened her eyes, heart still racing, and rolled her head to find herself lying in what appeared to be a small living room. Everything glittered. She pulled her arm out from under the blanket and felt the crown, bonded to her head. *How? I gave it to . . . gave it to . . .* Her eyes closed.

"Eva . . ."

Chloe's lips had barely moved, her voice no louder than the flames hissing on the hearth. A ribbon of smoke left the fireplace, snaked through the air, and entered the girl's mouth. She took in a long, sudden breath before exhaling what looked like fog, and she opened her eyes.

"Daughter of men," said a voice that reminded her of Aurèle's. It rang and faded away. "Rise."

No longer groggy, the girl sat up and saw that she was alone. A wane redheaded woman burst into the room, just before Chloe noticed the eyes glowing in the fire.

"Chloe!" gasped the woman and darted toward the bed with an outstretched arm.

"Who are *you*?" Chloe knocked the arm away while staring at the fire.

"Abrís."

The prophetess held out her arm again. Chloe glanced at the talon scars and then back at the fire.

"I am Lunen," said the voice from the fire. "An angel of the Raptor." The flames poured out from the hearth, swirling as they rose, lifting the eyes. A shadowy face formed around them.

"Angel?" said Chloe, scooting back on her bed. "You don't look like one. And where's Eva?"

"My body cannot pass into the Seen," said Lunen, "but my spirit stands in the fire. Those you love are in Sin Via."

"Sin Via! Why? We're supposed to go . . ." The girl's hand flew to her chest. Images of Lavian flooded her mind, his body like a fortress, lunging at her time and time again . . . lightning and shock waves roaring . . . The blade piercing her arm. The circle burning in the sand.

Had to be a dream! Chloe whipped the blankets back, wrestled her arm out of the robe that she was wearing, and looked down. There was a thick red scar from the Betrayer's Blade, right through one of the letters on her bicep. But the golden 𝕂 sparkled as though it were still alive.

"How?" she breathed. "I mean, I just remember being drawn to the beach."

"It was your time," said Lunen. "Whether you were led by the

spirit of our god or the will of the Serpent, the truth remains—you
have become like gold, refined by fire."

"Ni våpen mái jasamel avergade yú ilys prosvita,"* Chloe said,
still staring at the scar.

"It's okay," said Abrís and laid a hand on Chloe's shoulder.
"You're safe now."

"No one's safe!" said Lunen forcefully.

"Where are they?" said Chloe, panicking as she swung her legs
onto the floor. "Eva . . . *my ma* . . . Mercilus, J'san, Luther, Zane."
She rattled off their names to make sure he knew whom she meant.
"And why do I have the crown?"

"The lady never wanted to see you like this again," said Abrís.

"I know they're in Sin Via," said Chloe, who ignored her and
stalked toward the fire, "but what's happening?"

"War."

"War!" She stopped, faces flying through her mind—Eva,
Mercilus . . . visions of them dying. "Send me!"

"I will," said Lunen, and the quivering face nodded. "But you
must know the foe that you face."

"Quickly!"

"Lavian tried to kill you because the book's written on your
heart," said Abrís. "If you die, it dies." Chloe did not seem to be
listening as she yanked off her outer robe and threw it on the floor.
Her eyes caught her dagger, lying on a shelf by the window, which
she seized and stuffed in her waistband. "But there's another way he
can end his doom."

"How?" said Chloe over her shoulder, now standing in a
sleeveless tunic.

"By killing Estelle," said Lunen.

"*How?*"

---

* No weapon formed against you will prevail.

"Eva will explain everything," said Abrís hurriedly. "Just know there's a demon in Sin Via that's an Osprey. It mustn't escape!"

The girl stepped toward the fire and stopped. "But the gates are locked."

"Lavian has your blood."

Chloe blinked and a stunned look flitted across her face.

"Only the light can open the gates," said Abrís, "and Lavian has the blade—"

"From the fight," said Chloe numbly, looking at the scar in her arm. "And my blood as the light of the book." She gritted her teeth and stepped into the fire.

"One more thing!" called Abrís, the girl fading in the flames. "The demons in Sin Via need bodies. If the Titans arrive—"

She stopped as the fire fell to the floor. The girl was already gone.

———◆———

A fire was burning on the road beneath the Iron Peak, obscured with heavy clouds that hid the waning sun, and Eva emerged out of the flames. They were gone before she had taken a second step. The lady looked strong now, her body filling out its clothes, gray eyes peering over snowy cheeks that were no longer hollow. Zane came alongside her as she approached a large group of people that already stood outside the gates of Sin Via.

"We're too late," said the bald mountain of a man on their left. He was ignored as Eva swiftly considered the figures staring back at her, their breath smoking in the frigid air. They were mostly men that looked capable enough, dressed in furs and leathers, though two tall solemn-looking women stood with them.

Mercilus flashed a sword in his fist and gestured at the footprints in the gravel. They were all pointing forward. "They're still inside."

"He must have opened the fire," said Eva militantly, looking at

Snakehive's body. "It will burn until we close the doors. The city's surrounded by rock and thrown into Oblivion. The gates are the only way out.

"You, you, and you." Eva pointed at the women and then to a young man with a chiseled face and black windswept hair. "Come with me and mine. We face the onslaught.

"You"—she pointed to the eight or nine men on her left—"shut the northern door. Two on the gate, the rest form a shield around them. Everyone else, close the southern door."

The lady walked boldly toward the gates and flashed a sword, her newfound ranks making way as they shed their coats. "Trap them inside," she said to no one in particular, "and destroy them all."

J'san and Mercilus flanked their lady, followed by Luther and Zane. More swords appeared, the company pacing behind them. No one broke step as they crossed through the fire, into Sin Via.

"REAP IT!"

Wings ruptured from Eva's spine as she threw her sword, the missile hurtling end over end and impaling a Demon twenty yards away. The sword exploded in his stone-covered chest and reduced the figure to ashes. Screams echoed in the darkness as the enemy flashed their shields, but not before two more swords found their marks: down went a pair of Demons.

"The gates!" Eva yelled, and the men ran to close the doors under a barrage of lightning. Thunder cracked and boomed as the shields obliterated the bolts in clouds of livid sparks. Fighters sent flames through the air, the whiplike fires coiling around several Demons who burned but kept fighting until swords were plunged through their bodies.

The lady had chosen well; the women were poised, the black-haired man agile. They stood together, shoulder to shoulder, opposite the line of Demons storming toward them.

"Yeah!" yelled Luther, and the men rushed forward, J'san running

through a lightning bolt that he smashed with his shield, colliding with a six-armed Demon and plunging a sword through its throat.

Luther and Mercilus flew to meet the Demons that had risen into the air. Zane fought in front of Eva, who cried as she blocked a bolt inches from her face. The lady never saw the one thrown behind her, but the man she had chosen chopped the streaking blur. Thunder roared and Eva whirled around, cut the head off a lizard-like Demon, and shouted at him, *"Why aren't the gates closed?"*

"I don't know!"

Several men had their shoulders pressed against the doors, driving their legs, but the gates wouldn't budge. An unearthly scream rang in the distance.

"Why die in this place?" shrieked a Demon. "Let Tannin finish them!"

His fellows echoed the cry, and the Demons retreated into the city, the man beside Eva staring after them.

"Where'd they go?"

"It doesn't matter!"

The lady wheeled around as Luther landed beside her. She paid no attention to the threadlike flashes that spun around the dead or the white lights rising from their bodies, only that their number had been cut in half and that the gates were still open. "Close the—"

She saw it now. Above the brilliant glare of the fire, seething around the gates, were two soft blue and silver glows. The massive bald man, who had been pressing his shoulder against one of the doors, straightened up and followed Eva's gaze. Malströn and Ishva were suspended about a hundred feet above the gates, using their magic to hold the doors in place. Eva barked at the two fighters hovering over her.

"Mercilus, J'san!" She looked over at the man who had saved her life. "And you, what's your name?"

"Dez."

"Go with them. Cut down the goddess—she's weak—then the

god." The lady looked back at the men standing around the doors, their bodies shining now, wings folded, and slashed the air with her fist. *"And close those gates!"*

The assassins began their ascent, Mercilus leading the way as Malströn watched them coming for Ishva.

"Tannin!" cried the goddess, her voice carrying across the city. "Come quickly!"

And before the band had climbed halfway, Eva cried out. Tannin fell like a ghost from the sky, illuminated by the light of the Osprey perched on his head, and crashed a short distance from the gates.

The dragon furled its wings and flung its tail, forcing Luther, Zane, Eva, and the women with her to scatter like pigeons as it sailed under their feet. "Eva!" said Tannin, the lady and her fighters touching down. The dragon's mouth had moved, but the voices belonged to the spirits within, the screech of a thousand birds. "We know who you are, Lady of Sin Via! You, who turned on us and Lord Amanyára!"

Eva reversed the grip on her sword and slung it like a spear. The white core flew through the air and gave Tannin but a second to duck before it zipped past the Osprey. "Speak his name again, and I'll rip out your tongue!"

"No!" shrieked another voice, and the dragon drew back its head. "If the bird dies . . ."

Xoar came gliding out of the darkness and landed beside Tannin. The chalice glittered in his claws then faded, becoming shadowy and translucent. Mosca alighted beside him, and the outlines of the Demons emerged from the billows, spreading out on either side of the dragon. They were barely visible in the shadows, but the lavalike substance that dripped from their mouths gave them away.

A blue light flickered on the spider latched to Xoar's skull, and Cyca's voice came from the Demon's mouth. "What good is it to destroy ourselves, daughter of the Morning Star? Let us pass and you shall live!"

"Live?" said J'san, who had descended with Dez and Mercilus and was hovering over his lady. "You'll kill Estelle, and the world—"

"You believe Jezul?" Xoar shouted over him. "We seek to end our doom, and nothing more! What's our fate to you, son of dust?" He nodded at Eva and said, "Do not think, daughter, that you will escape Sin Via again."

The lady looked as though she had left the land of the living, carried to a recess in her mind.

"It is you who will not escape," said Mercilus waspishly. "I will cut off your head, and you will wander in ashes forever."

The Demons issued long and eerie sighs, and several backed away.

"Dreamers!" shrieked Cyca, and Xoar looked over his shoulder at the Demons behind him. "We have the dragon—we are more than they!"

"There are more of you," said Eva, finding her voice, "but you must kill us all. I have only to kill the Osprey. And when it dies, Lavian will kill your mind. Your memories will be devoured by serpents, your dreams ripped apart by rats. You will know nothing but pain, feel nothing but fire—scream only for ice."

Xoar stood in silence, the spider bathing in the truth. The gods hovered over the gates. The Demons did not move.

"Stand down," Cyca hissed at last. "And you will see your daughter one more day—"

Eva finished the sentence by throwing a sword in his direction. Xoar raised a shield that destroyed the sword in a splash of golden-white sparks, and the Demons retaliated by hurling jets of lightning.

There was war in Sin Via. Everyone with Eva threw swords and issued tongues of fire at the Osprey, forcing the bird to dive from Tannin's skull and disappear behind the dragon. The Demons hurtled into the air, the Osprey zooming back into view and trailing behind them as they raced toward the gates.

"Look out!" shouted Mercilus, shielding the lady from behind as Malströn rained down halos from the sky. More of Eva's men soared over and joined Luther, Zane, and Dez who flew to meet the Demons. Luther was the first to plunge through the enemy line, his shield shattering from taking four bolts at once. The fighter grabbed Xoar by the wing, spun him around, and cut off his head. The spider let go of the skull as it fell through the air and landed on the Osprey. Xoar's body hit the ground, the chalice clanging into the rubble. Several more Demons burst into flame and crashed into the ruins, Zane with them, unable to open his wings as he grappled with a batlike Demon.

"*BIRD, BIRD!*" bellowed Dez and J'san, the Osprey dodging their swords as it sped for the gates. But before they could give chase, Tannin spewed a river of lightning that pelted their shields and drove them back through the air.

Eva sped toward the gates, where she turned and hovered as the last line of defense. She flung a sword that crushed Mosca, his ashes raining, and flashed another: the Osprey was streaking toward her. The lady knew she couldn't miss and had no sooner raised her arm than Chloe burst through the fire behind her, shooting into the air the moment the wings burst from her back. The girl slammed the crown on Eva's head, who nearly forgot to flap her wings as she watched Chloe flying for the bird.

The girl unleashed a light wave at the Osprey, who fired lightning from its mouth; the two forces met with an explosion that stunned the bird and sent it reeling into the cliffs. The brilliant body smashed against the wall and fell into the ruins below.

Tannin screamed, the blue light from his mouth flashing in the darkness. Chloe pulled up and retreated frantically in the air. *My god!*

The monster issued another stream of lightning at Chloe, who zigzagged beneath it and was rocked by a blast behind her, showered in what felt like bits of glass.

"Watch your back!"

Chloe's head whipped around. Mercilus was holding a shield and smashed an oncoming halo, thrown from the god above. Eva climbed into the sky and sent a light wave that destroyed the goddess beside him. Chloe faced Tannin in time to dodge another blast then looked at Eva, her head turning back and forth as though it were on a swivel. J'san cut down a Demon as a large man closed the northern door. Eva was fighting the god with halos above.

"Eva's got him!" shouted Mercilus. "Let's take the dragon!"

"All right!"

Chloe drifted behind Mercilus as he threw his sword at Tannin, the fiery blade windmilling through the air and spearing the monster through its jaw. The beast snapped its head and shrieked, flames pouring from the wound. Mercilus moved out of Chloe's way to give her a clean shot at the dragon. The girl fired at his head and missed, diving as the beast swatted at them with its wing.

Tannin arched its neck and saw Malströn explode, hit by a light wave, then spotted J'san racing to shut the southern door. The dragon lunged forward and skidded to a halt ten paces before the gates, snapped its tail, and struck J'san in midair. The fighter went sprawling into the ashes and was immediately hit by lightning as a Demon swooped overhead. A thin golden light flashed around J'san's body, the white light of his soul swallowed in the glare of ultraviolet rays. More figures rushed to close the door, the Demons to meet them, but Tannin consumed them all with lightning. His tail came sailing once more and wedged between the doors.

Chloe resurfaced and had seen the dragon was fast but not as fast as she. Mercilus had her back as the girl rose higher, even with Tannin's chest, but was shoved out of the way as she fired. The light wave veered and missed the dragon.

"Get back!" screamed Eva and unleashed a stream of light that burned a hole through Tannin's shoulder. The lady looked murderously at Mercilus, the dragon shrieking and snapping its head.

"Get her out of here!"

Fury boiled in Chloe's veins. For a second, she wanted to fight Eva more than the dragon, but something about its moonlike eyes, turning in their direction, caused the women to forget each other. Tannin fought like a chained dog, refusing to pull his tail from between the doors.

Chloe dodged Mercilus's arm as he reached out to pull her away and threw her hand at the dragon. A light wave shot through the air and struck the beast in the chest. He shrieked again, another hole in his body, but would not fall. He sent lightning, but the girl had read his eyes and was already gone, diving down and skimming across the ground. Seconds later, she was climbing and about to strike again when she saw a gleaming body streaking to her right, three Demons leading the way.

The Osprey!

Chloe and Mercilus sped in the same direction, determined to cut them off before they could turn toward the gates. The Demons glided around Tannin's wing, just inside the cliffs, but were met by Mercilus and Chloe. Shots erupted, Mercilus flashing shield after shield to cover the girl who fired seven or eight light waves. The first Demon flashed a shield before he was hit; the others burst into flame. The Osprey cut back, the spider still clinging to its back, zooming to Chloe's left. The girl opened her wings, flipped in the air, and kicked her feet against the wall. A second later, she was speeding in the opposite direction.

Chloe shot past Eva as she flew over the dragon's head, unsure if she was feeling the heat from Tannin's breath or her mother's raging eyes. Mercilus struggled to keep up, the cliff rushing toward them as Luther and Dez rose into the air, Luther banking left to join Chloe while Dez leveled off with Eva.

"I got outside!" shouted Luther, pointing at two Demons who had risen out of nowhere and were now leading the bird. The fighter soared upward, speared the outer Demon with his body, and drove

him into the wall. Mercilus collided with the inside Demon, leaving
Chloe one on one with the Osprey.

She fired and missed.

"Dammit!"

Chloe flew higher for a second shot, but the Osprey raced away,
its glowing body fading into the city. Chloe was about to chase after
it when Mercilus grabbed her by the wing.

"Let it go!" He looked back at Tannin's tail, lodged between the
doors. "Gotta close the gates!"

"Maybe he'll follow us!"

Chloe fired a light wave that blew a hole in Tannin's head, just
beneath his eyes. She, Luther, and Mercilus flew into the city as the
dragon screamed, but the beast wouldn't move.

Chloe was circling to strike again when she gave a small shout.

"You okay?" said Luther, trailing her left wing.

But she gave no answer. Why had she not realized it before?
True, Chloe had never seen Tannin's face, not before this day, but
she had looked into the billows and listened to their screams . . . had
watched them drift over midnight scales, swirling around frosted
horns that cascaded down a dragon's back. She had witnessed the
scene beneath her in dreams long ago. Chloe knew the secret of
his heart, had seen it torn from the beast in the sea, dripping with
despair, and sown in the midnight dragon . . . beneath the seventh
horn.

She dove for the dragon's neck, Eva screaming, but the girl
paid no attention. There was no fear in her veins, only fire, her eyes
burning like the sun, lips pressed in a scowl. Tannin didn't see the
girl as he fought with Dez and Eva, who were breaking him down,
piece by piece. The lady was swatted through the air, wing broken,
and tumbled to the ground.

Dez dove to help her up, but the lady waved him away. "Get
her!" she shouted, pointing at Chloe. He hovered a second longer.

"Now!"

Chloe landed on Tannin's back, anchored her arm around the seventh horn, and nearly went flying as the monster reeled, snapping its jaws and firing lightning over his shoulder, unable to hit the girl. Mercilus killed the last of the Demons as Dez dove out of nowhere to pull the girl away, but Luther sacked him in the air. Chloe flashed a sword in her hand that looked more like a spear and plunged it through Tannin's scales. She knew the blade had reached its heart—she could feel its despair. Fire poured through her veins, surged through the sword, and emptied into the heart of the dragon. Tannin convulsed and staggered backward, dragging his tail out from between the doors. The girl grew weak, her very essence draining from her soul, but she would not let go. *I'll ride you to the ground.* . . .

The dragon pitched, flames rising through its scales, screamed the scream of legions, and fell to the earth. His body split as it crashed, tossing Chloe, who flipped and slammed to the ground. Her head burst in pain as she rolled onto her side, choking as though she were about to vomit.

"Get up!" Eva cried, scooping the girl in her arms. Mercilus appeared at her side, and they lifted Chloe into the air.

"*Eva!*"

Zane stumbled through the ruins, a wide gash across his abdomen, his skin burned from lying in the ashes. Eva looked down at him as he tried running toward the gate and then at Tannin's burning remains. The Osprey burst through the flames as though it had come out of the beast. Eva flung out her arm, pinning Chloe to her body with the other, and fired a light wave that forced the bird to dive then another, which missed and hit the cliff with an earsplitting blast. Knowing that he wouldn't reach the door in time, Zane threw a sword as he ran. The Osprey completed a barrel roll as it passed harmlessly overhead, zipped through the gate, and was gone.

Eva landed with Chloe and Mercilus, who let go as the girl leaned her head against her mother's shoulder, staggering, head swimming. The women clung to each other as Zane approached from the opposite direction, Luther and Dez alighting on their right.

They stood in suffocating silence, unable to think or feel, the crown shining brightly on Eva's head, the fire swirling magnificently around the gates.

"My lady," came a woman's voice. Everyone looked toward the dragon and found one of the women from their ranks, kneeling beside an impression in the ashes where a body had lain. Her eyes dimmed. "I'm sorry that we failed. The one with me"—her timid voice broke—"was my sister. I go to be with her." She drew a dagger from her belt.

"*No!*"

Luther and Mercilus jumped forward, but it was too late. The woman had fallen on the weapon, the ground hammering the hilt with a muffled clink and driving the blade through her heart. Instantly, a tongue of warm light whirled around her head and spread down to her feet. A white glow rose into the air, and she was gone.

Chloe trembled uncontrollably and nearly slipped through her mother's arm as Eva threw a light wave at the cliffs, then another and another.

CHAPTER 22

THE CRY, THE VOICE, AND THE VOW

E va strode through the gate and the fire that veiled it, holding Chloe so tightly that the two appeared as one, returning to a world that was colder and darker than before. Their wings dissolved into thin air, skin faded and the light vanished from their eyes. Their mouths steamed like chimneys. The women stood back and waited as Dez, Mercilus, Zane, and Luther emerged. Chloe was steady now, her head clearing, though she couldn't remember anything that had happened after she hit the ground. Judging by the defeated looks, however, she could tell the Osprey had escaped.

Luther was the last to leave. He gripped the iron ring on the open door with both hands and leaned back with all his might. Chloe had been about to ask for J'san when the door began to close, and a cruel and empty sensation crept through her body. She dropped her gaze and gave a start. Two tiny eyes were lying on the ground, staring back at her through the fire. She let go of Eva, crouched down, and picked up the Betrayer's Blade.

"Leave it," said Eva quietly, tilting her head toward the gates as the girl rose.

Chloe trembled, knowing what she held in her hand: the weapon of Lavian that was fashioned against her from the beginning that

killed her father and held her mother for seventeen years. But wasn't
that why she couldn't let it go? It somehow tied her family together.

Slipping her other hand behind her back and pulling out her
knife, Chloe twisted her torso to block her hands from view, switched
the hilts, and pitched her own dagger through the door. She sheathed
the Betrayer's Blade under her tunic, Eva watching the door close
with an empty clang. The flames were gone. Eva turned to Chloe,
who wanted to look away, lifted the crown off her head, and held it
out to the girl. Dez peered intently from behind.

"First, Zane," said Chloe.

Eva's face was expressionless, but she looked at the fighter and
nodded. He came forward and bowed. "My lady."

Eva placed the crown on his head, and his wounds were healed
within seconds, his blackened skin restored. Chloe wondered why
her own scar had remained from her fight with Lavian, but the
thought was swept away as Zane placed the crown on her head.

They shivered, but no one seemed tempted to pick up the
scattered coats that were lying on the ground. No one except Eva,
who strode over, snatched one up, and drew her dagger. The lady
cut away the lining and began tearing the cloth into strips while
the others circled Chloe, who glanced at the stranger, his own eyes
weighing the girl and her crown. Dez lowered his head in respect
but did not look away.

Mercilus took Chloe into his arms and she laid her head against
his chest.

"Good to have you back," he said, trying not to sound afraid.
But it would not have mattered if he had. Peace was spreading
through the girl, one that had nothing to do with his voice but his
touch. But the peace began to fade as Luther moved closer.

"You left your mark, girl," he said then groaned and looked up
to heaven. "We all did."

"What is it?" said Chloe, looking up into Mercilus's face. "Lunen told me something about killing Estelle . . . and Abrís said the bird couldn't escape. But why? What happens now?"

He gave no answer but flashed a look at Zane before he could speak. There was a silence, broken every now and then by the sound of tearing fabric.

"You're a warrior like your mother," said Zane, and he laid a hand on her shoulder. "You came when you didn't have to."

Mercilus let go and stepped away. Eva marched back to Chloe and began wrapping the black strips of cloth around the crown, violently, as though she hated its light. The atmosphere grew darker with every pass that she made.

"You're Dez, right?" Chloe heard Luther saying to the stranger. "Yes."

The girl studied Dez out of the corner of her eye, her head jerking slightly as Eva tied the covering in place. His dark eyes were squinting through the cold, his lips downturned, yet relaxed, as though they had been forged by a life of suffering.

"You're a helluva fighter."

"Thank you," he said in low tones.

"Tem e Raptorren endi," Chloe shivered, and the air grew warm. Eva put an arm around her daughter, and they set off together down the desolate road.

"You're free to go," Eva called to Dez, not bothering to look at him as they walked away.

"He's not a dog," Chloe said angrily, coming to a halt. Eva spun to face the girl, eyes smoldering, but Chloe looked back at Dez.

"You can come with us. I'm Chloe."

He bowed his head, but the lady would not relent.

"I say no."

"But he's—"

"Nothing!" said Eva, cutting across her.

"What's your problem? Why are you acting like this?"

"Not now, Chloe," said Mercilus, who caught her elbow and tugged her back. He looked at Eva. "She doesn't know."

The girl stopped at the sight of Eva's watery eyes.

"Ev—I mean, Ma . . . What's wrong?"

Eva was about to turn away, the lady not bothering to wipe away the large tear that ran down her cheek, when she caught herself and looked at Dez. "Thank you . . . for saving me."

"My honor," he said, and this time, it was Chloe who drew her mother close.

"What's wrong?" she asked again.

But the lady could only shake her head and took the girl by the wrist. The two set off again, Zane, Luther, and Mercilus trailing with Dez behind. There were no voices as they walked down the valley, only Eva whispering in Chloe's ear, telling her about the Osprey, how Lavian would use it to kill the Angel of the Sun, how the Earth would return to emptiness, and that all men—even they—would die.

The girl said nothing, unable to believe what she was hearing. Would the crown still preserve her life if the Earth were destroyed? Would she exist in space, in emptiness alone? But the girl didn't want to live. *Not without Eva and Mercilus.* A foreboding feeling was filling Chloe's chest, for the crown was telling her its secret of secrets. She would not have to live without the ones she loved. There was a way to destroy the crown and her own life with it.

They saw no living thing as they walked on. There was no movement, no wind, no sound but for the gravel crunching beneath their feet. The darkness was deepening when the valley gave way, its walls shrinking until they were merely boulders heaped upon boulders. The figures came into the open and turned south across the dusty plains. The clouds were broken here and there, stained with bloodred hues and growing darker by the minute. The sky looked forlorn, a giant canvas painting their despair for all to see. Eva wandered, not knowing what to do, and something about the setting sun broke her spirit. It was as though it too had forsaken them.

The lady let go of Chloe and fell to her knees. She slammed her fists on the ground and pressed her forehead against the frozen earth. Chloe dropped beside her, wrapped herself around her mother, and together they sobbed. They had found each other only to die.

The men drew close, each of them kneeling, Luther resting his head on Mercilus's shoulder. Hours seemed to pass before Eva spoke in a broken voice.

> *My god, my god! How I've run from this place, yet it clings to me and brings me back. How I tried—and believed—that I could rise above the sins of my past. But somehow I fall and return to the nothingness I was before.*

> *I failed. I'm sorry that I'm not enough. I know that I am dust . . . that I'm not perfect, and that darkness lives in me. I only ask that you search my heart, and know that I love you.*

> *Remember me, O God. When I've been erased from the earth, remember me. As powerless as I was, remember that my greatest joy was fighting for you. And when I'm gone, remember that I loved you.*

The words echoed in Chloe's heart, the girl crying not for herself, but for Eva. How she wished she could ease her mother's pain. The men stared blankly at the ground; there was nothing they could do.

Suddenly, the earth shook, and the air swirled around them, winds the girl could not control with the crown because they belonged to someone greater. There was a light that closed their eyes and a voice like an ocean.

*Eva! I have heard you and have searched your heart. You
speak of darkness, but I see none. Your failures? I have
searched for them but cannot find them. You love me,
and this is all I see. I see you—and remember you.*

*Now this is what I will do, for I am God—the god of
gods—and no one can stand before me. I am the Alpha
and the Omega, the one who stands on the head of the
Serpent and accomplishes all that he desires. I will erase
your wretchedness and remove your sadness. But I will
never erase your life. Have I not written your name on
my heart? Has not my Raptor come for you and marked
you as my own? You will reign with me in heaven and on
Earth. You will be my daughter, and I will be your king.*

*Rise! For my word will not be broken. I will make the
place of darkness your place of victory. In the place you
fall, I will lift you up. I will make you a conqueror, and
you will see me when I come for you. I will glorify you
before your enemies, and they will know that you are
mine. Now search my heart, and know that I love you.*

It ended as quickly as it began. The earth and air were calm, the
veiling light no longer there. The horizon looked more dismal now,
but no one seemed to care. The despair that had seized their hearts
had been destroyed. They rose in silence, Chloe taking Eva by the
elbow and pulling her to her feet.

"We have to find the Osprey," said Luther, his voice shaking
them from their dreamlike state. "Whatever it takes."

"We won't find it before it reaches Lavian," said Eva. She faced
the afterglow on the horizon. "The sun's nearly gone. . . . They can't
strike Estelle before nightfall."

"The angels will fight for him," said Zane.

"But can they win?" said Mercilus doubtfully. "Lavian only has to kill Estelle and it's over."

"It's my fault," Chloe muttered. "I don't know how I missed—"

"Don't!" said Eva, and the girl closed her mouth.

"What about the chalice?" asked Dez. "The angel that came to me, the one who brought me to Sin Via, said the Osprey gets its power from the chalice. If we destroy it—"

"We'll never find it," said Mercilus firmly. "It became invisible."

"What chalice?" said Chloe.

"You know the Osprey's clothed in light?" said Eva.

"Yeah."

"It was given its body by the magic of a chalice. If we could destroy it, the Osprey dies."

"Lavian will strike Estelle at first light," said Zane. "We have until dawn."

"We don't even have that long," said Mercilus. "There's just a few hours before the sun rises over Magón. Lavian will strike before Estelle even crosses our sky. We won't find it."

"We don't need to," said Chloe. She went on, feeling their confusion in the darkness. "Before I woke, I saw the Darkness looming over me. I looked into its eyes, and there was Linden and all its spirits—ravens hatching from crystal balls, serpents leaving the wands of the dead, and spiders swarming golden goblets. They were terrified of me. Of my voice. They dove into the water, but couldn't swim away, then rose into the air and fell back to the ground."

"What does it mean?" said Mercilus flatly.

"That when I speak, all darkness will be destroyed. Not just what we've seen hanging over Linden, but all its magic—lying under the water, buried beneath the surface, and hidden in the grave."

"And the chalice?" said Eva.

"Everything. Nothing will escape the light."

"The place of darkness will be your place of victory," said Eva, repeating the words of the voice. "We go to Mayko then. To the Temple of Death."

The others murmured in agreement, but for Dez.

"I don't understand."

Eva wavered for a few moments, as though wondering whether to trust him. "You've seen the Darkness?" she said at last.

"I have."

"My daughter will break it," said Eva, unable to hide the pride in her voice. "You can fight with us and set Linden free or stay behind."

Dez didn't answer as Chloe opened her arms, his jaw sagging as billowy clouds descended, swirling and flattening until they touched the ground and froze. Six sheets of ice glittered in front of the girl.

"Come on!"

Chloe and Eva each stepped onto a disc that was no wider than a pair of angel wings. Zane, Luther, and Mercilus did the same, and their boots froze to the sheets beneath their feet. Dez ventured gingerly onto the ice.

Seconds later, a wall of wind stormed across the plains, coming for Chloe and her band who leaned forward and covered their eyes. It struck and launched them into the air. Luther and Mercilus nearly flipped before balancing themselves on their frozen wings, rising higher and turning their shoulders into the wind as another blast hurled them forward through the sky. Chloe shouted and the air grew warm around their bodies. They soared upward and onward, bursting through the clouds and flying toward a silvery moon. The girl leaned right, streaking over the mountains, looked down at Sin Via, and knew they would not be defeated again.

CHAPTER 23

THE TEMPLE OF DEATH

A full moon shone over the plains of Mayko, nestled between Hexe Buttes and the Mountains of Eternum. Giant faces were carved into the cliffs that overlooked a behemoth black stone structure, alone in the fields, all pillars and archways with spires that reached for the stars. Four ancient roads cut across the plains and converged at the temple from the north, south, east, and west. A skiff of snow covered the earth. Not a blade of grass stirred in the night.

Chloe and her party glided over the bluffs and landed on the plains to the west, within a hundred yards of the temple, the ice melting under their feet.

"Chloe, what are we looking for?" said Zane.

"I don't really know. The angels told me something about standing on a white stone . . ." Her thought trailed away, and she looked at Eva. "I thought you said there was going to be an army."

The lady shot her a look that said, *How do you expect me to know everything?*

"They want us inside," said Mercilus. "Out here, we'd destroy them with the crown." He looked at the temple. "In there, we'll cave ourselves in."

"At least we won't need a lot of time," said Chloe. "Ten minutes, maybe. I can see the words in my mind, a few pages, different from the rest. They end in something that looks like a door. When I finish, it opens and the light destroys the darkness."

"It ain't about them anyway," said Luther. "It's about us." He smacked Zane on the shoulder and glanced around at the rest. "Let's just do what we do."

"He's right," said Eva quietly. "We stay together and do what we do."

Mercilus put his hand on top of Chloe's head and turned it in his direction. "This is what you were made for. End it." He moved away before she could reply, and Eva took his place.

The lady hugged her daughter, and the women whispered in each other's ears, nodding fervently until they broke apart.

"Let's go," said Eva. The party set off.

They walked shoulder to shoulder, the women in the middle, down the western road that sparkled like a carpet under the snow. Soon, they arrived at the steps, which were wide enough for an army, and took them to a sprawling terrace decorated with snowdrifts. A row of pillars faced them on the opposite side, a gaping arch beyond. Zane led the way as they crept past the crumbling moss-covered sculptures of planets, angels, and beasts. But it was a body in the middle, drenched in moonlight, whose pale stone was untouched by the hands of time that made them stop: Lavian, but not the Serpent that they knew.

The angel was standing on a pedestal of stars, his face smooth and fair, eyes filled with diamonds. Long hair flowed down his back, and a golden crown adorned his head. Despite the statue's glory, Chloe could tell that it was Lavian by the shape of his torso, the contour of his wings, and the way that he held the lightning in his fists. Engraved beneath his feet was the inscription,

THE TEMPLE OF THE SON OF THE DAWN
AND THE HOUSE OF THE GOD OF THIS AGE

How long they stood there, wondering how such a majestic figure could have become the Serpent, no one knew.

"Let's go," said Luther finally, not bothering to lower his voice.

"*Shh!*"

Eva was glaring as if he had awakened whatever was inside.

"What? We can't go through this place readin' each other's minds." Luther made a fist, and a brilliant sword exploded in the darkness. The rest did the same as he turned and walked with Zane, past the columns, into the temple.

Chloe and Eva followed, with Mercilus and Dez trailing behind. The girl glanced at a large set of eyes carved over the archway, and a moment later, she was through, creeping under a low ceiling suspended by a network of pillars. Her mouth was dry, hardly daring to breathe as she strained her ears. Putrid smells were everywhere, and throngs of the largest, hairiest spiders that any of them had ever seen fled the light, rattling the weapons and armor that littered the floor as they scurried into the shadows.

Blasphemies were etched upon the walls and ceiling. They passed slowly through an arch above which was written LAVIAN IS THE STAR MOST HIGH. The air grew fouler and reminded Chloe of rotting meat. They moved ahead through a second arch and found themselves standing inside an enormous hall. Zane and Luther stopped. Chloe stifled a shriek as she and Eva seized each other by the arm and froze, Mercilus and Dez stumbling into their backs.

"No!" breathed Eva, looking around in horror. Human heads were on every step that lined the walls, their eyes and mouths open, contorted, as though issuing silent screams. Decapitated bodies hung upside down from the balconies above, though Chloe wasn't sure what was holding them in place. Their abdomens were torn apart, their skin half eaten away.

Zane ventured into the hall, picking his way over the fallen lampstands as Luther followed cautiously behind. They moved toward a massive archway that led to another room, but Zane crouched before he got there and held his sword over a frozen puddle. The liquid instantly melted, and he picked something off the ground that he examined in the sword light. He rose a few seconds later and returned with Luther, the others coming to meet them.

"The twenty-third enforcer, commissioned by Ley," said Zane and held out a lead crescent covered in blood.

"Impossible!" said Eva. She released Chloe's arm and waved a hand emphatically toward the bodies. "Look at this! Can't be more than a few days old."

"Let's keep moving," said Mercilus, looking around at the dark floor. "There isn't a white stone, so this can't be it."

"Chloe, have you seen this place in your mind?" said Eva. "Do you know where to go?"

"No," said the girl. Her eyes flitted to a row of six or seven bodies, the holes in their bellies large enough for a person to crawl through. She looked away. Then back again. "Never anything like this."

Bats suddenly flew out of every open door that lined the hall, screeching. Chloe and her team ducked as they zoomed over their heads, through the arch behind them, and vanished into the night.

"Listen!"

The figures straightened up as Dez extinguished his sword to lessen the noise of the flames. Eva, Chloe, and Mercilus did the same, and they heard small *clip-clops* seeping into the hall.

"One horse, one rider," whispered Dez. He ignited a sword and waved it toward a passage on their left. Eva and Mercilus clenched their hands and raised swords with the others. Chloe lifted her fists, covered in white-hot lights. The hoofbeats were slow and methodical, echoing in the chamber and growing louder until a dark horse emerged from the door, paced a few yards into the room, and stopped. Its rider wore nothing—paper-thin flesh stained with blood, a wispy mane of white hair falling to his waist. His nose and eyes were gone.

"We have not come to destroy you," he said, speaking through a strangled voice and jet-black fangs. "First you must pass through the wall and find death on the other side. It will do its part, and we will do ours."

"Like that?" scorned Eva. "We follow *you?*"

"Like that." He had whispered, but his voice somehow filled the hall. *"Come through the wall and find the white stone, but will she stand and stand alone?* What will you do, daughter of men? Stay here? Soon the sun will rise, and the Serpent will kill Estelle. Choose any door. They all lead to us."

Chloe's face hardened as he wheeled his horse around, the beast as wasted as its rider, and disappeared down the passage he had come. She dropped her hands, and the hoofbeats died away.

"He's right, we can't stay here." The girl squeezed her way past Dez and Mercilus, walked two steps in the direction of the rider's door, then changed her mind and headed for a corridor in the corner. Zane and Luther hurried to overtake her as the rest followed quickly behind.

Chloe stretched out her arm and held Luther back. "I'm going first."

"Chloe."

The girl faced Eva, and the party halted. "It's too narrow. . . . I can't fight with someone standing in front of me. I'm the strongest, I lead," Chloe added when Eva opened her mouth.

Zane and Mercilus leaned in as though preparing to split the two apart. Dez raised an eyebrow and looked at Luther, his face unreadable, then back at Chloe and Eva. To everyone's surprise, the lady nodded weakly.

Chloe's face didn't soften as she set off again. Her mind was on the other side of the wall, preparing for whatever lay ahead. She flashed a shield in her hand and edged through the doorway. The black stone passage could not have been more than four feet wide and felt strangely warm. A hand touched her hip, and the orange light from Eva's sword pushed the darkness farther down the corridor. The girl blinked.

I didn't mean it like that. . . .

The passage shone brightly now, the men filing inside, but the air became foggy as the swords brushed the damp walls. Chloe hadn't gone far when the passage veered right. She stopped, poked her head round the corner, and stiffened.

"What is it?" said Eva, pressing against Chloe and craning her neck to get a better look. But the girl said nothing as her mother cursed softly to herself. Large sections of the walls had been cut away and crammed with dead bodies, covered in thin layers of flesh and streaked with blood, stacked so tightly they were gruesome walls in themselves.

Chloe edged around the bend and moved along the passage, descending now. Twice, she almost shot a light wave down the corridor, swearing that she had seen something move. Chloe edged around another corner, bodies as far as she could see, and felt as though she had somehow joined them—they whose lives had been wiped away.

"We should be on the ground soon," Eva whispered as they moved on, Chloe barely nodding, her eyes locked on the darkness ahead. This time, the passage seemed to go on forever; and there were whispers, voices, if only in her mind. She eventually made a turn and came to a dead end.

"Now what?" said Mercilus.

"No way I'm stayin' here," said Luther.

"Shut up!"

Eva stopped as the wall opened on their right, the bodies drifting apart like sliding doors and showing a vast room with an earthen floor. Wide bone-colored pillars supported a low stone ceiling. A yellow serpent was lying on the altar within, thicker than Luther's arm. It had a single smoking eye and a black fin that ran down its back. In front of the altar was a great white stone, flat, square, and gleaming in the sword light.

They all looked at each other and then crossed the threshold. The bodies closed behind them.

No one took notice of Venus, who stood on a pedestal against the far wall, wearing an iron gown and silver mask. The snake had lowered itself onto the white stone and was rising on its tail.

"I got it," said Mercilus and was about to throw his sword when the wall of bodies opened behind Venus.

The devourers streamed through the gap, led by the rider, and salivated at the lives before them. Before Chloe could do more than look around, Zane fell over dead. Eva cried out; her fingers went black, the darkness spreading instantly along her arms, toward her face, which became like ashes. The lady fell on her knees with Mercilus, Luther, and Dez, and their swords vanished. The room would have been swallowed in darkness if it weren't for the letters that glimmered on Chloe's arm.

"*MA!*"

The girl was paralyzed. She wanted to give the crown to them all, but the devourers were upon them—hunched men that prowled like beasts, horses bearing fangs, and monsters soaked in earth—sweeping around the altar. Chloe opened her arms and smacked her fists together. A lens of light arched over her body and flashed across the room, smashing everything in its path and leaving a dozen devourers burning in its wake. Two pillars crumbled, and the ceiling caved where they had been, the serpent slithering out of sight. The rest scattered, rasping and whimpering, then crawled forward again.

Afraid of collapsing the room, Chloe ripped off the crown's cover, and the light destroyed every shadow. The devourers cowered and shrieked for Venus, who stepped down from her pedestal, stone hair sculpted as though it were flying in the wind. The goddess raised her scepter, and Eva gasped as Chloe lifted the crown from her head.

"Keep it! They're using us!"

Chloe rallied at the sound of Eva's voice, but hope vanished at the sight of Luther, lying motionless on the ground. Dez and Mercilus were still writhing, unable to breathe. She threw two light waves at Venus who broke them with her scepter, the shock waves cracking the pillars around her.

"Let them go!" Chloe screamed.

"An army I do not need," moaned Venus, her voice between that of a woman and a man. "I have been given the hand of death, to kill by fevers and famines and plagues. One will live and the rest must die."

Chloe's mind raced. If she gave the crown to Eva, her own life would be taken. She didn't care about herself, but her mother would die if anything happened to her. And if Chloe died now, the Darkness would never be broken. Their deaths would be in vain. The blasphemies on Venus's arm flickered as the goddess slashed her scepter through the air. Mercilus convulsed, and his body became rigid. Chloe looked at Venus and saw her reflection in the silvery mask. She knew what she would do: destroy the Darkness and then herself.

But Eva's still alive. . . .

She stooped to pull Eva to her feet when Dez flung a sword from the ground; it clipped the snake that had come flying through the air. Chloe straightened as the creature ignited, spun like a windmill, and wrapped itself around her body. The devourers hissed, still cowering as they cheered on the fight. The girl staggered, her arms pinned against her side, ribs about to snap as the snake tightened like a vise. Her right knee hit the ground; but she yelled, full of rage and despair, and forced herself back onto her feet.

Venus laughed madly and swung her scepter, killing Dez who had already slumped to the ground. "Your blood is mine!"

"Jae ilys ihlo akhánokam yú, vur A id gyle yú!"*

The snake choked Chloe off, but it was too late. The letters flashed on her arm, and the light cut the beast in half. The carcass burned wildly as it fell, and Chloe struck Venus before it ever hit the ground. Fissures spiderwebbed through her frame, and the goddess reeled against a pillar, shattering, her scepter skidding across the floor.

"*LET'S GO!*" shrieked Chloe and dragged Eva forward as the devourers dug through the bodies, trying to escape. The girl laid her mother on the white stone, stood over her, and began to speak.

"Sai înzengen zod raimae, cy raimae zod Deo. Sai eyam id lunan . . . cy lunan sijar sai jørnesh . . ."†

A river of light streamed down Chloe's arm, over her hand, and was caught in a sudden whirlwind. A second torrent burst through her talon scars and fed the storm, which spooled into a cyclone. Chloe never stopped speaking the words from her heart and could scarcely see through the light as it raged like never before. It bored through the ceiling, screaming like it hated the darkness. It consumed the pillars, the devourers, Venus, and her scepter; and instantly, the spell over Eva was broken. The plague gave way, and the lady could breathe freely again, her skin the color of the white sands of Sai.

Chloe pulled her arms against her body and crossed her fists before her face. The cyclone contracted and spun with greater speed until the earth trembled.

"A ta'el yú sindsiban, yú ilys exa hesbaen engorii. . . ."‡

Eva picked herself up off the stone and stared at her daughter, beautiful, fearless, and stronger than the world. Chloe flung her arms away from her body, and the cyclone opened, shredding the

---

* They will not overcome you, for I am with you!
† In the beginning was the Word, and the Word was God. In him is light, and the light shines in the darkness.
‡ I tell you the truth, you will see heaven open.

temple and showering the plains in its ruins. Light towered into the sky, words raining from the dreamer's mouth. The night became day as another cyclone descended from Zaphon and reached toward the girl, who stood in death but not alone.

CHAPTER 24

SUNDOWN AT DAWN

Lavian stormed along the battlements of his fortress beneath crimson stars that littered the darkness. Small groups of angels scattered out of his way as he passed, rage flaring in those orange and ominous eyes. It wasn't until he had reached the foot of Cain's Tower that he stopped and stared into space.

"Curse Cyca, I'll lick his lying tongue!" he hissed. "The worm should have been here by now!"

"Does he have the spirit?" asked an angel that drew near, his voice as shrill as the wind.

"Not if he's as worthless as you!"

Lavian turned to the angels that stood beside him, and something about the pale blue light emanating from his mouth made them stand back. "Madra, it is because of wraiths like you that we fail. Jezul prevails because of his legions."

He paused as the darkness released two thick vapors that entered his nostrils. There was a faint rumble, which might have been thunder, and the Serpent murmured as though he had heard a voice.

"They are more cunning than mine, but one day I will face him alone . . . *tssss* . . . and who will save him then?"

The Serpent had no sooner looked away than a voice echoed from above.

"The girl flies for Mayko!" said Balim, gliding through the darkness and landing in their midst. "Father," he went on hurriedly, "she will not fall to Venus!"

There was a burst of lightning, and the angel fell with a sickening thud. The light of his soul flashed through the floor, plummeted through space, and disappeared into the Earth below.

"The girl is where I want her," said Lavian, who murmured as though his mind was detached. The tip of his tail slithered through the bleeding hole in Balim's body, which he lifted and threw over the wall. "I know your thoughts." Lavian looked back at the angels who shuddered. "That I should make a weapon, like the Betrayer's Blade, and take the girl alive. Hold her like Eva, who was bound for seventeen years. True, I could have made another like the first . . . yessss . . . I could have held the girl for a thousand years, but all magic can be broken. I have told you, witches, that I seek to end our doom and not delay it. I fight only to win."

Lavian held out his hand, unsteadily, as though contemplating whether to kill them all; then a shout made him wheel around in time to see a violet flame in the distance. What appeared to be a little white star came streaking out from the light, and the fire was gone. Lavian rose on his tail, angels flocking to his side as the oncoming speck took shape. Soon they could make out the beating wings of a bird.

"The Osprey!" cried Madra, and a roar went up from the angels. The light from the bird grew brighter and illuminated the horrid faces along the battlements, eyes glittering as though they had been filled with ice. Lavian reached out, and the Osprey landed on his arm with a scream. The angels thundered with glee and the stars flickered, but the pupils narrowed in Lavian's eyes.

The Serpent snatched the tarantula that was clinging to the bird and held it before his face. "And the chalice?"

The creature breathed its response so that none but the Serpent could hear. The celebrations stopped as Lavian crunched the spider in his fist, the body releasing its spirit as the Snake flung it into space.

"We have the Osprey," Lavian called out, "but the chalice is lost."

"Curse Cyca!" yelled a voice from the horde.

"Yessss," said Lavian coldly. "Curse the worm!" He looked down at the Earth where two lifeless patches were surrounded by a radiant mosaic. "The Osprey dies if they break the Darkness, but the light has not yet risen. We need the spirit till dawn, then no more."

"It will be the end of an age," said the quivering voice of an angel, and murmurs rose around him. "No longer held beneath the stars of God, no longer chained by the shadow of tomorrow."

"We are the Fallen!" shouted Madra. *"Who will erase our name!"*

These words were greeted with a mad shout, the angels erupting until Lavian rose on his tail and raised a fist.

"Tssss!"

The voices ceased.

"Do not think Jezul will let his word fail," said Lavian ruthlessly. "No, not easily, for he is like me—a warrior to the end."

Lavian lowered himself and turned his attention toward the Osprey, staring through its eyes into the emptiness within. Drawing the bird to his mouth, he said,

> *Take now, Osprey, this venom mine,*
> *That chills and kills a soul divine;*
> *And strike Estelle but once not twice—*
> *And turn his light, his blood to ice!*

The Snake sank his fangs through the Osprey. The bird twitched violently, flapped its wings, and stiffened. For a few seconds, nothing happened; then fangs descended from its beak, hanging like white shadows, its talons became razors, and a blue light shone from its mouth as it struggled to breathe. Lavian opened his mouth and placed the bird on his shoulder, which appeared as calm as before.

"Kael, Gallica, bring me your legions," he said. Two figures stepped forward, their wings shaped with wide, sweeping arcs like blades. "We pass through the fires to Magón. The rest of you will come to me when you find me on the Mountains of Eternum."

"*OUR GOD!*" they yelled. The Serpent rose into the air, the Osprey clinging to his shoulder as he sped for the top of the fortress. In less than a minute, Lavian was soaring toward his throne room, where the wall ahead of him became a waterfall. The Snake shot through the torrent, into the room, and landed in front of the black ring. He slithered forward and swung his fist through the crystal frame, which burst and showered the floor with glittering shards. The Serpent picked a piece off the ground and held it over his eyes. The sliver dug into his face, trails of blood oozing down his skull, covering his sockets so they were hidden from view.

Lavian moved down the row of violet fires and disappeared through the flame by his throne. Kael, Gallica, and their legions pelted through the water a split second later, the procession snatching up the fragments on the floor, covering their eyes and vanishing through the fires.

———◆———

A wave of violet flame ripped across the middle heavens, over the eastern rim of the world, beyond the Drothenn Sea, and tore the atmosphere in two. A black hole opened, and Lavian and his angels zoomed out into the darkness. Dawn was minutes away.

"Hide the Osprey!" cried Gallica. Droves of angels flocked around Lavian as their bodies became obsidian. Within seconds, the radiant creature was hidden, and the sea lay in darkness to the west and Magón beyond. The fire disappeared, and the red quivering stars went black, leaving the angels hovering without a trace.

"With me!" shouted Kael, and he sped off with his angels, something like a greenish comet appearing high above them, infecting the darkness as it fell toward Earth. It wasn't long before the brilliant mass slowed and transformed into a gemstone tower with no windows and gates of light, looming where the violet flames had been minutes before.

A flash of fire erupted in the heavens, just beside the tower and a little to the north. A river of jeweled angels spilled into space, wings thundering as the gates began to open, releasing pink, orange, and bronze beams of light.

"Kashe kavar!" shouted Aurèle. The angels split, a thousand following Eyewing and circling the tower like a school of fish, while thousands more trailed Aurèle and Capella, who flanked the gates on either side. They spread out and formed what looked like a swarming wall of insects as the Angel of the Sun stepped through the gates.

Estelle's body glistened like crystal, draped in a golden veil. He walked westward through the heavens, eyes closed, as he had since the day he was created. There had been wars and famine, peace, and love, a time for everything under the sun. Some ended anon, others lasted ages, but there had always been the hope of tomorrow. The sun must rise—ever it must rise—and so Estelle walked on, needing no wings, striding on the rays of light that came from his body. His veil trailed from the tower, tumbled past his feet, and dangled over the Earth below. A new day dawned.

The gates closed silently behind him, and the tower flickered; the angels drifted away as it plummeted through space and then surrounded the Angel of the Sun. He held out his right hand, and sunbeams passed through the Unseen realm into the world of men, the oceans sparkling somewhere far below.

Eyewing flew ahead of the swarming angels to escape the light of their bodies but found nothing. He circled behind Estelle, flying further into the darkness, and was about to return when he saw it—a glimmer that was gone.

"Draaken!" he bellowed and threw his sword at the place where he'd seen the light. A blue light shield flared, and the sword exploded in a cloud of sparks. Instantly, fire and lightning, light shields, and blasts filled the atmosphere. It was war in the heavens, green and white lights rising and falling as bodies shattered and souls were released.

There were glimpses of the Osprey as Dark Angels maneuvered around Lavian, their bodies reflecting the light of the bird. The Serpent retreated, and Aurèle charged, fire streaming from his eyes into the arms of the Fallen. Droves of jeweled bodies followed him, blazing in the light of their swords, while Cappella hung back with his angels and guarded Estelle.

"Vur mocce!" Lavian pumped a fist toward the Earth, and red stars rained from above but were obliterated by clear stars that fell from somewhere higher. The explosions could be felt a galaxy away. A blizzard of sparks began drifting over the angels that made it difficult to see. Lavian retreated further, shining in the light of the Osprey, pulling the angels farther away.

Another wingbeat and Lavian grabbed the bird from his shoulder and spun his tail around it like a cocoon. The light of the Osprey vanished; and Lavian dove through the fray, broke free, and plunged toward the Earth.

The Snake resurfaced seconds later, joining Kael and his angels who were looming in front of Estelle. It was as though the darkness had carried him through time. They peered through the snowstorm of shattered stars, thickening now, barely able to see the battle ahead. Just as Lavian lunged forward, however, a shock wave rocked the heavens. The Snake struggled to stay upright as he wheeled around and saw a funnel of light descending over Linden.

"We're too late!" screamed Kael, looking down at the Earth where another cyclone of fiery light was climbing into the atmosphere.

"Never!" shrieked Lavian, and the Serpent—that dragon of old—spun away from the light and raced toward Estelle.

Aurèle killed two Dark Angels and turned. He had felt the darkness shift. The archangel made for Estelle while Lavian, Kael, and his angels sped from the opposite direction, invisible in the shadows of space.

Lavian drew near, Estelle's reflection flashing in the crystal over his eyes. He glanced back, the funnels nearly touching, dipped his wing as he unraveled his tail, and slung the Osprey toward Estelle. Gallica and his angels banked hard to their left, circling north, and lashed Capella and his angels with lightning.

"Falkón!" shouted Capella, and his angels drifted north, away from Estelle. The Osprey zoomed like an arrow, its starlike body camouflaged by the raining sparks. The bird folded its wings and stretched out its talons, just as Aurèle swooped around the Angel of the Sun. Carried by the darkness once more, Lavian suddenly appeared and smashed into Aurèle.

And the archangel fought the Dragon. Strength versus strength, power versus power, their crystal wings glinting and gleaming as each dodged the other's strikes. Lavian threw an errant bolt that exploded inches beside Estelle, and the Serpent edged away, as though afraid of touching the veil. The Snake cut off Aurèle's right arm. The archangel flashed a sword in the opposite hand, flipped to avoid a light wave, and severed Lavian's tail as it sailed for his head. Aurèle turned toward his brother, but not before the Osprey had smashed through the veil, hitting Estelle with such force that it plunged through his chest and exited on the other side.

"My will, my throne!" screamed Lavian. Aurèle watched in disbelief as venom surged through Estelle, the angel clutching his throat as the Osprey returned to Lavian and landed on his shoulder. The Serpent drifted away, tongue flickering as Estelle lifted his face and turned to ice.

"Aurèle!" Lavian yelled over the booming blasts and cries, the war still raging. The angel looked back at the Serpent, whose tail regenerated as his own arm returned, translucent but thickening.

"You were never enough!"

Lavian threw a bolt that Aurèle blocked and shouted, "Watch the world die!"

The rays of Estelle dimmed. His body had just started sinking into space when Kael dove out of nowhere, opened a bladelike wing, and cut off his head. A white light rose from the angel's body as it crumbled out of sight.

Time stopped on Earth.

The oceans neither rose nor fell, and no shadow moved. Every tree stood frozen. There was no wind. And then the seas began to churn, raging against shores that could no longer keep them at bay. Skies melted as light merged with darkness, the Seen with the Unseen and time with eternity. The world was sliding into emptiness, into what it was before.

"My god!" Kael shouted victoriously. He swooped in front of Lavian and smacked him on the chest as Aurèle retreated with his angels.

But Lavian shoved Kael away. Although the light from Linden had fallen back to Earth, the funnel from Zaphon continued to burn.

CHAPTER 25

WHEN THE MORNING STAR COMES FOR HIS OWN

Chloe's heart grew cold, the light no longer flowing through her veins, and the cyclone tumbled to the Earth.

"What's happening?" said Eva, her voice trembling as she searched Chloe's face for an answer.

"I . . . I don't know . . ."

The girl's mind returned to the world around her, the last wisps of light dying away. She stood amid a sea of ruins, and the sky dimmed but was not dark; it was as though it were confused, unable to discern between night and day. "I don't feel it anymore."

"They've killed Estelle," said Eva bitterly. She stepped forward and flung her arms around Chloe, even as lightning struck the buttes over a hideous face carved in the rock. They looked up and saw Lavian, tail dangling over the precipice, the Osprey perched on his shoulder. A streak of purple flame opened the sky above the Serpent, his angels gliding like bats through the hole and landing on Hexe Buttes and the Mountains of Eternum. They stood along the ridges and stared down at Chloe and Eva through the jagged crystals over their eyes. The fire in the sky vanished.

Chloe wanted to fall. There was no way of escape; the Seen and

Unseen had become one. They couldn't pass through the fire. They couldn't fly away.

"Why are they here?" said Chloe, angry and afraid. "They've already won." Tears ran down her face: she had trusted her god and was a fool for believing.

"He's come for the crown," said Eva, speaking into her ear. "Don't ever take it off. . . . *Promise me.*" She squeezed her daughter so tightly that Chloe couldn't breathe. "I never thought my girl would be like you."

The lady shoved herself away, opened her arms, and shouted, "*LAVIAN!*" And before Chloe had realized what her mother had done—killing herself so her daughter couldn't give her the crown— there was a flash of bluish light, and Eva crumpled, a hole in her chest.

"*No!*"

Chloe dove to Eva's side, snatched the crown, and pressed it on the lady's head with all her might. She let go, but it thudded to the ground. Chloe picked it up and tried again and again.

The ground trembled and made it impossible for her to hold the crown steadily on Eva's head. She gave up as the earth split miles to the east, and she lay on top of her mother, arms wrapped around her neck. Almost instantly, water gushed from the chasm and spread onto the plains. There was a deep and thunderous sound as a distant mountain crumbled like sand; the angels on its peak rose into the sky and landed on the neighboring ridge. Lavian watched a moment longer as creation slipped away then gave the Osprey to Gallica and launched himself from the precipice, soared across the plains, and landed in front of Chloe.

"Now you know the curse of the crown," he hissed, slithering over the ruins and as he came closer. The girl didn't look up, sobbing; she knew what she had to do, but couldn't let go of Eva. The dark waters gurgled as they rose like a tide over the ruins, marching toward the white stone. "You want to be with her, but cannot join her because the crown will not let you die. Now you see that life is a curse . . . *yessss* . . . because it keeps you from the ones that you love."

The freezing water reached the place where the women lay. They began covering Eva, her body quickly growing cold. Chloe hardly noticed the biting water as it rose slowly around them, wishing that she were dead. "End the pain!" hissed the Serpent smoothly. "End it now and be with her. . . . Give me the crown, and I will give you death."

And Chloe realized that Lavian didn't know the secret of the crown—that it can be broken by the one who wears it, that its light will leave, and once it grows dark will give up its life. *He thinks I need him to die.*

But the girl said nothing, and the Serpent pressed on. "It's your fault that your mother is dead." He had reached her side, never pulling his gaze from the crown, lying in the water next to Eva's head. "Because of you, she no longer wore the crown. If she had, she would have lived . . . but she gave it to you, because you are weak.

"Do you think you defeated me when you fought me on Mount Nin?" he breathed, circling slowly around Chloe. "No, dreamer, I came not to destroy you, but to harm you. I knew that when Eva saw you crushed, but not destroyed, she would fear for your life and give you the crown."

"Liar!" choked Chloe. She pushed herself up, just enough to keep her head above the water, and stared into Eva's face. It glowed in the light of the crown, quivering beneath the ripples as Lavian slithered past.

"Liar?" he said quietly. "Search your heart, and know my words are true. Your mother was strong and would never have given it to me. But you are weak. I knew you were the only one to whom she would give the crown, and once you had it, you would give it to me."

"Why?" Chloe shouted hoarsely. Another mountain crumbled onto the plains, which now looked like a shallow sea. "Why did you kill her? You've already won!"

"And will win!" Lavian stopped moving and yelled down at the girl, her head bent inches over the water. "I am forever! The most vile and vicious that's ever been. There's no one like me! You're an overcomer? *I overcame!* I'm the destroyer, I'm the devourer, I'm darkness, and death lives in me. My power is transcendent, my throne, preeminent. I want your heart, I want your life, I want your crown. *Give it to me!*"

The angels stood unmoving as Lavian's voice echoed. Chloe could scarcely see Eva's face through the water and her own wall of tears. She convulsed with the sobs, the pain slashing her heart *like a knife.*

Chloe picked up the crown, sat up straight, and put her other hand beneath her tunic. Lavian rocked as she lifted the crown out of the water, the wet band like molten gold, holding life and no longer wanting it. "Dên di soni benachad,"* said Chloe mechanically.

And in one shaky movement, she raised the dagger from the water and plunged it through the opposite arm. Blood ran like a river down her forearm and over the crown. The band opened and she threw it away.

"Take it!"

Chloe expected Lavian to scream, to kill her as he had Eva. But he stared at the Betrayer's Blade, its eyes burning in the hilt. "The weapon fashioned against you will prosper," he hissed. "The Serpent wins."

Watching the crown where it lay, growing dim as its light escaped through the water, Chloe's strength left her, gasping now, the water churning around her neck.

And then off to the east, a torrent of water gushed through a gap in the mountains. It surged across the plains, curled along the buttes, and stormed toward Chloe and Lavian. The sea had risen from the south.

---

* To die is gain.

"Skin for skin," said Lavian, as the earth slid further into emptiness.

"Moj Deo, moj Deo, wayshem vor yú vurstel mocce?"* Chloe whispered in a daze.

And before Lavian could react, a star smashed into the plains behind the girl. The explosion passed harmlessly through Chloe and hurled Lavian backward through the air. With what little strength she had, Chloe looked over her shoulder and saw a rising column of smoke, the water strangely calm around it. And what might have been hope flickered in her eyes. His skin covered in writing that glittered like gold, his lips pressed together in fury, beneath those flaming eyes, Jezul came out of the billows, walking on the water.

Tongues of light came from his feet and snaked toward her through the water like eels. They reached the girl in seconds and swirled around her body. One tied itself around the knife wound in her arm, and the bleeding stopped. She suddenly felt warm, could feel her heart beating again; he was coming for her. He had both arrived and had always been.

Jezul had not taken more than five or six steps when Mount Mammon erupted behind him. Chloe gaped in fear as a fountain of ashes and dazzling lava rose into the air, but the god never broke step. Lavian burst from the groundwater in the distance and climbed through the air as the tidal wave passed beneath him.

"To the fire!" shouted the Serpent, and his angels obeyed. Those standing on the peaks beside Mount Mammon took off and dove into the lava, giving up their spirits. Instantly, it flowed like a river down the mountain and plunged into the waters that covered the plains. Somewhere in the curtain of steam, the lava rose, coiled, and shot forward like a brilliant stream of venom that corkscrewed through the air. The lava jet flew at the tidal wave that barreled from the east, pinning Jezul and Chloe between them.

---

* My God, my God, why have you forsaken me?

"Look out!" Chloe cried, not knowing what else to say as she struggled to rise, but the earth shook so violently that she fell back on her knees. Jezul reached her a second later, lowered his head, and closed his eyes.

The Morning Star breathed in, crossed his right arm over his chest, and flung it at the tidal wave. The wall of water exploded before it could wipe them away, reeling as though it had been hit by a mountain. He flashed his left arm at the torrent of lava, which erupted with a sonic boom so that Chloe thought her head had been split in half.

The sea fled to the east and the lava to the west. Jezul opened his eyes and looked at the Fallen then drove a fist toward the earth—the shock wave forced the waters of the deep back into the Underworld. He spun in the opposite direction, flashed his arms over his face, and raised them in a sweeping motion. The wrecked mountains rose from the earth and stood where they had since the beginning of time. The waters of the deep receded, and the Morning Star pulled his fists to his sides. The chasm closed.

Jezul lifted his eyes toward Zaphon and shouted, "A ilys ihlo valeren uniq yú unimdad mocce!"* Then he caught Chloe's upper arm, pulled her to her feet, and held her head against his chest. They were standing on the white stone, wet grass shimmering softly in front of them like an enchanted dream. Shallow lakes were scattered across the plains. A small pool lay beside them, its water trapped by the ruins, covering Eva's body.

"I didn't think you'd come," said Chloe, hating the words. Standing in his arms, she wondered how she could have doubted.

But Jezul said nothing as he pulled the dagger from her arm. The blade burst into ashes, and the wound healed at once, though the scar remained. He looked into the girl's face, and she did not

---

* I will not lose any you gave me!

look away as a warm, electric sensation spread through her. She saw that he still loved her.

Chloe would have stood there until her own life withered and was swept away, but Lavian appeared out of nowhere and landed to the east. The angels glided down from the ridges and amassed on the plains like a shadow behind their god, a shadow that became a sea of lightning, bolts flashing in their fists. The Snake kept his distance, Gallica standing right behind him with the Osprey on his shoulder.

"Jezul," said Lavian in that swarming voice, low and vacillating, carried on a breeze. "I know what is written—'Yú ain e Alpha enå Omega, înzeng cy deya.'* I came to kill Estelle, this is true, for when he falls, the world falls with it. But he only carried time in his hands, and you are time itself, the one who still remains.

"I came not to destroy the Earth, but to show the girl is faithless. I knew that if she saw her world falling around her, she would no longer believe."

The clenching in Chloe's stomach intensified. Jezul was silent, keeping an arm around the girl.

"Have I not shown you her heart, Son of God?" said Lavian. "How she preferred dying over living for you? How quickly they turn, *brother*. . . . Unlike me, who served you for a thousand years."

Lavian swayed, his mouth moving yet making no sound.

"You know that Linden is mine, for it was given to me by its first king," he resumed, unable to hide the venom in his voice. "Do not those who live in darkness belong to me? Am I not their god? Yet," he hissed, "I will give you Linden—and remove its darkness—for the girl. Only one faithless life, Morning Star, for the lives of many."

Chloe shivered and gripped Jezul with all her strength. *Wouldn't it be worth it, my life for theirs?*

"I came not for the many, but for the one," said Jezul. "I came for the girl and for her alone."

---

* You are the Alpha and Omega, the beginning and end.

"You came for her?" leered Lavian. "She doubted you."

"Tra jae ain inshonel, A ilys permanera iishonel."* Jezul looked long at Lavian. "This will be a sign to you that I am faithful and true. Through the one, the many shall live, and through the girl, I will save the faces of men."

"Through the girl," echoed Lavian, his tail gliding in a wide, figure-eight pattern beneath him. "I know what you will do for Eva . . . *yessss* . . . for you've made her your promise, and your promise cannot be broken . . ."

And a confused, yet enchanted feeling came over Chloe.

"But you have sewn your word in the heart of the girl, and when she dies, it dies. Yet you have said that your word will never die. Even if you raise her again, Morning Star, has not your word been broken? *Yessss!* For it perished, even for a moment. Today the girl will fall, and when she dies, your word will return to you void."

Lavian crossed his fists in front of his chest and looked to heaven. "Darkness unto darkness!"

"And light unto light," said Jezul. He stepped forward and stretched out his arms. "Choose now your god!"

And the girl watched, mesmerized, as creation came alive. The ground rumbled, the noise magnified by the terrifying sound of crunching rocks as the mountains broke away and rose into the air. They soared over Chloe and Jezul and hovered in pairs behind them, save Mount Mammon, which joined the Northern Sea as it rushed over the buttes for Lavian. Its waters arched over the angels like an immense rainbow, waves upon waves, crashing back and forth. The four winds screamed around Lavian. The storm clouds rallied for Jezul.

The sky thickened and tore itself apart. Chloe looked up and saw the Darkness, bleeding with stars, but it was being penetrated

---

* If they are unfaithful, I will remain faithful.

by a funnel of light that whirled above her. And something about the light said that it wasn't over.

"Yeah, yeah, *yeah!*" she shouted, pumping her fist three times in the air. The writing on her arm was burning. The fire and the light, the rage and the hate had returned.

Jezul stared at the Dark Angels, and the sword of Life erupted in his fist. Its flames were red and whispered for the Dragon. He never broke his gaze, even as dazzling white stars appeared above the darkness and rained past the Fallen stars. They grew no larger as they came, gathering to form Leo and Aquila. The constellations were soon thrashing like wolves, high over Chloe and Jezul, though not before the red stars had fallen to form Draco and Scorpius, streaking toward Lavian. More white stars descended, bringing Taurus to Jezul. The last of the blood stars plummeted, and Centaurus paced over Lavian.

Chloe flashed a sword in her fist and stood beside Jezul, her eyes burning, looking only at Lavian. She would throw his heart to the dogs.

"No!" Jezul took Chloe by the wrist. "He's mine! Break the Darkness . . . *Break it!*" he said again when the girl wouldn't move.

Chloe opened her hand, and the sword vanished. Lavian licked the air, lightning in each hand. Jezul looked back at the makeshift pool where the lady lay, keeping his body between the girl and the Fallen. "Eva! Stand with me!"

There was a white flash beneath the ice, and Chloe's heart beat wildly. Her eyes were burning, but she didn't blink, not wanting to miss what a voice was telling her she would see—a prodigy that would end her despair.

And Eva rose, as though in slow motion, her head and shoulders breaking through the ice. Her body was made of diamonds, her hair trailing like a waterfall as she stood to her feet. Her eyes were no longer gray, but shadows and light that discerned good from evil. She stepped over the rubble and walked toward Jezul, more glorious than gold, for gold was the dress that she wore. Light emanated from her body, and stars welled in her hands. She was as perfect as the god who called her.

Chloe wanted to run to her but was afraid to touch the goddess. The lady walked forward and took Chloe by the arm.

"I am with you forever," she said. Her voice was immortal; there was no fear or sadness in her being, only power.

Chloe nodded and was unable to fight back the tears as she stood between her mother and Jezul. The Morning Star looked at Eva then stared at the Fallen. There was nothing more to say. Each knew what he must do. Eva let go of Chloe and moved forward with Jezul, the girl standing behind them, on the white stone.

Lavian looked over his shoulder at the Osprey, saying, "Kill the dreamer."

The bird jumped from Gallica's shoulder, circled in the air, and flew toward the back of Lavian's army. Chloe watched the radiant figure fade away, zooming through a corridor of seas: the water arching overhead and the ocean of angels beneath.

The girl furrowed her brow, took a deep breath, and began speaking the words in her heart. "Karnal børgen karnal, ak Ånepra børgen ånepra. . . ."* Light gushed from the writing and scars on her arms, instantly exploding into a vortex around her.

Whether it was the light rising around the girl or that the Osprey was safely away, the Serpent struck. *"Destroyers!"* Lavian threw a lightning bolt at Jezul that the waters chased, curling downward over the angels and hitting the plains as they raced toward Chloe. Jezul smashed the bolt with his fist as Eva threw her arm forward. Two mountains responded, one soaring on either side of the rising light—the four winds fought to hold them back but in vain. Eva and Jezul floated into the air, just before the mountains smashed

---

* Flesh gives birth to flesh, but the Spirit gives birth to spirit.

into the sea, spraying water into heaven as they sank into the earth. There was an earthquake but the ground inside the light was still.

"A ta'el yú sindsiban, za tenen hil mái za wosti . . ."*

The girl pressed on and stretched out her arms, the cyclone expanding around her.

"Dên deya!" yelled Jezul, who spun as he issued flames from his hand that opened the sky above him. He ran through the air at the Fallen, rising out of the sea, and the Raptor zoomed out of the burning sky like a sunbeam, followed by a tide of shining angels.

Chloe never heard the roar of the angels that pounded the atmosphere like breaking waves, couldn't see Jezul swarmed by Dark Angels, or Eva fighting Mount Mammon. Her mind was lost in the light.

Outside the cyclone, fire and lightning flew endlessly, white and green flashes decorating the sky. Eva hammered the sea with mountain after mountain and then called tornados from the storm clouds, casting them at Mount Mammon as the volcano erupted again. The funnels caught the gushing lava and spewed it over the Fallen, who spiraled into the sea.

Aquila battled Draco in the heavens, stars crushing stars with blasts that showered the sky with glassy shards. Leo and Taurus flung Scorpius through the funnel over Chloe, the constellation severed by the light.

Dark Angels were beginning to break through the onslaught but were consumed the moment they flew into the light. More angels came, hurling lightning at the girl, but the bolts were devoured: The cyclone had become too strong, its peak closed so that no one could enter from above.

Eva never saw the Dragon plunging through the sky behind her. He folded his wings and dove through the ground.

---

* I tell you the truth, we speak of what we know.

"Vur nasii agaben Deo morlin . . . mái hvi unimdad hvis Soen e unem. . . ."*

Chloe's voice was swallowed by the cyclone that towered into the heavens and nearly touched the light from Zaphon. She was halfway through the final verse when the earth split beneath the stone, which tipped and jerked her mind to the world around her. She stopped and steadied herself then froze. Lavian had risen from the rift, ten yards in front of her, inside the howling light.

He lunged before Chloe could react, her mind still coming back to herself, but another figure flashed through the wall and tackled Lavian. The bodies tumbled to the ground and were up in an instant, Lavian launching to his left and snapping his tail at Chloe, Jezul diving and taking the strike with his shoulder. He was back on his feet as Lavian fired at Chloe, swinging his fist and crushing the bolt with a shock wave. Lavian coiled and threw two more bolts, one from each hand, both smashed by Jezul.

Lavian shrieked and turned his attention away from Chloe, who, no longer lost inside her head, had fired a light wave that severed his wing. The Serpent whipped his tail around Jezul who caught him by the throat, spun, and slammed him to the ground. The earth crumbled and dragged the limp body into the chasm, tail unraveling around Jezul and sinking out of sight.

"Are you all right?" Chloe shouted to Jezul. But as she stepped toward the blood-soaked figure, the Osprey pelted through the cyclone behind her. Chloe saw Jezul's eyes flicker and wheeled around. The Raptor burst through the opposite wall, collided with the bird, and tore its head from its body.

Jezul clenched his fists as the Osprey burst into flames. The Raptor circled the perimeter of the cyclone and landed on his shoulder.

"Now!" yelled Jezul, staring into Chloe's face.

---

* For God so loved the world that he gave his only Son.

The girl never wavered. "Duenshi credae ilys ihlo di, ak vor emsata atim."* And it was finished.

The cyclones touched in the heavens, and the light from Zaphon and Linden united. Chloe's eyes lingered on the Morning Star a second longer then saw a blinding flash. The cyclones unwound, and a supernova destroyed the Darkness.

Chloe felt the frozen ground pressing against her body. She could see only shadows, unable to tell whether her eyes were open. The roaring in her brain was quickly fading; she could hear distant voices, cheering, then suddenly she could see. Chloe was suspended high over Linden, her country a gleaming bed of jewels, but something even more glorious came into view: the faces of men whose eyes were filled with light. Cities and towns flitted before her, filled with young and old, weak and well, save Sin Via. The haunt had been erased, a lake of gold resting in its place. The shadows returned, and the voices faded away.

Chloe opened her eyes and found herself lying amid the temple ruins, alone on the plains. She shivered as a breeze rattled the grass, grass that no longer glittered with beads of water. The Mountains of Eternum were standing in their proper place. The girl got slowly to her feet and raised a hand to shield her eyes.

"The sun," she murmured, squinting at the heavenly body as it hung over the horizon, basking in a soft blue sky. *But how?*

"Chloe."

The girl turned to find Jezul standing behind her. His hair was as white as the snow that lined the mountains; though the writing still shimmered on his body, his eyes no longer blazed.

He moved forward and took her into his arms. She closed her eyes and began to cry. No one had loved her enough to die for her— no one except Eva and the thought of her made the tears stream even more.

---

* Whoever believes in him shall not perish but have eternal life.

Minutes passed before Jezul lifted her face, and the girl returned his gaze, not bothering to wipe her eyes. He touched the wound where she had plunged the Betrayer's Blade. "You are strong," he said. "The one I made you to be and are becoming still."

But the girl pressed her forehead against his chest. "No," she said softly. "What Lavian said is true. I'm not like . . . like Eva."

"Is true?" repeated Jezul, now tracing the scar along her upper arm, the one from her fight with Lavian. "Only light is true. The power of the crown came from its light and was able to heal all wounds. But the wound that would have ended in death leaves a scar. They are your glory, a testament of the blows that were destined to kill you, but failed. No, daughter, the Serpent came for your life on Mount Nin. You fought him and won."

Chloe looked up, her eyes narrowed, and her mouth trembled. Triumph flitted across her face.

"I'm sorry that I destroyed the crown," she said and stepped back. The girl seemed taller now. "I mean, that was true. What he said. That I didn't wanna live anymore"—her voice broke, but she didn't look away—"and I didn't want him to have it . . . and now it's gone."

"This was the Serpent's plan, that you give him the crown. Lavian knew that if he killed Estelle, I would restore creation. See now," he said, looking into the sun. "I have put a new angel in the heavens, and he will govern time until I return. When my god himself will be the light of the world."

"What about everyone else?" said Chloe fearfully. "I mean, the floods and everything. Eva said . . ." She paused. A breeze rattled the grass and sighed into silence. "She said that everyone would die."

"There are secrets that even angels do not know," said Jezul, "for they have not always been. They knew that if Estelle dies, the earth would return to what it was before, formless and void, and the bodies of men would be no more. But mankind existed before the foundation of the world. Their days were written in me."

"So no one died then?" she said hurriedly, not trying to understand what she'd just heard. The Truth was standing before her.

"No!" He looked slightly defiant, and the girl was dizzy with relief. "While you and Eva were standing on the white stone, the spirits of men were given to me, and their bodies returned to the womb of Earth—the place where they were formed before the dawn of time. This was the vision you saw, the eve you found the book."

"But that was so long ago!"

Jezul smiled. "I showed you the future, but even now, they walk in the world of men, their bodies returned to them, their time away less than a dream."

"So it really was about making me . . . *Oh!*" Chloe threw a trembling hand over her mouth. "If I would have died by the blade . . ."

"The weapon fashioned against you would have prospered. My word would have failed. You destroyed the crown and thwarted the plot of the Serpent, but struck yourself with the Betrayer's Blade."

"I'm so sorry! I never thought—"

"Peace," he said, and the girl lowered her hand. "You will shine with me forever, long after the darkness is gone. I will not remember your doubt, unbelief, or sins, only that you loved me.

"Forget what is behind," he said, and a cloud layer moved over the plains from the south, "and look to what will come." A single ray of light pierced the clouds and fell on Jezul. His body glowed, and the writing blazed on his skin. His hair was melting into the light. He opened his arms, translucent now, and a line of fire erupted behind him.

"One more land is bound in darkness, held by the Dragon. When it falls, the head of the Snake falls with it."

"I'll go," Chloe whispered. Her eyes were closed. She knew that he was leaving and couldn't bear to be alone.

"Through you, the end will come. At the voice of another, Magón will fall."

"And Lavian . . . will I see him again?" said Chloe, glancing up.

"You will. And darkness itself. It will hate you and come for you because I have set you apart from all who walk the Earth. The light in you cannot be hidden."

"But I don't have the book of Magón." *And how can I do it alone?* She gasped. Something had pulled back the veil of her heart. Jezul's voice came again, this time from a long way away. "The Raptor will come for you and lead you the way you should go. But will I leave you an orphan?"

At these words, a diamond flashed, high above the sun, and fell toward the Earth as though it could not fall fast enough. There was an explosion behind Chloe—like that of the Morning Star when he had smashed into the Earth—and the girl bent low, covering her head as a shock wave rolled through her body. She straightened up, turned around, and stared into a million flecks of light, swirling, rising slowly into the air.

And when the girl thought she could cry no more, Eva emerged from the cloud—not the goddess whose body was made of diamonds, but the woman of flesh, the one whom Chloe had first seen in Carnecia, who held her those nights they fled Lavian. The one that she loved.

"Ma!"

The women rushed toward each other, Chloe hardly noticing the golden letters written below Eva's collarbone: *EVLIN CE ENÅ VICTUS.** Within seconds, they collided, locked in an iron-clad hug, pulling at each other's hair, weeping.

"Eva," said Jezul. The women looked in his direction, their heads pressed together. He was nearly lost to view, transforming into light. "Go to La Cade and anoint Deangelo, son of Holm, king over Linden. I will give you the power of creation once more, not through the crown, but through your blood. You will give the people a sign,

---

* More than a conqueror.

and summer will come in winter. They will believe your word and serve Deangelo as king. Tell him that I will raise his throne. He will be the last king of Linden, for I am coming soon, and when I come, the end comes with me."

No sooner had he finished than the ray pulsed and he was gone, leaving Chloe and Eva to stare into the fire. They held each other fast, each lost somewhere in her mind until a flurry of snow broke their trance.

"Let's go," said Eva softly.

Clinging to Eva, Chloe walked a few paces toward the flames and stopped.

"I'll try," she whispered, looking at the clouds.

"Try what?"

"To forget what's behind."

They stood a moment longer and strode through the fire, the girl knowing that she'd never forget the day the Morning Star came. The explosion was still ringing in her heart.

CPSIA information can be obtained
at www.ICGtesting.com
Printed in the USA
BVHW042102070623
665585BV00001B/4